UNTIL YOUR FATHER COMES HOME

UNTIL YOUR FATHER COMES HOME

MEAGHAN DWYER

This is a work of fiction. Names, characters, places, and incidents either are a product of the author's imagination or are used fictiously. Any resemblance to actual persons, living or dead, business establishments, events, or locales is entirely coincidental.

Library of Congress Control Number: 2026914209

ISBN 979-8-9889851-3-6 (ebook)

ISBN 979-8-9889851-5-0 (paperback)

ISBN 979-8-9889851-4-3 (hardcover)

Cover Design: Miblart

First Edition: July 2026

Published by Carpenter Books, LLC.

meaghandwyerbooks.com

1

October 12th, 1958, Pocono Lake, Pennsylvania

Clara Haggard left her bedroom and approached the front door of her cabin, staring out the window into the vastness of the woods. Red, brown, and orange leaves radiated under the sunlight, the trees watching her in unison. She gripped the doorknob so hard that it hurt. *There is no one out there*, she told herself. The cabin existed far away from civilization. No one would find her here. She opened the door to find the covered porch empty except for two rocking chairs. Chimes moved with the gentle breeze as she took a step. Paper crinkled under her shoe. Her eyebrows furrowed as she collected the familiar newspaper sitting on her doorstep. *The Flatbush Times*. She had never subscribed to that paper, and they didn't make deliveries this far out.

PSYCHOPATH STILL AT LARGE, MANHUNT UNDERWAY

Below the headline, there was a black-and-white portrait of a young woman wearing a dress with a cinched waist and a puffy skirt. The lady smiled with straight teeth and long hair, looking happy and in her late teens. Clara clenched the paper, nearly tearing it apart. There had to be someone spying on her; someone had left this paper on the doorstep for her. She returned inside and locked the door. After staring at the front page for a moment longer, she threw it into the garbage.

She walked past the tan loveseat in the living room that faced a wood-burning fireplace, along with a matching upholstered chair and end table. A couple of throw blankets were folded underneath the coffee table, and a bookshelf was bolted against the opposite wall, full of her favorite books arranged by color. She continued walking into the kitchen, up to the calendar hanging on the wall. The cabinets and countertop matched the wooden walls and floors. Another day crossed off.

Clara cracked a few eggs and turned on the gas stove, blue flames flickering under the pan. After whisking the eggs, she placed a couple pieces of bacon next to them. Sizzling, they filled the air with the most delicious scent. A bang came from the living room, causing Clara to drop the whisk. Drops of egg yolk splattered over the floor and on the side of the oven.

Not again. Her jaw tightened.

The end table lay on its side, while the rest of the room looked to be in order. Clara checked the front door, locked. One of the windows was open, though. Perhaps a gust of wind pushed over the end table? It was lightweight. Probably nothing. After taking deep breaths and standing it upright, Clara returned to the kitchen and finished making breakfast. She sat on a stool next to the counter, facing a wide window.

Too much time on her hands. Too much time to think. Alone with her thoughts. Nothing but peace and quiet. No noise from cars racing up and down the street, their horns blaring at one another. No police or ambulance sirens. Only the sounds of the leaves moving in the wind and birds chirping. Brooklyn had always been a better fit for her.

After eating and cleaning the kitchen, Clara walked out the

front door and locked it, putting a bag over her shoulder with some water, a pen, and a notepad. She took sunglasses off the collar of her gray dress, put them over her brown eyes, and pulled her long brown hair into a ponytail. No fuss. She climbed the hill for the 77th time.

Hundreds of birds flew from one tree to another on the branches above her. They chirped loudly, planning their escape to the south. Narrow beams of sunlight seeped between the branches and found her. The hill needed a river streaming down it, then it would be complete.

The bare spot at the top of the hill was her destination, where there was a small section that housed her garden with a couple of tomatoes remaining. Clara picked them and placed them inside her backpack. The plants would be dead soon enough. After setting her backpack on the ground, she lay on the grass and closed her eyes, taking deep breaths. The rapidly approaching winter would offer her no escape. No, she couldn't think about that now.

She sat up and took in the view. The curved hills, the trees, the strange shapes of the clouds. If she screamed, no one would be around to hear it. Or at least she hoped not.

Clara took out a pen and paper, thinking about what she should write to her mother. She did this once a day, every morning, while sitting on this hill or in the cabin if the weather kept her inside. She rested her hand on the page before shaking her pen. It must be running out of ink. Nothing to update her on. Every day was one and the same. No excitement or fun, all serious and dull. That was the purpose of this. Her purgatory.

Dear Mom,

Someone is watching me. I know it. Their eyes pierce through my body as I walk past a window or go on a hike. It's been 77 days since I escaped Brooklyn. No, escape isn't the right word. I moved here to find peace. But that doesn't seem to matter. My head feels like it's been cut off from my body with a pair of scissors, dissociated from what's occurring around me while still having a lingering connection. I know I'm meant to suffer; this is my purgatory. And I will suffer here until the end. I'm so sorry I had to leave. I miss you every day. I think about Dad every day. Tell him I'm sorry if you get a chance.

I do love this cabin, and I've found a routine that suits me. I've tried experimenting with new recipes, I've read so many books, and I draw nearly every day. Please send me a letter back, Mom. I'd love to hear from you. I need to know you're okay.

Love always,

Clara

She had sent seventy-six letters to her mother so far; all similar. The letters would never stop. No matter that her mother refused to write her back, she would continue reaching out. Clara returned the letter and pen to her bag. After spending an hour in the sun, down the hill she went.

When she laid her eyes on the cabin once again, her body tensed and her breaths became short. Her leg hesitated before lifting her foot onto the first step that led to the charming front porch. Clara braced herself for what could be waiting for her inside as she swung open the door. The family room was in complete disarray. Her books were thrown from the bookshelf all over the floor, some open and some closed. Her end table was tipped over again, and the blankets she had neatly folded on the back of the couch were on the floor. A teardrop streamed down Clara's cheek.

Clara picked her bookshelf off the floor and put it against the wall. Grabbing her screwdriver, she had to once again bolt the bookshelf to the wall. Her heart hammered in her chest, and she couldn't stop her eyes from welling up. Her home must be organized. Her home should always be clean; Clara lived there alone. She picked up the books one by one and organized them by color on the bookshelf. One book didn't belong.

The Executioners by John D. MacDonald. She never purchased this book; someone must have placed it there. She could go into town once every two weeks, and the only store she was allowed to go into was the grocery store. Anywhere else was against the rules.

Maybe she did buy that book and had forgotten about it until now. *Yes, I must have bought it*, she thought, placing the book on the shelf with the others.

The last book on the floor was *The 4:50 from Paddington* by Agatha Christie, one of her favorite novels. The spine was ripped, the pages falling out. *It's not a big deal*, she told herself. *It's only a book.* She sandwiched it in between two other books on the shelf. *From this point of view, the book looks whole.* Time to move on. She picked up her end table and blankets off of the floor, folding them neatly and stuffing them under her rectangular coffee table. All right, well, everything was where it should be.

That shouldn't have happened.

Let's do that again.

Clara approached the cabin after her hike and gave it a small smile, a sense of calm washing over her. It was her sanctuary in the woods, and she enjoyed living there. She always felt so alone in Brooklyn, although she was constantly surrounded by crowds of people. It was a process coming to terms with living with herself, but she came to a deeper understanding of the inner workings of her mind. For better or for worse.

The woods were quiet and tranquil as she entered her perfectly neat cabin. The family room was organized to her liking, looking the same as how she had left it. She walked to her lovely bookshelf and pulled *The 4:50 from Paddington* by Agatha Christie off the top shelf. It was one of her favorites. Not to mention it was in mint condition.

Clara picked up the book to find the pages falling out of the spine. *No, it is not broken!* No, the book was not broken.

Again.

She picked up the book to find it as new as the day she had purchased it. She returned it to the shelf. Clara made sure to care for her books, as they were her proudest possessions. Time to make herself a cup of tea. Clara paced in the kitchen with her arms crossed, waiting for the water to boil. The tea kettle screamed, the water ready to be poured. After making her tea, Clara sat on the upholstered chair in the living room, setting the tea on the end table. Her journal sat on her coffee table, and Clara stared at it, picked it up, and opened it to the next blank page. She readied her pen to sketch.

The image of the young girl from the newspaper. The alleged psychopath, according to the journalist who wrote it. That was presumptuous of him. Clara drew the lady's high cheekbones, heart-shaped face, and a strained smile, adding a few tears on her cheeks. She drew her in a lacy black dress and had her wear a matching veil covering her forehead. The lady held a cigarette in one hand with smoke rising from it, while she clenched a knife with the other. Standing on top of the bones of the men she murdered.

Clara stopped drawing. She slammed her journal shut and tossed it onto the coffee table, along with her pen. It was time to run a bath. The day molded into night, and darkness surrounded Clara's cabin as she went into the bathroom. Steam rose from the water, filling the room and fogging up the mirror. She took off her gray dress and undergarments, climbing inside the tub. She leaned her head back, closing her eyes and breathing in the heavy, misty air. Nothing could beat a soothing bath after a long day. She hummed "Hush, Little Baby," a song her mother sang to her every night when she was little. Why didn't her mother ever write her back? Clara would never turn her back on her mother. She would die before it could ever come to that.

The thought escaped her when someone knocked on her bathroom door. She sat up in the bathtub, gripping the sides. The locked doorknob twisted and turned. Clara froze, holding her breath as the water rippled. The small gap between the door and floor revealed a shadow of shoes. Clara shut her eyes, turning her head to face the back wall. She reopened them, moving her gaze slowly over to the door where the shadow had vanished.

Clara crawled out of the tub, putting on her nightgown and bracing herself for who might have been standing there. She opened the door slowly, and there was no one. The water in the tub drained as she stepped into the kitchen. The window was left open, letting in a chilly breeze. As she went to close it, she halted. Fog in the shape of a mouth was left on it. Someone had breathed on that window. Clara slammed it shut, checking every inch of the cabin to ensure no one was hiding. The front and back doors remained locked.

Clara crossed her arms and let out a sigh. Her bedroom door was cracked open, leading to a dark and small room. She didn't like closing the door. Every creak made her jump from bed. Exhausted, but her body still refused to let her fall asleep.

It was too cold for comfort in the cabin. She lay in bed, covering herself with a heavy quilt. The woods provided a chilling breeze, somehow permeating through the thick walls. She stared at the ceiling blankly, trying not to think about any of her victims. Some of them pleaded with her to let them live before taking their last breaths. They deserved it; Clara shouldn't feel sorry. Except for one of them. She should have let him live. Why hadn't she let him live?

Taking deep breaths, Clara closed her eyes for a moment. She reopened them to find a man hovering above her, his body horizontal to hers. His face was a few feet away and his eyes were sunken, round, and black, and his mouth hung open. He looked young with his hair shaved, wearing white pajamas. Blood soaked through his shirt from his chest and dripped onto her quilt.

Frozen. Holding her breath. Too frightened to scream. Eyes shut. Body shaking. *Please be gone. Please be gone!* Eyes opened. The man disappeared, along with the blood on her quilt. Her heart beat out of her chest as she tried desperately to catch her breath. The air was too thick. She put her shaking right hand over her chest and turned on the lamp with the other, nearly knocking it off the nightstand. She wanted to leave the room, but someone might be waiting for her on the other side of her bedroom door.

After a few moments, she opened it to find no one and walked into the kitchen to get some water. She could barely hold the glass steady enough to drink from it. She turned on all the lights, checking to make sure the back door was locked, the closets were empty, and no one lay under the beds. As Clara double checked the front door lock, the newspaper sat on top of the garbage, staring at her. The psychopath on the loose, the authorities hunting her down. She picked it up again and stared at the young woman on the front cover.

The young woman was her.

2

Three Months Earlier, July 11th, 1958, Brooklyn, NY

Oliver Anderson waited by the coffeemaker in the break room, putting his hands in his pockets and checking the clock. Thirty minutes to go until the weekend. The coffee dripped as a couple of men walked by him, talking about how much they were sweating. Oliver wrinkled his nose; they really were sweating. After pouring himself a cup, he started to clean out the residue inside the coffeemaker when he remembered that wasn't his job anymore. So back to his desk he went. A coworker cut him off, causing Oliver to almost spill some of the drink on his white shirt.

"No, that's fine," he whispered after the man didn't acknowledge him. "Thanks for apologizing, though!"

He returned to his desk, taking a sip and placing the mug on the chipped, wobbly desk. He straightened his pens and pencils so they were parallel with his typewriter, and he fixed the pile of completed cards. One more obituary left to go.

Martha Taylor (née Black). Born on September 7th, 1876, passed away on July 7th, 1958. Survived by her eight

children, Rebecca, Mary, James, John, Helen, William, Charles, and Walter, twenty-two grandchildren, and five great-grandchildren. She will be greatly missed. Funeral service at St. Catherine of Sienna at 10 o'clock on July 14th. Interment at Holy Cross Cemetery.

Done.

He typed every last obituary from the pile on his desk since lunch, so he sat back in his chair and took a cleansing breath, fixing his curly brown hair.

The noise in the large room consisted of typewriters, ringing telephones, and men discussing subjects ranging from politics, sports, and the weather. The air smelled musty, probably due to the high humidity and heat. Men kept walking to the windows for relief, only to remember they didn't open. The breeze would be too hot anyway. Oliver doubted it would cool the place down one bit. The hanging lights didn't help either, as heat radiated from them. Oliver moved his desk over as much as he could, so that a light didn't hang directly over him. The rich managers were tucked away in spacious offices, while the rest were placed in tiny cubicles on a large floor. Everyone seemed to know everyone's business.

That was why Oliver always kept his mouth shut.

"A couple more deaths!" said his assistant, Alex, bringing Oliver a new stack and slamming it onto his desk. The break was short-lived, but it was nice while it lasted.

"You're joking," Oliver said, shaking his head.

"You're working at a good pace, though. The last guy was always way behind, and that's why he was thrown out onto the street."

"Thanks for the reminder." Oliver joked as Alex hit him on his back.

"Any plans this weekend?" Alex shifted from one foot to the other.

"I think I'll spend some time with my brother and his family."

"That's nice."

"What are you up to?"

"Listening to the Dodgers games." Alex smiled. "I better get going. I need to mail out a letter for Frank."

Alex ran away while Oliver chuckled to himself. Oliver had recently been promoted to the obituaries department at the *Flatbush Times.* He sighed and stared at the pile. When he finished one pile, another came. He shouldn't complain, though. It had taken him a few years to be promoted to this position.

But it was tedious. Writing down the correct spelling of their names, the correct birthdays and death dates, the correct spelling of their relatives, and writing about their lives which always meant they were outstanding citizens, prospered in their work, and were the best family men and housewives to have ever lived. Most of it had to be bullshit, but their obituary would be in a popular newspaper in one of the largest cities in the world. If you're going to go out, might as well go out with a bang.

Oh, and another thing. The horrible penmanship. Deciphering the handwritten notes was a tall order.

Oliver should be thankful for this promotion. Increased pay and no more handwashing mugs, and sometimes cleaning the bathrooms, as well as having to kiss up to the bosses who mocked him and told him he would never make it as a reporter. He still wrote during his free time...

Having a job typing obituaries was not the kind of writing he had in mind, but he had to start somewhere. Oliver cracked his knuckles and picked up the next note.

Robert Cassidy Jr., known as Robby. Born on October 1st, 1907, and passed away on July 2nd, 1958. Survived by his loving wife, Cindy, their three children, Linda Smith, Robert Cassidy III, John Cassidy, and five grandchildren.

At least they didn't include his grandchildren's names. And their names were common and easy to spell. Oliver should be able to type it out in no time. He didn't need to include the cause of death, but he couldn't stop himself from reading them.

Cause of death: Robert Cassidy Jr. suffered blunt force trauma to the head after being impaled by a sign hanging over the entrance to Devin's Tool Shop.

Oliver grimaced. What a horrible way to die.

Done. Next.

Bernhard Altenhofen.

Great. That was one hell of a name. He began typing, reading his name letter by letter and triple-checking his work. He would never want to misspell someone's name in their obituary; that would be a disrespectful act. They included a copy of the man's death record. His cause of death: *stabbing himself in the heart.*

"Oh, no," he sighed. "Sorry, Bernie."

He started typing out the name, feeling washed over with guilt. The poor man killed himself, and it might have been because his name was hard to spell.

Poor guy.

Bernhard Altenhofen, known as Bernie. Born on June 21st, 1923, and died on July 5th, 1958. He is survived by his wife, Lena, six brothers, mother Brenda, and father Heinrich. A gifted golfer. He will be missed. Funeral service at Church of the Holy Innocents on July 15th at 10 o'clock, and will be laid to rest in Holy Cross Cemetery.

Oliver finished typing details about the date and time of the funeral and placed it in the "finished" bin. His assistant, Alex, would take Oliver's work to the next department at the end of the day. Speaking of the end of the day, he looked at his clock to find five o'clock had finally come. He drank the rest of the coffee and collected his belongings.

"See you later, Alex," Oliver said as he walked by Alex's desk and handed him his day's work.

"See you Monday!" Alex waved after adjusting his glasses. "Have a good weekend!"

"Thanks, you too!"

Oliver approached the elevator, surrounded by other men, and waited; the down-arrow button already pressed. He worked on the sixth floor. Taking the stairs was manageable but inconvenient, especially in ninety-degree heat. The elevator arrived, and at least ten men piled inside. With the number of men trying to squeeze into the elevator, the weight had to be straining. Oliver had typed an obituary a couple weeks ago about a man who got onto a supposedly up-to-code elevator, but the steel wires snapped as he and six of his friends rode it. The elevator plummeted to the ground floor and killed him instantly. With that in mind, Oliver opted to take the stairs. Though he didn't want to sweat through his suit, it was better than the alternative. As he reached the ground floor, the elevator dinged and everyone poured out and went their separate ways.

Oh, no, Oliver thought. He had already made eye contact with her; it was too late. The receptionist approached Oliver, fixing her blonde hair. She always perked up at the sight of him, adjusting her clothes and rubbing her lips together. "Hi, Oliver. How was your shift today?"

"It went well, how was yours?" he asked politely.

"Good. We're always busy and hustling." She giggled. "Any plans tonight?"

That was a hint, but he would not be taking it. "Yes, I'm visiting my brother, sister-in-law, and nephew."

"That's nice. I might head to the beach this weekend, maybe Coney Island. Have you ever been?"

"Yes, many times. It's great there, you'll have fun with your friends."

"Thanks!" She flipped her hair over her shoulder.

There was a pause between them.

"I better get going."

"Okay." She waved at him. "See you Monday!"

"Have a nice weekend!"

"Thank you, Oliver, you too!"

He pushed open the entrance doors, revealing a bustling city with crowded sidewalks and streets. Horns, sirens, and chatter from non-stop car and foot traffic. Oliver thought it was rude of himself to dread speaking with her every morning and evening, but he made an effort to be polite.

Oliver walked around groups of young families, teens giggling and smoking, and old men complaining about the loudness of radios in cars as they drove by. One never knew the type of people they would run into and meet in Brooklyn. Oliver guessed that was what made it more exciting.

Leo's Pizzeria was on his way to his brother's apartment, so he wrestled his way around the flow of traffic and stopped inside. After the man in front of him received his pizza, Oliver approached the counter.

"Hello, Oliver!" Leo said, scratching his bald head and holding a notepad and pen. "What can I get for you?"

Oliver gave him a smile. "Hi, Leo. I'll have a medium cheese pizza, please, half pepperoni."

The counter was almost as tall as Leo as he wrote down the order. Smoke came out of the large pizza oven behind him, and flour was everywhere, ending up on Oliver's sleeves. Workers raced around the kitchen. One spun dough in the air, while another poured sauce over the dough and spread it around. Men sat at the few tables in the closet-sized restaurant, chatting or reading newspapers. Oliver didn't know how they could stand the heat. It must be a hundred degrees in this place.

"Sure, that'll be $1.50, please." Leo's shirt was full of sweat and grease. Oliver handed him the money, and Leo placed it in his cash register. He told the order to a young man, giving him the instructions in Italian. He turned to Oliver again. "Say, how's George doing? Such a great kid."

"He's doing well, I think," Oliver nodded. "He's seeing the best doctors in the city."

"Is the pizza for him?"

"Yeah, I'm on my way to Marcus's apartment."

"Take the money back, it's on the house!"

Oliver waved his hand. "No, no, no, but thank you for the gesture. It's very kind of you."

"Send him my best, Oliver," he said, handing the box of pizza to him.

"I will, Leo. Thank you."

He traveled a few more blocks to his brother's apartment complex, standing in front of the entrance and pressing the buzzer. It didn't make a sound; it still must be broken. A resident walked out, holding the door open for him, and he thanked her and stepped inside. With no option for an elevator, he climbed the stairs that creaked like his feet would fall straight through, and wood pieces chipped off them. *I'm definitely sweating now*, Oliver thought, reaching the fourth floor. A door slammed inside his brother's apartment. He held out his fist for a couple seconds before knocking on their apartment door a few times, and Marcus whipped it open.

"Oliver, you shouldn't have!" Marcus said, taking the pizza. Oliver followed him into his one-bedroom apartment, which had peeling wallpaper and scratched hardwood floors. The kitchen had white cabinets that needed another coat of paint. Marcus set the box on the green counter and opened it, taking a piece for himself.

"How's George doing today?" Oliver asked.

Marcus wiped his mouth with a paper towel, running his other hand through his black, poker-straight hair. "He's hanging in there, and he loves the summer heat; it makes him feel better. Nancy said he got a good night's sleep last night, so his energy seems to be a little better today. I guess he did well in his lessons."

"That's good."

Marcus walked to the mirror hanging on the wall by the front door. He combed his mustache, adjusted his tie, and picked out a hat from the coat rack. "I have to get going."

Oliver leaned against the kitchen counter and crossed his arms. "Where do you have to go?"

"I have an urgent meeting with a patient."

"A patient?" asked Oliver, lowering his voice. "On a Friday night after you've finished your shift?"

"Yeah," Marcus smirked, opening the door. "Her name's Melissa, she's a special case. I'll see you later."

The door closed as Oliver shook his head and rubbed his eyelids.

Nancy stepped into the kitchen and leaned against the counter. Her eyes were swollen and red, and her ivory dress looked like it was a faint yellow. "Hi, Ollie!"

"Hey, Nance. Is everything all right?"

Maybe it was Nancy who slammed the door earlier.

"Yeah, everything's fine. We-we just got into a little bit of an argument, that's all. You didn't have to bring us supper. You're too much!"

Nancy changed the subject; she probably didn't want to discuss it further.

"Oh, stop it! I'm making the big bucks now, remember?" Oliver said. If only that were the case. Yes, he made more now than he ever has, but that wasn't saying much.

She nodded, touching Oliver's arm briefly and giving him a smile. "Well, you're going to make George's day."

"He is my favorite nephew."

Nancy giggled as they walked into the living room. That always made her laugh. Oliver turned his attention to George, who sat on the tan couch under a large window, hitting cars together. "I brought some pizza, George! Are you hungry?"

"Yeah, I want pizza!"

"Let me get you a slice!"

Oliver grabbed a slice of pizza and a napkin, then handed them to him. George grinned at Oliver, taking a bite. Oliver rubbed George's brown hair, getting a laugh out of him. He sat beside him.

"You're going to get so big and strong, and you'll be ready to take on kindergarten!"

"You really think so?"

"I really do." Oliver took a slice and accepted a glass of water from Nancy. She sat on the other side of George, stroking his hair. She fixed her curled brown hair; it matched her eyes. "How is it, George?"

"Good!"

"So, it's been a couple months now since starting this new job, right?" she asked, standing and leaning against the opposite wall. Oliver nodded. "How is it going?"

"It's going well," he said. "I hope I'll be able to continue moving up. The work is tedious and not at all creative or investigative, but I do get to read about some strange deaths, so I guess that's something."

"Oh, like what? Just spare George's ears from hearing details."

"A man was recently stabbed through the heart." Oliver made a funny face and pretended to stab himself with the crust of his pizza. George laughed. Oliver had to make light of it; he didn't want George to have nightmares.

Nancy shook her head. "You promised me you would share any weird deaths, yet this is the first one you've told me about."

"Some of them are disturbing."

"And?"

Oliver chuckled as she raised her eyebrows at him.

"Let me get you some napkins, George," she said.

As Nancy returned from the kitchen, Oliver stood, crumpling the napkin in his hand. "Well, I'd better get going."

Her smile faded for a moment, and she fixed her posture. "Oh, all right. Can I talk to you in the hallway for a second?"

"Sure. See you later, George!"

"Bye, Uncle Ollie!" George waved to him. Oliver patted him on his head again before he and Nancy left the apartment and stood in the narrow hallway. She shut the door so George couldn't overhear her. She held out a check Oliver had written her and Marcus, but Oliver didn't take it.

"We're not taking this," she said.

"Come on, Nance. I can afford it, I'm making the big bucks now."

Nancy didn't laugh this time. "No. It's a wonderful gesture that we appreciate, but we're making out okay on our own. Since downsizing, we have had enough money to get George the best doctors in the city."

"Marcus is stubborn."

"You know him too well." She showed off her dimples. "You're a great brother to him, and a great uncle to George. Take the check, Ollie."

He sighed as she continued to move the check over his hand. He took it, placing it in his pocket. "If you ever need anything, let me know."

"I will, thank you. Marcus is trying to get George an appointment next Friday, and you should see the resume of this doctor. They think it must be psychological. I finally have some hope again."

"I've been praying for him. He's such a great kid, it'll work out."

"Thank you, Ollie." She touched his shoulder, her eyes becoming glossy. "Have fun tonight, you deserve it!"

"I could stay longer if you want," he offered.

"No, Ollie, go have fun! We'll see you around."

Nancy hugged him tightly. Oliver walked down the hallway toward the stairwell, looking back once at Nancy as she returned to her apartment. He headed down the stairwell and through the front entrance out onto the sidewalk, once again maneuvering around the crowds. His apartment was a five-minute walk from theirs, making it easy to check in on George. He enjoyed bringing him surprises to brighten his day.

In his complex, he took the elevator to the seventh floor, walked down the hallway to his apartment, and passed Fluffy, an orange cat lying in front of his neighbor's door. Oliver petted him briefly before picking up the newspaper on his doormat. He unlocked his door, set down his briefcase and keys, and flipped through the pages to the obituaries. One day he would make it to the front page and write stories as a proper journalist. One of the seniors in those positions would have to die first. Still, he had to pinch himself that the words he typed made it into a popular paper. *One day, one day.*

Oliver's one-bedroom apartment was spotless. There was a single red couch with end tables opposite a table with a record player and a pile of records. This led into the small but open dark brown kitchen, where Oliver made a pot of coffee. His windows overlooked the brick building next door. Oliver hadn't bought a kitchen table yet. He had a list of things to buy to make it homey.

He washed his face in the blue sink in the bathroom, combed his hair and changed into a tan suit. Oliver took a sip of coffee, then slammed his mug onto the counter. Coffee splashed onto his bright blue counters and black-and-white tiled flooring. Marcus shouldn't be putting him in this position. Oliver cleaned the mess and tidied himself up. The time was 5:50 p.m. He left for Grayson's Pub, one of Marcus's usual hangouts.

3

July 11th, 1958, Brooklyn, NY

A fist pounded against Clara Haggard's townhouse door. Well, her parents' townhouse door. Well, technically, her father's townhouse door. He was out doing God knows what, but that worked in her favor on an evening like this. Clara rolled her eyes, leaning a broom against the wall in the kitchen. She didn't have time to explain herself, already telling her friends that she didn't want to go out with them tonight. They never liked to take no for an answer.

"I'm coming!" Clara yelled as she sprinted through the orderly kitchen and living room to open the door. Kate smiled, one hand on her hip and the other holding a cigarette, her white teeth a stark contrast to her deep red lipstick. Betty stood beside her, holding a purse. Both of their hair was curled, and they wore brightly colored dresses, mint green and pink.

"Clara, are you coming or what?" Kate said, fixing her poofy skirt.

Clara shook her head. The grandfather clock ticked in the

corner of the living room, the time inching closer to six. "I told you I can't. I have plans tonight."

"Be more specific."

"That's as specific as I want to be." Clara crossed her arms. Kate tilted her head and crossed her arms, imitating her.

"You never hang out with us anymore!" Betty said.

"Who are you seeing?" Kate asked.

"Kate, come on! I have things to do."

Kate inhaled her cigarette. "Who are you seeing? I asked you a question."

"I'm not seeing anyone. You would be the first to know, I promise."

"I don't believe you!" Betty yelled, pointing her finger at Clara. "Liar, liar!"

Clara moved a strand of her hair behind her shoulder as Betty laughed. "Oh, stop! I'm telling the truth."

"All right, yeah, sure," Kate sighed, looking at Betty with a frown. "You're going to miss out on a wild night."

"Have a good time!" Clara forced a smile as she waved them goodbye. As soon as Kate and Betty turned and descended the stairs leading to the street, Clara's smile washed away. They had no idea how easy they had it. So naïve, so clueless. Maybe that was how eighteen-year-olds were supposed to be. Clara closed the door and climbed the stairs to her bathroom. It was time to get ready. She lifted a loose white tile from the floor and took out her makeup case, setting it on the green countertop. She stared at herself in the large mirror, putting on bright red lipstick, black eyeliner, and dark gray eyeshadow, then put on minimal blush to her cheeks. Returning the makeup case under the tile, she curled her hair and put on a black taffeta dress with a fitted bodice and a full skirt, puckering her lips in the mirror. She tied a black ribbon in her hair and inserted a hair clip to hold her bangs back. Clara posed in front of the mirror, then left the bathroom and walked down the stairs.

Someone knocked on the front door. Was it Kate and Betty

again? *You've got to be kidding me.* The clock kept ticking. As she reached to open the door, Clara's mother burst in, carrying several grocery bags.

"Hi, Mom," Clara said. "Do you need help with those bags?"

"Hi, honey," she said, walking through the spacious living room to the kitchen table and setting them down. "No, I'm fine. Thanks for cleaning the floors, but you didn't have to do that!"

"You're welcome." Clara took the groceries out of the bag, putting them in their proper place in the cabinets or the shiny white refrigerator: cereal, bread, milk, and TV dinners. Her mother handed her a bag of apples, which Clara arranged in a wooden bowl on the red-tiled counter by the sink.

"I see you're ready to go out with your friends, huh?" her mother asked.

Clara turned to her, tensing up, then nodding and relaxing her shoulders. "Yeah, Kate practically begged me to go with her."

"I'm glad you're spending some time out of the house. You're so young, you should enjoy it!" Her mother tugged at her dress. "I love that dress!"

"Thanks, Mom!" Clara gave her a hug and headed toward the door.

"Don't be out too late. Be back before your father comes home."

"I will!"

"And don't get into too much trouble!" she joked.

"Yeah, sure!" Clara put on her black gloves and grabbed her purse off the front table, and headed out the door.

Ah, the streets of New York, how wonderful they are.

The heat was getting worse with each passing day, but Clara didn't mind it. The heat brought her sanity, allowing her to focus on the task at hand. She carried her boxy black purse in her right hand and tapped her heels against the pavement. Clara put on her sunglasses and lit a cigarette. She would live in this city until the day she died. The electric energy, the never-ending noise, the distractions. She inhaled her cigarette as she walked among the crowds on the sidewalk to her destination, Grayson's Pub. Kate was right in accusing Clara of lying because Clara did have a date tonight. A special someone she had met briefly a couple times before.

As Clara passed by a newspaper stand, she jerked her neck toward it and stepped backward. The headline caught her attention as she squinted to read it.

BERNHARD ALTENHOFEN'S DEATH RULED A HOMICIDE

Below, it read: ***Investigators following leads after Bernhard Altenhofen found dead with a stab wound in his chest on July 5th. Police have begun interviewing family and friends of Altenhofen but have no top suspects at this time as the investigation continues. If you have any information about Altenhofen or this case, do not hesitate to contact the New York Police Department.***

Bernie Altenhofen's picture was on the page, showing a scruffy beard and a round-shaped face with a good head of hair. He looked to be in his thirties at most.

"Sad about that young man, huh?" the worker asked.

"Yeah," she said, looking away from his portrait.

The older man stroked his white beard, sitting on a stool by the stand. "There's some sick people in this city."

"Yeah," Clara repeated quietly, inhaling her cigarette before dropping it on the ground and pressing it with her heel. She moved along to the bar.

Grayson's Pub was an average hole-in-the-wall with great drinks and friendly bartenders. There were exposed brick walls, scratched hardwood floors, and a darkened atmosphere with most light coming through the front windows. The teenagers, too young to drink, sat in booths, drinking soda pops and gossiping about their classmates' love lives. Clara smirked, gazing around the room for her special someone. She sat at the bar alone, having not found him, and glanced at a clock. *6:15 p.m. Shit.* They were supposed to meet at six; she hoped she didn't miss him. Men sat at the bar, talking so loudly it was easy to overhear their conversations. Clara tuned them out.

"Can I get you anything, miss?" the bartender asked.

"I'm fine for now, thanks."

The back door opened, and a bell rang. There he was, standing six feet one with a groomed mustache and a black hat matching his suit. Her sweetheart, her man. She gave him a smile and tapped her fingers on the countertop. He sat next to her, took off his hat, and rubbed his hair. Clara fought the urge to roll her eyes. He had his wedding ring on. How silly of her to expect him to take it off.

"Are you Melissa?" he asked, taking out a cigarette and smoking.

"I am," Clara said. "Are you Marcus?"

He nodded, smoke pouring out of his mouth and nostrils.

"What's wrong, my darling?" she asked, resting her chin on her hand. Men loved to be stared at in awe and given a woman's full attention, making them feel like the most interesting man alive. Clara would hang on his every word like she needed them to breathe.

"Nothing important. Family drama."

"Don't get me started on family drama. I also have my fill." Clara held out her hand, and Marcus handed her his cigarette. She inhaled it and handed it back. "But that's not why we're here, now are we?"

Marcus chuckled.

"You have such long legs." He stroked up and down her leg under her skirt.

Clara crossed her legs, glancing around the bar. No one seemed to be paying attention to them. "Where do you want to go?"

"I have a nice place."

He started to stand, but she placed her hand on his chest. "Where are you going? I'm not going anywhere until we've had a few drinks."

Marcus smiled and gestured to the bartender to come over. He ordered whiskey, and she could order a beer.

"Did I mention I'm a psychiatrist?" he asked.

"No, but that sounds interesting."

"Oh, it's fascinating. It's the one area in my life I got right. A patient of mine finally fell asleep last night after staying up for nearly two weeks. It was wonderful to witness, and she felt much better and more relaxed the next day. I'm hoping I go into work on Monday and hear that she slept well tonight and the next two nights. I can't wait to see her progress."

Clara leaned forward. "Why did she stay awake for so long?"

"Her mind simply wouldn't allow her to sleep. The mind is powerful; it can ruin you."

A man approached Marcus, slapping him on the back. His thick eyebrows matched his mustache. He leaned in toward Marcus's ear as the bartender handed Marcus and Clara their drinks.

"I'm still waiting on $300," the man said. "You're running out of time, Marcus."

"I said I'll get it to you," Marcus snapped.

"I'm counting on that." The man hit Marcus across his back and walked out of the pub. Clara stared at the bar counter until the door slammed shut.

"Thank you," Clara said to the bartender. He glanced at Marcus for a second and moved on to other customers.

"What was that all about?" she asked, running her fingers through Marcus's hair.

He shrugged. "Nothing."

The clock ticked in the corner. 6:30 p.m. Clara slowly sipped her beer, while Marcus ordered one drink after another. Spending time studying men at bars gave her useful information. Men could be overpowered by a woman half their size when they were tipsy. Men also couldn't have too many drinks; some men became angry drunks. Marcus had to be in the sweet spot: loopy, but still having his faculties.

The clock chimed at 7 p.m. Marcus had four drinks, the perfect amount for a man of his size. The next step was getting to his apartment.

"Ready to go?" Clara asked, as a smile crept onto Marcus's face. He tossed money onto the counter, gripping her hand tightly and leading her out the door onto the busy sidewalk. The sun scorched the earth as Clara squinted and held her hand over her eyes. Marcus gestured toward a sparkling blue Corvette and opened the passenger door for her. She climbed inside and sat on the white leather seat as he closed the door for her. The heat from the seats permeated through her dress as Marcus sat in the driver's seat and turned the key.

"What a gorgeous car!" She rolled the window down and stuck her arm outside it, moving her hand around in the hot air. Marcus turned the radio louder, playing "Jailhouse Rock" by Elvis Presley and pulling away from the bar. Clara leaned her head back on the seat as Marcus took out a cigarette and handed Clara the lighter. She lit it while he held it in his mouth. She lit one herself and exhaled the smoke, watching it leave the car and into the city air.

"Is this place private?" Clara asked. But of course she knew exactly where he was taking her.

"No one knows about it except me. I'm sure you won't tell a soul about it or what's about to happen, right Melissa?"

"Of course not. Not a soul."

He parked on the street next to an upscale apartment complex not too far from her father's townhouse and turned off the car. Marcus walked over to her side and opened the door for her. Reaching his arm out toward her, she took it with a smile. His hand was steady and firm, as he helped her out of the car and into the building. They took the elevator to the fifth floor in silence, and once they reached his place, he opened the door to a nicely furnished apartment. It had black-and-white checkered flooring with blue cabinets and matching countertops. Two couches and a blue table with leather chairs complimented the floral wallpaper. A spacious, two-bedroom apartment.

"This is beautiful," she said, looking around. The place was spotless.

Marcus turned to her, gripping her shoulders, his fingertips digging into her skin. He leaned over and kissed her as she moved backward. Clara held his tie to prevent herself from falling over. He tried to move the zipper of her dress downward, but thankfully, it was stubborn. Clara took a step backward.

As they kissed, she guided him into the kitchen. She sat on the countertop as he kissed her neck and moved closer to her. Clara glanced around herself. A knife set sat on the counter by the refrigerator. She reached out, stretching as far as possible, for the largest knife in the collection. Marcus kissed her on the mouth again, as her fingers barely touched the largest knife in the knife set. He grabbed her hip with one hand, putting his other hand up her skirt. Clara kicked his legs as a reflex, pushing him away from her.

"You must think I'm stupid, don't you?" He laughed. "I recognized you the moment I saw you. You're an unhinged psychopath. You're sick. I've had patients just like you." Clara gasped with widened eyes as Marcus smiled at her, took a few steps backward, and tried to steady himself. "If you don't give me what I came here for, I can walk you right to your father's front door and tell him all about our meetup."

She stuttered, trying to catch her breath. "What if I tell your wife?"

"I'll tell her you're one of my patients who fantasizes about me. She'll never believe you, Clara."

Clara moved further back on the counter at the sound of her name, the back of her head hitting against the cabinet. "I can tell my father you assaulted me!"

Marcus waved and grinned. "Your father will never believe you, either."

Her heart felt like it could break through her ribs. This has never happened before.

"You're going to give me what you promised," he said, moving closer to her again. The stench of his whiskey breath climbed her nostrils.

Clara shook her head. He approached her, grabbing her wrist and dragging her off the counter. She elbowed him in his gut, causing him to bend over and put his hands over his stomach. She tried to reach for the knife again, but he wrapped his arm around her neck and slammed the back of her head onto the kitchen counter. He crushed her neck, trying to pull her toward a bedroom. Clara bit his wrist, and he grimaced, letting her go. She pulled a knife out of the set and raised it high, stabbing him. The knife broke the skin and went through his chest, blood gushing from it.

Clara backed away from him. Marcus fell flat on his back with his arms flailing and blood pouring out from his chest and spreading over the floor.

Clara let out a sigh of relief, backing away from his body as his muscles twitched. It was done at last. Now she had to leave. She dropped the knife onto the floor, it collided harshly with the tiled floors and chipped one. She ran into the bathroom and gripped the porcelain sink, staring at her reflection. Her makeup was smeared across her face, and the tears dragged her mascara and eyeliner down her cheeks. Clara removed her gloves, shoving them into her purse, and glided her fingers over the imprints of Marcus's fingertips on her neck, wincing. Her wrists had scratch marks on them from his fingernails, and her dress was torn on the left shoulder.

Clara took deep breaths, holding her stomach. *You can do this. You can do this.* It had never gone that far before. He tried to drag her into the bedroom... No, no time to think about it. The most important part was that he was dead, and her work for tonight was complete. Her hands shook as she turned on the two faucets. She washed her face, taking off all her makeup and cleaning up around her eyes with a few tissues. She tried to neaten her hair, laying it on her shoulders to cover the tear in her dress and the marks on her neck.

That wouldn't be good enough. Her dress had blood stains on it. It being black didn't hide it well enough, not for during the daylight. Clara stuffed the tissues in her purse and put on her gloves again. She couldn't walk down the busy streets with blood splattered on her dress. She sprinted past Marcus's body who lay beside puddles of blood, into the bedroom and threw open a closet. His bare clothing essentials hung inside: one pair of pants, one dress shirt, a couple of blazers and ties, and a trench coat. The trench coat, it was. She threw it on, buttoning it and tying the belt around her waist. It was huge on her; the sleeves were far longer than her arms, the length of it reaching her ankles. She didn't have a choice; there was no better option.

Two people knew about their meetup tonight, and one of them was dead, so she would leave his body and the murder weapon as-is. No need to complicate things further; she needed to get out of this apartment.

Clara walked past Marcus's body again, her heels tapping and his blood continuing to spread over the tiles, and closed the door. The world blurred around her as she walked speedily down the hallway, bypassing the elevator for the stairs. Her heels echoed through the stairwell as she made her way to the bottom floor. The sun hadn't set as she left the apartment complex and passed his shiny blue Corvette in the street. Marcus would never drive it to cheat on his wife ever again. Clara put on her sunglasses and kept her head down, checking her watch. 8:00. Hopefully, her mother was correct in saying that her father wouldn't be home until 9.

Only one way to find out.

4

The streets of New York City were empty with steam rising from the manholes on the sidewalks and the sun beating down on them. *Where is everyone? Not a sound,* Oliver thought. The brick buildings stood tall on either side of the street with no cars in sight. The traffic light turned from red to green, but no one was around to heed it. A man appeared before Oliver, stepping toward him on the sidewalk. He was young, looked to be around fifty, wearing a tailored beige suit. He waved toward Oliver as if he knew him. Oliver waved back reluctantly, standing still. The man continued toward him then stopped. Oliver tried to figure out what the man was waiting for. A metal sign swung above the man's head for Devin's Tool Shop, its rusty metal scraping against the thin pole sticking out from above the entrance with every breeze. Oliver gasped, his body freezing.

"MOVE!" Oliver ran toward him. "Sir, you need to move!"

It was too late. The sign dropped, splitting the man's skull into two, his eyes, nose, and his brain falling onto the sidewalk in front him. The faceless man remained standing. He reached out toward Oliver and walked toward him as Oliver backed away.

Oliver jolted upward from bed with the piercing sound of his telephone ringing on the wall. He rubbed his eyes and yawned. The ringing stopped. He drifted off to sleep last night after hours of tossing and turning, thinking about the last argument he had with his brother. He lay in bed again, staring at the ceiling with his hands folded over his stomach. Oliver didn't want to get out of bed, but the phone rang a second time. He jumped and ran into the kitchen, picking it up. "Hello?"

"Ollie..." It was Nancy, her voice shaky. She was crying.

"What's wrong?" Oliver asked, holding his breath.

"It-It's Marcus, Ollie. I'm so worried. He's still not home. I called the hospital, and they said he never came in last night. This has never happened before; I-I have no idea where he is."

"Nance, it'll be all right," he said, placing his other hand on the wall and crossing his legs. "I'll go to his hangouts and see if I can find any information."

"Should I call the police?"

"I don't think we need to get them involved yet. Stay strong for George, you don't want to get him all worried."

Nancy took a deep breath. "You're right. I'm sorry, Ollie, I'm on edge that's all. I have a terrible feeling."

"Don't be sorry. I'll find him, I promise."

"Thank you."

"I'll keep you updated."

They said goodbye, and Oliver hung up the phone, hanging his head and sighing. This was bound to happen. Nancy was probably up all night, waiting for Marcus to come home. He could picture her lying in bed, wide awake. Eventually, she would get out of bed and pace the floor to try to get rid of her nervous energy. Her eyes welling up, her hands shaking. She called him at the crack of dawn, waiting until it was an acceptable time to call. Oliver clenched his fists. How many times over the years did he have to tell Marcus to behave? Marcus engaged in such deplorable behavior, and Oliver always had to clean up his mess.

After marrying Nancy, Marcus would return home before midnight to keep a facade that Marcus went out to bars to drink with friends, nothing more. Not only did it not work, Oliver told him it would catch up with him, eventually. That was what Oliver said when he confronted his brother last night at Grayson's Pub. Oliver pressed his hand against his forehead, his mind drifting back to the previous evening.

* * *

Oliver arrived at Grayson's Pub at 6:00 p.m. last night. The bar roared as groups of teens laughed, sitting in the circular booths against the right wall, while men chatted loudly at the bar. A couple elderly men sat at the end, playing cards and smoking, and a few young men played darts in the corner, cheering after one of them hit the bullseye. *Where was he? There he was.* Marcus sat at the bar alone, checking at his watch and smoking a cigarette. Oliver took a deep breath, bracing himself. This wasn't the first time he had confronted his brother about his cheating on Nancy. With Nancy in earshot, Oliver had to resort to dirty looks and subtle jabs of disapproval. He could never sit on the sidelines and watch, though that was what Marcus expected. Oliver adjusted his jacket and squared his shoulders before approaching his older brother and tapping him on the shoulder.

"Oh, Oliver!" Marcus said, shaking his hand. "What are you doing here?"

"I thought you were seeing a patient."

"What makes you think I'm not?" He smirked, pressing his cigarette into an ashtray.

"Let's talk."

"Go ahead."

Oliver pointed to the back door.

Marcus waved dismissively. "I don't have time for this, my patient should be here any minute."

"I'm not asking."

Marcus chuckled. "Fine, make it quick."

Oliver followed Marcus out the back door into an alley. He waited as a worker in another restaurant took out the trash. Loose garbage was scattered on the ground, emitting a rotten smell and smoke poured out of vents from different buildings. Once the door slammed shut, Oliver pushed Marcus backward. Marcus kept his balance, trying to conceal a smug grin.

"What the hell is wrong with you?" Oliver yelled.

"Come on, Oliver—"

"Stop it! How can you do this to George?" The words had been building over the years poured out of his mouth like a faucet that couldn't be turned off. "He looks up to you, and he's sick, Marcus! You should be spending every moment you can with Nancy and George when you're not at work. You take them for granted. How can you keep doing this to Nancy? She's a great wife to you and loves you."

"She never–" Marcus stopped himself. "You have no idea, Oliver, what I've been going through. My life has been hell."

"You think I give a shit? There are no excuses for this. You've been cheating on her from the second you married her, and it's disgraceful. Stop doing this to Nancy!"

Marcus's face tensed. "Oh, and you're so perfect with what you've been doing?"

"I never said I was perfect," Oliver paused, glaring at him. "What are you saying?"

"You know exactly what I'm saying."

"Say it," said Oliver, stepping closer to Marcus. "Say it to my face."

Marcus stared at the ground and said nothing as Oliver's face was a few inches away from his.

"Mom and Dad would've despised the man you've become," Oliver said. "What you're doing is going to come and bite you in the ass, and I won't be there to pick up after you like I always have." Oliver's shoulders tensed as blood rushed to his face. He stormed away from Marcus, wondering why he bothered. His brother was a lost cause; he would never care about his family.

* * *

Oliver snapped out of it, returning to the present, and punched the kitchen wall, his fist breaking through the wallpaper and wallboard. His hand stung. He shook it and rubbed it then ran cold water over it in the sink for a few seconds.

He showered and got dressed, putting on a navy blue collared shirt and tan pants and combed his hair, before he grabbed his wallet and keys. The cat lay again on the doormat of his neighbor's apartment as Oliver passed by him, taking the elevator and leaving the building. Nancy didn't deserve to panic like this. Marcus had been doing terrible things behind her back, asking for trouble. Oliver knew this would happen. He knew it.

This was the one time he desperately wanted to be wrong.

Elvis's music blasted out of the teenagers' flashy convertibles and the sidewalks were full of people. He made his way across the street, passing a newsstand where a group gathered in front of it, speaking in hushed tones. He ignored them; his surroundings were only a distraction.

The front door of Grayson's Pub was locked, so Oliver pounded on it, waving to a man who cleaned behind the counter. The worker looked less than pleased, wiping glasses with a towel. Oliver put his hands in his pockets and waited. Maybe the worker thought he would leave if he was ignored. *Not happening.* He knocked again a few times. The bartender looked at Oliver again, finally setting down his towel and approaching the door. He unlocked it and cracked it open.

"We're closed for another hour," said the bartender, starting to close the door again.

"I'm not here for drinks," Oliver said quickly as the worker stopped. "Did you work last night? My brother came here, and he didn't come home. I'm trying to track him down."

"I didn't, but Arthur did. He owns the place; I can grab him." He opened the door, waiting for Oliver to enter before closing and locking it.

Oliver thanked him, approaching the bar and resting his hands on the wooden counter. He took deep breaths, staring out the wide window overlooking the street. People walked by, enjoying their day. Oliver had spent too many mornings tracking down Marcus before he was married; this reminded him of those days. Nancy didn't deserve this. Marcus had a child at home, a child who desperately needed him. And he chose to abandon him.

"Sir?" said a man, approaching him from the kitchen and slouching over the counter. Looked to be in his mid-fifties with graying hair and wrinkles around his eyes.

Oliver snapped out of it and turned to him. "Hi, I'm looking for my brother who came here last night. I have a picture of him."

He took out his wallet and handed it to the man who studied it, taking his glasses off his shirt and placing them on the tip of his nose.

"His name's Marcus. Do you recognize him?"

"Oh, yeah! Marcus Anderson, right?"

Oliver took the picture back. "That's right."

"Yeah, he comes here almost every night. He's an excellent tipper, so he's quite popular around here with our guys."

"Was he with anyone last night?" he asked.

"He was getting handsy with a girl. I've never seen her before, but he brings a new one each time, so that's not a surprise." The man laughed.

Oliver clenched his jaw. "Did he mention where he was going?"

"No, he took off in his fancy Corvette with her." He pointed to the street.

"A blue Corvette, right?" The car that Marcus was supposed to sell to pay off George's medical bills. Yet he never sold it.

"Yeah, it's bright blue with white leather seats. He keeps it in perfect condition, tells me about all the work he does on it. It's a beautiful car. He once showed it to me after I complimented him on it."

Oliver nodded, putting the picture in his wallet. "Which way did he leave?"

"He went that way," he said, pointing to the right. "That's all I know."

"And he never came back?"

"No."

"Thanks for your help."

"Don't mention it. I'll let you out."

The man unlocked the door, slamming it behind Oliver after he left. Dread washed over Oliver as he walked a few blocks down the street to the right, looking up and down at apartment buildings and townhouses. He stopped at the next block. The street had a few groups of people, a small family, a couple of teenage girls, and two older men. Marcus, Nancy, and George used to live here before they sold their apartment and downsized to help with the medical bills. Or so Marcus told him.

Then he'd learned the truth—that Marcus kept the apartment. That was why Marcus and Nancy had so little and struggled to pay their bills. It hadn't made sense before. Marcus had an important job as a top psychiatrist at Sinclair Hospital Psychiatric Ward, and the rent of their current apartment was low. Marcus liked to gamble, but that didn't explain why they were in debt. Nancy lived in a shitty apartment, worrying about making ends meet, while Marcus kept a fancy car to attract women and a second apartment for hooking up with them. No matter how many times Oliver complained and confronted Marcus, he refused to change. Oliver wrote the check to help Nancy and George, though he knew she would be too proud to accept it. Oliver stopped in his tracks.

The blue corvette was parked in front of it.

Marcus never left that apartment last night.

Oliver's breaths became short as he walked inside, hitting the elevator button several times. Once it beeped and the doors opened, he entered and pressed the button for the fifth floor a few times. Oliver fidgeted with his hands and tapped his right foot against the carpeted floor. The doors opened, and he ran down the hallway to apartment 513.

He knocked on the apartment door. "Marcus! Marcus, are you in there?"

No response.

He tried opening the door but remembered they locked when closed.

An idea popped into his head. He walked next door and knocked. An old lady named Marilyn lived there who used to make cookies for George. She was always kind and positive as Oliver frequently ran into her while visiting his brother. He needed something to pick the lock.

Marilyn opened the door, adjusting her glasses with one hand, while the other held onto a cane to steady herself.

"Hello Oliver!" Her face brightened at the sight of him, giving him a wide smile. "I haven't seen you in a long time. How have you been doing, young man?"

"Hello Marilyn, I'm well. How are you?"

"I'm good, thanks for asking!"

"Have you seen Marcus lately?" he asked.

"Yes, a few days ago. He got my mail for me, such a nice fella."

"Can I borrow a paperclip? I'm worried about Marcus, and I don't have a key."

"Of course! Let me fetch one for you."

She left the door open, walking away slowly. Minutes passed by, and she hadn't returned. Oliver checked his watch, it had been nearly ten minutes. He scratched the back of his head and put his hands on his hips. He was close to pacing again.

At last, she returned, handing him the paperclip. "Here you are, my dear."

As he thanked her and walked away, she continued, "I did hear a loud thump last night like somebody fell over. I knocked on his door to make sure he was all right, and I thought I heard someone say 'I'm okay'."

"Thank you, Marilyn."

"Let me know if you need anything else. Do you want some breakfast? I can make you some breakfast. You need to put on some weight, Oliver."

"I'm fine," he said, too distracted to laugh it off as he usually would. "Thanks again."

She shut the door, as Oliver walked back to Marcus's apartment and jammed the sharp end of the paperclip into the lock and jiggled it. He kept trying to turn the knob to no avail.

"Dammit!" he whispered, taking a step back.

"Oliver, I made some pancakes," Marilyn said, standing by her door.

Come on, not now, Oliver thought, sighing before turning to her. "Thank you, Marilyn, but I'm not hungry."

"Are you sure? I have plenty."

"Yes, I'm sure. Thank you."

"All right, dear." She closed her door again.

Oliver took a deep breath and tried again, moving the sharp end of the paperclip inside the lock again and turning the knob. He pushed the creaky door open.

The apartment looked identical to when Marcus and Nancy "moved out" even though the furniture was in the same place. A low couch with red upholstery sat in the center of the room with a matching armchair beside it, and the radio used to stand opposite the couch. Before Marcus married Nancy, Oliver would pull up to Marcus's apartment in his Ford Mainline, opening the door for him, and pulling him out. Oliver would wrap Marcus's arm around his shoulders, kicking the car door shut with his foot. Marcus's feet struggled to keep up with Oliver as he dragged him into the apartment building, to the elevator, down the hall, and into the apartment. After managing to open the door, Oliver would bring Marcus to his bed. Marcus would plop down as if gravity were too heavy for his body. Oliver took off Marcus's shoes and laid the blanket over him. Oliver would sigh and shake his head, leaving him and heading back home. Too many nights like that to count.

Oliver took a step forward into the apartment. Two legs stuck out from behind the couch wearing black pants and dress shoes. He couldn't make a sound as his throat felt like it was closing up.

He slowly walked around the couch and backed up, running into a silver kitchen chair and knocking it over. His brother lay on the floor. Blood covered his chest and dried up on the tiled floors around him. The back of his head was cracked open, his eyes were wide and bloodshot, his mouth hung open, and his palms faced the ceiling as his arms lay on the floor on either side of him. Oliver collapsed onto his knees and put his head into his hands. He wanted to scream but his lungs deflated, making it impossible to make a sound.

Please, no. His eyes welled up. *No please!*

"I didn't mean it, Marcus!" he whispered. "I swear I didn't mean it!"

He looked away and when he did, the murder weapon appeared before him, lying on the floor along with pieces of chipped tile, all covered with blood. Someone stabbed his brother right through the heart, dropped the murder weapon, and fled. Oliver shook as he couldn't bear to look at his brother. He had been left alone in that state all night.

Oh, God. Nancy and George.

Oh my God, he thought, covering his mouth with his hand after seeing his brother again. He looked away at the sight of his brother lying on the floor, drenched in blood. Oliver collected himself, approaching Marcus's body.

Oliver had to call the police. He crawled to the phone in the kitchen, pulling himself up by the kitchen counter, and dialed the police department. He described in detail how he found his brother dead, how his brother was the victim of a homicide. After Oliver provided the address, the dispatcher said police were on their way.

"Thank you," he said, hanging up the phone.

He teared up, staring at Marcus again and guilt washing over him. He could've prevented this; he could've done more to bring Marcus home.

"I killed my brother."

5

Clara halted before her townhouse, taking off her gloves and putting them into her purse. She searched for her father's car. It was nowhere to be seen, her father hadn't returned home yet. She opened the front door and slowly closed it, trying to reduce the creaking. A pan slammed down onto the counter in the kitchen as she took a step up the creaky stairs. *Shit*, she thought, stopping before taking another. Creak. *These damn stairs.* Another step. Creak.

"Clara, honey, is that you?" her mother asked.

Clara held her breath, gripping the thick railing with one hand and her purse with the other. *Please don't come to the stairs. Please don't come to the damn stairs.*

"Yeah, it's me," Clara said with a shaky voice. "We finished early, so I'm going to take a bath."

"All right. Your father will be home soon, so wash off your makeup."

"I will." She gave a deep sigh of relief, climbing the rest of the stairs, running into the bathroom, and locking the door behind her.

Clara turned the faucet of her claw-foot bathtub, the water

pouring inside. Steam filled the room and fogged up her mirror. She stared at herself. She formed a fist, wanting to punch the mirror and shatter it. Instead, Clara relaxed her hand and rolled her eyes.

She took off Marcus's trench coat, revealing dried spots of Marcus's blood on her dress. Clara whipped it off over her head, throwing the coat and dress against the floor before kicking them into the corner. The blood-stained tissues and gloves in her purse also needed to be discarded.

Clara would have to get rid of everything somehow without her mother noticing. She interlocked her fingers and placed her hands on top of her head, removing the ribbon from her hair. *Everything's fine.* No one would ever suspect her of any wrongdoing. She's an ideal citizen, born to be a mother and homemaker. An innocent young woman.

There's some sick people in this city, said the newsstand worker.

You're sick, Marcus's voice said in her head.

She shook her head.

"I am not sick," she whispered, grinding her teeth.

Clara took out her bath salts from the cabinet and put some into her tub. She sighed, sitting on the edge and moving her right hand through the scalding hot water. As she sat inside, a burning sensation coursed through her whole body. Burning. Once she adjusted to the water temperature, it felt lovely. Clara rested her head back and closed her eyes.

You're sick, Clara.

She slid further down and let her head go underwater. She liked to play a game: how long she could hold her breath before she would drown. The counting started.

1... 2... 3...

Everyone remembered their first. Clara's first kill was Peter Donavan.

7... 8... 9...

She waited outside of Danny's Restaurant, leaning back on the brick wall with her left leg crossed over her right, smoking a cigarette and wearing her black dress. That same black dress was now drenched in blood and needed to be discarded somehow without her father seeing.

13... 14... 15...

Peter sat in the driver's seat of his car, taking off his wedding ring and placing it into the glove compartment. He rubbed his hands together and fixed his blond hair, looking into the rearview mirror. *Awe. He must've never cheated on his wife before.* He wore a tan trench coat similar to the black one Clara stole from Marcus's apartment to hide her bloody dress.

20... 21... 22...

The trench coat she also needed to discard without her father seeing.

27... 28... 29...

Clara smirked as Peter stood in front of Danny's Restaurant, his head turning right to left, left to right, looking for her in the crowds of people passing by. Clara crossed the street, taking off her sunglasses and smiling.

"Are you Peter?" Clara asked, placing her hand over her heart.

"I am." He nodded. "You can call me Pete if you'd like."

"My name's Patricia."

His eyes sparkled. "I like that name."

Patricia must be the name of his wife. The wife he was perfectly fine cheating on. What a loving husband, her name brought a smile to his face. *How sweet.* At least Clara was younger than his wife probably was, right?

35... 36... 37...

Clara stared into his blue eyes. Barely taller than her, he was five feet seven inches, and his arms were thinner than twigs. He wore a gold ring with a scarlet stone on his pinky. This man had never seen a day in combat; he must be a draft dodger. He got his daddy to bail him out, perfectly fine sending poor men in his place. With her secret weapon, she didn't foresee any complications to her plan.

40... 41... 42...

"Let's go 'round back," he said, leading her around the restaurant through the backdoor. One had two choices when walking through, a staircase or a hallway leading to the restaurant. The floors, walls, and stairs were dark, the only light coming through the open door. Clara followed him upstairs to an abandoned attic at the top of the restaurant. Nice and private.

"I used to hang out with my friends here to drink and smoke while I was in high school," Peter said, gesturing around with his back turned to her. Big mistake. "We used to finish our classes and escape to this place. The restaurant was abandoned at the time, but this new restaurant never uses this space."

Now he used the room for other endeavors.

50... 51... 52...

The attic was full of spider webs and had one small, circular window. Plywood flooring and exposed insulated walls with a single lightbulb dangling from the angled ceiling. Someone could only stand straight in the middle. Peter overlooked the street. He fiddled with his pinky ring. He seemed to start having regrets, as if he didn't know if he could go through with it.

Awe, he has a conscience.

100... 101... 102...

Clara picked up a knife, sneaking from behind him. Thank goodness the plywood didn't creak. The knife penetrated his back, tearing through his skin, and inserted itself between his ribs. His lung was punctured as Peter collapsed on his knees, holding his neck and gasping for air. He couldn't form any words as he fell over onto his back and breathed his last.

Clara held the blood-soaked knife, staring at his lifeless body on the floor, and the corner of her lips curled. Calmness washed over her. That man's life rested in her hands, and she could take it away. And take it away, she did.

One step closer.

110... 111... 112...

Two weeks later, her hair whipped against her face for the fifth time as she leaned against the railing by the stairs leading to the subway. Clara pulled a cigarette out of her purse and smoked, waiting for Bernie to show up. Men carrying briefcases passed by, arriving in their neighborhood after a long day of work. Clara didn't bother looking for her man; he would find her. These men didn't think they needed to change their names. *Pathetic.*

120... 121... 122...

Bernie approached her with a smile, wearing a brown suit that matched his thick beard. His forehead wrinkled whenever he moved his eyebrows. Clara lifted her sunglasses before holding her hand out for him to take. His hand squeezed hers, leading her into Schmidt's Bar and Restaurant. Unlike Peter, Bernie stood over six feet tall with broad shoulders. Alcohol needed to give her a hand this time.

She sat beside him at the bar, opting for a Coca-Cola, while Bernie slammed one beer after another.

"Have you ever played golf?" he asked, turning to her.

"No." Clara shook her head, leaning toward him. "I would love to learn more about it, though."

"So, there's eighteen holes, a front nine and a back nine. A par is how many shots it should take you to get the hole, and the lower the score you have, the better."

Clara leaned in closer, ignoring every word he said. "So interesting!"

"Yeah!" His face lit up, flushing. "I shot an 89, not too bad! I got some pars and a couple birdies. On one par three, I nearly got a hole-in-one, but it lipped out!"

"No way!" She rested her hand on his arm.

"Yeah," he said proudly. He took another sip of beer. "Have you heard of Arnold Palmer?"

"Of course, I'm sure you're as good as he is."

Bernie tried to conceal a smile by drinking his beer again. "No, I wish! I would love to see him play live someday, though."

Maybe in the afterlife. Clara smiled and nodded along.

130... 131... 132...

Bernie's hand became unsteady as he held his beer, and his speech slurred. He was ready.

"Ready to go?" Clara asked.

He nodded, tripping over the stool and catching himself. The bartender extended his hand. Bernie forgot to pay, so Clara paid for him. It was the least she could do.

"Better keep an eye on him," the bartender said.

Clara handed him the money. "Oh, I plan to."

One step closer.

141... 142... 143...

Her third murder was Marcus Anderson.

Clara's lungs pressed against her ribcage, ready to burst. Her body tried pulling her over the water, but she resisted. Her lips weakened as she pressed them together. *A few more seconds... a few more seconds... a few more...* Clara combed her hair with her fingers and opened her eyes underwater. Nothing in her hair. Where was her hair clip?

She jumped with water spilling over the edge of the bathtub, pulling herself up by the sides. The damn hair clip. Her eyes widened. Marcus must have taken it out of her hair while kissing her. Marcus set her up.

"That bastard!" she whispered, pressing her palms against her face. "Shit!"

Clara turned her head to her jewelry box on the counter. Her mother gave her those two hair clips. Maybe both of them were sitting there. *Please. Please.*

Climbing out of the bathtub, water dripped all over the floor as she opened the jewelry box to find one hair clip. She threw the box against the tile, causing the top to detach from the bottom. Clara wrapped a towel around herself and sat on the floor. She couldn't panic. No one would be able to narrow it down to her from a hair clip. But she would've rather left nothing at all.

Someone pounded on the floor, making Clara flinch and hold her hand over her chest.

"Clara, I heard a noise. Are you all right?" said her mother.

She took a deep breath. "Yeah, I'm fine. I just dropped my jewelry box."

"Oh, okay. Are you hungry?"

"Sure." Clara put her hand around her neck, trying to steady her voice. "When's dad coming home?"

"I'm not sure, he said he's running late again."

"I'll be down in ten minutes."

It'll be okay. She had time. She couldn't do anything about the hair clip now; it was out of her control.

"Okay." Her mother walked away and down the stairs, as Clara stood, wiping the steam off the mirror and staring at herself. She rested her hands on the counter and sighed. Her bloody dress and Marcus's trench coat lay in the corner. How was she going to get rid of them without anyone seeing?

Clara needed to get dressed first. She picked the evidence off the floor, taking it into her bedroom and stuffing it into the corner of her closet. She put on a casual blue sundress with a high waist and neckline and combed her hair with a brush from her nightstand. She went downstairs, walking through the cozy living room and into the kitchen. Her mother had cooked chicken with mashed potatoes and green beans as sides. Clara took a seat, even though her body resisted.

"I heated everything up," she said, putting a full plate in front of Clara.

"Thanks, Mom." Clara wasn't hungry, but her mother gestured for her to eat. She couldn't disobey her mother's orders. The grandfather clock ticked in the living room, reminding her of the seconds passing. The house was silent except for the traffic going up and down their street. The beeping of cars, Elvis music, and teenagers laughing before inhaling once more from their cigarettes. Normal teenagers. Clara could never be like one of them. She wondered what it was like to spend an evening with friends, dancing in dancing halls, and going to the show...

Meanwhile, evidence that would convict her in a murder trial and send her to the electric chair sat in the bottom of her closet. Throwing the dress and trench coat in the trash wouldn't be good enough, they needed to be destroyed along with the gloves and tissues in her purse.

"How were Kate and Betty?" her mother asked.

"What?" Clara said.

"How were Kate and Betty?" her mother repeated.

Clara swallowed a spoonful of mashed potatoes. "Oh, great. We had a great time."

"What did you do?"

"We went to the soda fountain and took a walk."

"Was Sam there?"

Clara had almost forgotten about him, his blond hair, brown eyes, and freckles on his cheeks. She'd had the biggest crush on him in high school, but she hadn't seen him since graduation. "Yeah, he was there. We danced together."

Her mother clapped and tucked a loose strand of Clara's hair behind her ear. "That's so exciting, Clara. I know you've been hoping for that for a long time."

"He's very kind."

Her mother rubbed Clara's forearm briefly. "I'm glad you had a nice evening."

"Have you seen any of your friends lately? How about Gloria?"

"No, not in a while. I just haven't been feeling myself."

Clara knew the feeling well.

Her mother leaned in toward her. "How have you been doing lately, honey? I worry about you, you know."

She stared into her mother's eyes and tried to stop herself from tearing up. Her mother had beautiful skin, smooth and free of wrinkles. Her brown eyes matched hers, and her lips were full and pink. Clara hoped she was half as glamorous as her. Her mother was the one person who truly understood her, how she wished she could tell her everything.

Her mother moved her chair closer to Clara and wrapped her arms around her. Clara leaned her head on her mother's shoulder and sighed. She couldn't shed a tear; she must remain stoic.

"Sometimes I can't control myself, no matter how hard I try," Clara confessed.

"You're a wonderful daughter, Clara, and I know how you feel. But things will get better, I promise." She turned to look Clara in the eye. "You can tell me anything, right?"

"Yes," she whispered.

"You're never alone. I'm always here."

Clara gave her a small smile as her eyes welled up.

Her mother kissed the top of her head. "You have so much to look forward to. If you give your father more time, he'll come around about college. Don't be too pushy or disrespectful, but remind him how much it would mean to you if he'd let you go. He has a soft spot for you."

If only that were true.

"Just stay on your best behavior." Her mother said, standing and pushing her chair under the table. "And eat your dinner."

"I am." Clara ate some more of her chicken.

"Do you mind if I go to bed?"

Clara looked at the clock. Almost 9:30 p.m. "No."

"Make sure everything is cleaned up for when your father comes home. Good night, dear."

"I will, good night."

Based on prior Friday nights, her father shouldn't be home for a couple more hours. Her mother's footsteps clicked up the stairs slowly, and her bedroom door slammed shut. Clara should wait at least ten minutes before sneaking the clothes downstairs and into the backyard. She ate another bite of chicken, staring at the clock as the second hand ticked.

Her fork tapped against the plate. The clock kept ticking, and

Clara waited. Not being able to sit still, she paced the first floor. Living room, dining room, kitchen. Kitchen, dining room, living room. Once ten minutes had passed, she went into the courtyard in the back of their townhouse. She poured some gasoline on their fire pit, then lit a cigarette and inhaled it a few times. After she threw it into the pit, the flame began consuming the wood.

She ran into the house but had to slow down her pace not to wake up her mother. As she carefully climbed the stairs into her bedroom, she opened the closet door to find the dress and trench coat sitting where she left them. Clara grabbed them, along with the tissues and gloves from her purse, holding them all close to her chest. Her parents' bedroom door was closed.

Someone knocked on the door as Clara froze on the stairs. It better not be her father. Sometimes he didn't get out his keys and unlock the door himself. Clara ran to the front hallway closet, stuffing the clothes inside. Her father wouldn't be wearing a coat in this heat, and he always kept his briefcase in his bedroom. Worst-case scenario, she would have to wait until her father went to bed. Clara tensed up and opened the door.

"Hi, Clara!" a young boy said. He was the son of their next-door neighbor.

"Hi, John. How are you?" Clara let out a sigh of relief, holding onto the edge of the door with one hand.

"Can you give us a cup of brown sugar, please? We ran out," he said.

"Sure!" She forced a smile, heading into the kitchen, and the boy stepped into the front hall. *Shit.* The clothes sat in the front closet as the clock kept ticking. She measured out a cup and poured it into a glass container, wrapping it with aluminum foil. As Clara returned to hand the boy the sugar, he began opening the door to the front hall closet. She sprinted to him, pressing against the door to close it, so he couldn't see anything inside. Nosy kid.

Clara tried to catch her breath as the boy stared at her. "Here you are!"

He took the sugar and thanked her. Clara closed and locked the front door, grabbed the clothes from the front closet, and returned outside. She threw them on top of the fire. The flames consumed the dress, trench coat, tissues, and gloves, reducing them to ash. She crossed her arms, backing away from the heat and wiping the sweat off her forehead. The evidence was gone. The only thing left was her hair clip, but she couldn't burn the other one.

* * *

Clara remembered that day well five years ago. She and her mother went shopping in Manhattan, going into boutiques and jewelry stores. The beautiful windows displayed the latest spring fashion, a lavender shirt, cream blouse, and a matching cropped jacket for women, along with a single-breasted suit and a light polo shirt for men. They walked past a window with a mannequin displaying a floral dress with a flared skirt with pretty pink flowers and mint green leaves, almost as if they were hand-painted on the dress. Her mother pulled on Clara and pointed at it.

"I love this dress!"

"Me too!" Clara said. They went inside to catch a better look. The dress was soft and comfortable. Clara's mother picked up a hanger and held it in front of Clara.

"Oh, this would look so nice on you!" She smiled, returning the hanger to the rack. Clara approached the showcase of hair accessories and jewelry. Her mother touched her shoulder as Clara studied the hair accessories through the glass. A black bow hair clip was on display.

"Would you like to get a couple as an early birthday present?"

"I would love that!"

* * *

No, Clara couldn't get rid of the other hair clip. Her mother would start asking her about them. Besides, nothing tied her to Marcus's death. No one would come looking for her.

She relaxed her shoulders and took a deep breath.

"What are you doing?"

Clara gasped and turned. Her father stood across from her, staring at her.

6

Oliver stood with one hand on his hip and the other under his chin. The next morning wasn't supposed to be like this. Usually, he would return to ensure Marcus was lying in bed. Oliver would wake him up, Marcus would complain about being hungover, and Oliver would rebuke his behavior. And they would repeat this routine the following weekend. Marcus's bed was empty and made, his shoes didn't lie on the floor next to it. Oliver couldn't wake him up. How badly he wished he could.

He paced the apartment, waiting for the police to arrive. His blood pressure rose every time sirens blared as they passed by the apartment. They must be getting a lot of calls today. Oliver fidgeted with his hands, avoiding looking at his brother's body lying on the floor on the other side of the apartment. He should be angry, furious even. He had a right to be. But his anger melted away at the sight of his brother. Oliver could've done more to prevent this; done more to help Nancy and George. Marcus didn't deserve to die, he was so young and had a son who adored him. But why did Marcus have to behave the way he did? He wouldn't have gotten himself killed if he had spent the night with his wife and son. Oliver walked on the tile floors. Back and forth, back and forth. Until someone pounded on the door.

He raced toward it, swinging it open to find two policemen and ambulance attendants wheeling a stretcher down the hallway. A thin man dressed in a gray suit and matching fedora stood in front of him. His nose was long and pointy, and his forehead had wrinkles.

"Have you walked around the apartment?" the man asked.

"Yes," Oliver replied. "In the living room and kitchen."

"What have you touched?"

"Um." Oliver turned briefly. "The kitchen counter and telephone."

The man nodded. "Please wait in the hallway. I will ask you more questions in a moment."

Oliver obeyed, leaving the apartment and standing across the hallway, while the detective entered Marcus's apartment and looked around. He took out a pen and notepad, approaching Marcus's body. The rest of the men waited in the hallway in silence, avoiding each other's gazes. The detective's pen clicked, and he flipped pages of his notebook to find a clean one.

He walked around Marcus's body, continuing to take detailed notes. He moved Marcus's jacket, searching his pockets. The detective pulled out Marcus's wallet, a pack of cigarettes, a lighter, and another small object that Oliver couldn't make out. A pile of cash was pulled out of and returned to the wallet. He studied the knife lying on the floor and turned toward the knife set on the kitchen counter, along with another knife that lay on the counter. He started writing again.

"Arthur, you may come in now," he said.

The man named Arthur passed by Oliver and entered the apartment, wearing a camera strapped around his shoulders. The light bulb clicked and flashed before it dropped onto the floor. Arthur took several pictures: different angles of Marcus, a few photos of the contents inside Marcus's pockets, and a few of the murder weapon on the floor and the knife on the countertop.

"All set, sir," Arthur said. The detective thanked him, and Arthur left the apartment, walking down the hall toward the elevator.

"The rest of you may come in now," the detective said.

The two police officers and two ambulance attendants rolled a stretcher into the room. The detective approached the ambulance attendants. After he cleared his throat, they adjusted their posture. "You may take the body now, and an autopsy should be performed." He turned to the two police officers. "I'm leaving. Exercise caution with the evidence. I will speak to you later, after I follow some leads."

"Yes, sir." The two police officers said simultaneously.

The detective set his sights on Oliver next, asking to speak with him at the end of the hall, opposite the elevator.

"The victim's name is Marcus Anderson?"

"Yes, sir."

The man wrote in his notepad. "Tell me about him."

"He's a psychiatrist at Sinclair Hospital's Psychiatric Ward. He has a wife named Nancy, and a son named George."

"Who are you?" he asked.

"His brother, Oliver."

"Any other siblings, parents?"

"No other siblings. Our parents passed away when we were young."

"Did he have any friends?"

"He's closest with Dr. Edward Taylor, but Marcus's wife, Nancy, would know more about that."

"Why did you come here this morning?" he asked.

"Nancy called me this morning, saying Marcus didn't come home last night, so I went around looking for him. I went to one of his usual bars, Grayson's Pub, where I talked to the owner. The owner said he left in a blue convertible with some woman. Marcus told me he was meeting someone named Melissa." The man raised his eyebrows. Oliver continued. "The owner pointed in the direction of this apartment building, and I knew he had kept this place."

"How did you know that?"

Oliver sighed. "Marcus told me a while ago."

"Did this owner say what this woman looked like?" he asked.

"No." Oliver shook his head.

"Where were you last night?"

"I visited Marcus, Nancy, and George after work, then I returned to my apartment to change my suit before going to Grayson's Pub to see Marcus. I knew he was meeting with some woman, and I tried to get him to go home instead of cheating on Nancy again."

"And then, what?"

"I went home."

"You went home?"

"Yes, sir, I went home," Oliver repeated as he resumed writing.

The detective's eyes narrowed at Oliver briefly. "You didn't see the young woman?"

"No, I didn't."

"Have you and your brother had any issues recently?"

The last words he had spoken to his brother before Marcus was stabbed to death were that their parents would despise him and how his behavior would come back to bite him. They might have been true, but harsh. Not the last words Oliver would ever want to say to his brother.

"I tried to get him to return to his wife and son, and he refused and wasn't happy that I tried interfering in his business."

"Thank you, Mr. Anderson. I will be in contact with you if I have any more questions."

Oliver nodded as the detective walked down the hallway with one of the police officers to the elevator. Oliver collected himself, stopping to look inside Marcus's apartment once more. The police officers used a rope to tie off the area in the kitchen where Marcus was found. The ambulance attendants lifted Marcus and placed him on the stretcher. They laid a sheet over him and rolled him out of his apartment. When they walked down the hallway toward the elevator, Marcus's left hand was exposed, hanging off the side. The remaining police officer in the apartment wrote down notes in his notepad. He adjusted his hat and pushed his glasses further up his nose.

Oliver stood in the doorway so as not to disturb the scene. "Hello, officer?"

No response.

"Officer, do you think they'll find the person who did this?"

The officer didn't look up. "It's a big city. Crime has been on the rise."

Oliver put his hands on his hips. That wasn't helpful. "Who could've done something like this?"

"That's what we'll try to figure out."

"What's the detective's name?"

The police officer sighed. "Detective Howard. You're lucky to have him. If anyone could find who did this, it's him."

Oliver nodded.

"Did you say your brother has a wife? Who should we break this news to?"

My God. Nancy and George. Oliver didn't want to break the news, but the thought of Nancy breaking down at the sight of a police officer standing on her doorstep made him shiver. Nancy would press tissues against her face while sliding down the wall and onto the floor. George would run over to her, confused and crying. No, Oliver had to be strong here. He had to be the one.

"He has a wife and son, but can I break the news to them?"

The police officer stuck his notepad into his shirt pocket, along with his pen. "Yes, you can. We'll investigate your brother's case as best we can. Sorry for your loss."

"Thanks," Oliver whispered, leaving the apartment and walking toward the elevator. He needed to break the news slowly, but all at once. *Nancy, I'm so sorry, but Marcus passed away.*

Decisions needed to be made. Should Oliver be the one to tell Nancy about how Marcus was killed, how his killer was still at large and might never be found, and that Marcus had kept the apartment and the car? The elevator doors opened, and he stepped inside. Nancy would find out Marcus had been murdered one way or another. The police would interview her soon. She would either learn through Oliver or the police.

Oliver left the apartment building, jerking his neck to the left. Police officers rummaged through Marcus's car with two police cars parked behind it, their lights flashing.

"I'm Oliver Anderson, Marcus's brother," he said to a police officer who looked to be his age.

"Hello, sir," he said, reaching out his hand to shake Oliver's.

Oliver shook it. "I was wondering what will happen with the apartment and the car."

"We shouldn't need to keep them for long. Did Mr. Anderson have a wife or children?"

"Yes, he has a wife and son."

"His wife will be notified, and the apartment and car will be returned to her."

Oliver shook his hand again. "Thank you, officer."

"Of course."

Oliver headed to Nancy's apartment. His brother lay on the floor with a stab wound to the chest. His head bashed against the tile flooring. Marcus must have fought until his last breath, the murderer fighting him and stabbing him, causing Marcus to fall backward. He was a strong, tall man, but he couldn't handle alcohol as well as his size would suggest. Still, it was hard to believe a woman would be able to overpower him.

And no solid evidence that would lead directly to his murderer.

Nothing.

But a small object in Marcus's pocket.

What could that object be?

Detective Howard studied it closely and laid it on the floor for the photographer to take pictures. One of the policemen collected the object and put it into a labeled bag. Oliver jumped backward onto the curb at the sound of the horn.

"What the hell is wrong with you?" the driver yelled through the rolled-down window.

Oliver didn't respond, waiting for the car to drive by and looking up and down the street before crossing. He would have to be there to console Nancy and George. Should he take Nancy out into the hallway? That wouldn't be private enough, but George couldn't witness her breaking down. If he saw his mother fall to her knees in anguish, he would never be the same. George was already dealing with enough from his illness. Nancy was already suffering enough watching her son fight against his illness. Where could he take her so they could talk alone?

He passed by Grayson's Pub, stopping dead as something through the window caught his eye. Detective Howard stood by the bar with his notepad and pen out, probably asking the owner about Marcus's whereabouts last night. The owner was animated, moving his hands in the air. He called over a bartender, introducing him to the detective. While Detective Howard continued to ask the bartender questions, the owner moved on with his day.

Oliver went into an antique store next door, stepping around furniture, pots, and decorations. The inventory was overwhelming for the tiny shop. He looked out the front window, concealing himself behind an eight-foot-tall bookshelf stacked with books, world globes, clocks, and other knick-knacks. After interviewing the bartender, the detective should walk by the window. Oliver had some questions to ask the bartender himself. Oliver coughed; this place needed some dusting.

"How are you doing today?"

Oliver flinched as he turned toward an elderly gentleman. "Fine, how are you?"

"Great! Please let me know if you need help finding anything. I'll be right behind the counter."

"Thank you." Oliver said, as the shop owner left his side. Oliver returned his attention to the window, gently spinning one of the globes. Detective Howard didn't waste any time; he should be out of the bar soon. He glanced back at the shop owner, but the old man wasn't paying any attention to him. The man sat behind the counter, organizing files. Out of the corner of his eye, Detective Howard passed by the window. He waited a few more minutes before leaving the shop and returning to Grayson's Pub.

Oliver whipped open the door and approached the counter, waving the bartender over. The man wiped the counter with a damp towel, putting it aside and giving Oliver his full attention.

Oliver rested his hands on the counter. "I'm sorry to bother you, but my brother, Marcus Anderson, was here last night. Have you heard about what happened to him?

"I'm sorry for your loss," the bartender said.

"Thank you. I was wondering if you could tell me anything about last night."

The man glanced at the ceiling. "He was here with a young woman. She only took a few sips, but he had several glasses of whisky. They talked and sat for about an hour, then left together."

"Nothing seemed strange?"

"Well, I did mention to the detective that a man came over to him and leaned real close to his ear, saying something like he owed him money and his time was up."

Oliver's eyes widened. "What happened after that?"

"Um, your brother said something about how he was going to pay him back, and that guy patted your brother on the back and walked out."

Oliver nodded with his mouth open.

"Can I get you anything?" The bartender gestured toward the bar.

"No, thank you, though. I appreciate it."

"Of course." He grabbed the towel again, cleaning off the counter as Oliver left Grayson's Pub into the hustle and bustle of Brooklyn. The sweltering heat and the burning of his skin under the sun didn't bother him. The crowds blurred around him as he walked down the sidewalk, rehearsing breaking the news to Nancy in his mind. He would mention how he died if she inquired about it, which she probably would.

Nance, Marcus is gone. No, that's not specific enough. She would ask him what he meant by "gone". *Nance, Marcus passed away last night.* That was probably the best way to put it. Nancy would ask how after that, but she would ask that question no matter how he started the conversation.

Marcus and Nancy's apartment was about a ten-minute walk away. The Brooklyn traffic was deadlocked while his mind couldn't stop racing. Oliver couldn't leave Nancy and George alone after delivering such news. They could live at his place for a while. George wasn't in school yet, so it might not be too difficult for them to move. Though, it might be challenging to make a huge change after learning about the loss of their husband and father.

Once Oliver reached the apartment complex, the building stood tall before him. He fidgeted with his hands and sighed, entering. His feet had weights strapped to them as he climbed the creaking stairs. He took several deep breaths, his stomach burning. He stared down the empty hallway, fixing his suit jacket and fiddling with his sleeves. Approaching the apartment, he shakily knocked on the door. A few seconds later, Nancy answered. Her face had lost all its color, her eyes were wide and tired. She didn't get any sleep last night.

Nancy didn't say a word, gesturing Oliver inside with one hand while holding her neck with the other.

"Where's George?" Oliver asked.

"Sleeping," she answered as they moved into the kitchen. Nancy leaned against the counter, crossing her arms and waiting for Oliver to tell her the news. She bit her lip.

"Are you sure George won't eavesdrop?"

"Let's go into the bedroom." They walked inside, passing George who slept on the couch, nestled under a blanket. Nancy closed the bedroom door slowly.

They both sat on the same side of the bed as Nancy stared at him, waiting to be told what had happened to her husband.

"Marcus has died," Oliver said quietly.

Nancy gasped, her mouth falling open. "What? What happened?"

"Someone killed him."

She blinked rapidly as her eyes locked on Oliver. She grabbed at the neckline of her dress. "What? Who?"

"The police are doing everything they can to find h-him." Oliver would spare her the details of Marcus getting handsy with a young woman, or a man demanding his money back. Nancy suspected (or knew) Marcus was unfaithful and loved gambling, but that didn't matter now. No reason to mention his infidelity yet. It would bring Nancy more pain.

"I need some time to think." She spoke as if she had trouble breathing and stood, walking toward the wall and returning to the bed. Nancy pressed the palm of her hand against her mouth, closed her eyes, and cried. Oliver grabbed tissues from the bathroom and handed them to her. He sat closer to her, wrapping his arm around her shoulders.

"I'm so sorry, Nance."

She dabbed her eyes and took a deep breath. "I knew when you came here alone that it wouldn't be good news, but I can't believe this..."

"I can't either."

Nancy shook her head, at a loss for words. "What about George?"

"You and George can stay at my place for a while, so you two aren't alone if you would like."

"I don't think that's a good idea right now." She looked at the closed bedroom door briefly. "I don't want to worry him. If we're moving in with you, he'll start asking questions. I'll have to tell him before the... funeral."

"I'll take care of everything, Nance. I'll do the bills, I'll make the arrangements, I'll take care of everything. You just need to focus on George."

Nancy wiped her eyes dry, fidgeting with a hole in her skirt. "Thank you, Ollie. You've always been wonderful. Thanks for your offer for us to stay with you. Maybe soon, but right now, I think George needs to stay here."

"I understand."

Nancy moved closer and hugged him. She rested her head on his shoulder and sighed. "Please find who did this, Ollie. Please."

"I will, Nance. I promise you."

Someone knocked on the front door as Oliver and Nancy turned toward the closed bedroom door.

"I'll get it," Oliver offered as he left the bedroom and opened the front door. Detective Howard stood there with his hands in his pockets and a poker face.

"Hello, Mr. Anderson," he said. "Is Mrs. Anderson here?"

"Yes."

The detective paused for a moment. "May I come in? I have some questions for her."

Oliver gestured him inside. "Yes, of course."

Detective Howard stepped inside, and Oliver led him to the kitchen table. He poked his head into the bedroom. "Detective Howard is here to talk to you," he said.

Nancy stood, nodding. Oliver picked George up, laying him on Nancy's bed, so Nancy could sit on the couch across from Detective Howard, who sat on a wooden chair.

"Hello, Mrs. Anderson," Detective Howard said, opening his notebook and readying his pen. "I am so sorry about the loss of your husband."

"Thank you," Nancy whispered.

The detective turned toward Oliver. "You may stay while I ask Mrs. Anderson a few questions."

Oliver sat beside Nancy. She took his hand and squeezed it while clenching tissues with the other.

"When was the last time you saw your husband?" he asked.

Nancy stuttered. Oliver could answer for her if she couldn't get the words out. The last time she saw Marcus was when he left the apartment yesterday evening for Grayson's Pub.

"I saw him leave Grayson's Pub with a young woman last night."

Oliver's eyes widened as Detective Howard's eyebrows rose.

"Where were you when you saw them leave Grayson's Pub?"

"Down the street. She wore a black dress and gloves and carried a black, box-shaped purse. She also had long brown hair. After they drove off in his blue Corvette, I went home."

"You went home?"

"Yes."

"Why did you follow him to Grayson's Pub?" he asked.

"He has a history of being unfaithful, and he told me he was going back to work to help a patient. I wanted to find out if he was telling the truth."

Detective Howard nodded. "Where was your son?"

"He was playing with a neighbor, so I asked the mother to watch him. I was gone for half an hour at most."

He looked to be writing every word down. "Has Mr. Anderson received any threats you're aware of?"

Nancy shook her head.

"Did he owe anyone any money?"

"I don't know." She spoke quietly as if speaking hurt her throat. "He took care of our finances. He did like to gamble; I'm not sure where."

"Are there financial troubles here?"

"Well, we-we've..." Nancy stuttered and teared up. "Our son, George, has medical issues, and we've had to pay for different opinions and treatments, none of which have amounted to anything yet."

Detective Howard wrote down more notes then locked eyes with her again. "I am sorry to hear that, Mrs. Anderson. Is there anything you would like to tell me? No detail is too small."

She shook her head.

"I'm sorry again for your loss, Mrs. Anderson. I will be in contact if I need any further information. If anything comes to mind for you, please do not hesitate to reach out to me." He handed her his business card.

He and Oliver stood, and Oliver walked him out, opening the door for him.

As Detective Howard left the apartment, Oliver's mind raced with Nancy's revelation. Nancy was there, standing down the street from Grayson's Pub. She saw the person who could have killed her husband. If someone couldn't confirm that she returned home right after watching Marcus and the young woman drive away, Nancy might be considered a suspect. Detective Howard knew of Marcus's infidelity, gambling, and the high-stress home situation of caring for their sick son. He could twist that into a motive, and police loved suspecting family members.

Another troubling thought struck his mind.

The killer might have seen her.

7

October 13th, 1958, Pocono Lake, Pennsylvania

Clara lay on the green grass on top of a tall hill, closing her eyes and allowing the sunshine to gaze down upon her. Her skin felt its warmth. No breeze today, which made the cool weather bearable. She paid close attention to the smells and sounds surrounding her. The scent of the grass and leaves, and the sounds of bumblebees flying from one flower to another and birds flying to different branches. The calmness and perfection of nature clashed with the cabin. She touched the tips of the blades of grass as hundreds of them pressed against her body.

Something moved next to her. Clara flinched, sitting up and raising her sunglasses. A rabbit stared at her, then returned into the woods. She lay on the grass again, trying to recapture the peace she had moments before, but last night weighed on her mind. She could picture that nightmare so clearly; it felt real. That man floated in midair, hanging above her and gazing down upon her with fiery eyes. The blood splattered from his chest, dripping one drop at a time onto her quilt before the floodgates opened and it became drenched. The thick liquid warmed the quilt and sheets, seeping through them onto her pajamas. He knew her. She was the reason he ended up that way. He wanted her to suffer. And her mind obliged.

She opened her eyes immediately and sat up again. *It's only a dream, Clara*, she thought over and over again. The front and back doors were locked. Nothing in the cabin was out of place, and there were no footprints or any physical evidence. Well, besides the fog on the window where someone might have breathed.

Clara yawned. She spent a few hours last night standing in her kitchen, cradling a cup of tea, followed by endless amounts of pacing between the kitchen and the living room. All of the lights stayed on throughout the night. *Oh, God.* The thought of having to fall asleep again tonight. But she must sleep; she couldn't keep going on without it. Her body wouldn't be able to resist much longer. How many nights could go by pacing through the cabin while the rest of the world slept? No, Clara couldn't think about it now. No need to think about it while the sun was out.

She took out her pen and paper from her backpack, shaking the pen and readying her hand.

Dear Mom,

I'm quickly deteriorating. No matter how I try to shut out the past, it seeps into my bones and my mind surrenders. I shouldn't be thinking about those men at all. I shouldn't be scared of them, yet I shiver at the nightmares I've been having. Is this remorse? This cabin is my purgatory, reliving my greatest sins until I admit what I did was wrong. But I did no wrong. Except for... I know I shouldn't have killed him. I wonder if he's behind all of this. If he is, I would understand. I don't deserve peace.

I can't control it here, like I couldn't control it in Brooklyn. A fresh start is a lie. You'll always be stuck with yourself and your old ways. I'm trying to change, but I can't, no matter how hard I try.

The weather is getting colder each day, the darkness creeping earlier and earlier. It's hard to be alone sometimes. Please send me something so I know you're receiving my letters, Mom. I need to know you're all right. Please, Mom, please. I love you very much. You must know that, Mom. Despite what I've done. I'm sorry for letting you down. I hope you find it in your heart to forgive me someday.

Love always,

Clara

She folded the letter and placed it in an envelope. Clara stayed on the hill for a few more minutes, bracing herself for her biweekly trip to the grocery store. The one store Clara was allowed to shop in, a thirty-minute drive away. She packed up her things and headed back to the cabin, walking down the hill and over the dead leaves, crumbling under her flats.

When Clara arrived at her cabin, she clenched her fists and fixed her back to a rigid posture. She forced a smile. Why wouldn't she be happy to see the cabin? It was so peaceful; she always found it exactly as she had left it. It was a joy to walk through the door.

She stepped onto the porch and let herself in, finding it perfectly organized and orderly. *Thank God*. She dropped her back-pack as she made her way to the bathroom and stared at herself in the mirror. Her makeup case sat on the counter, tempting her, as she tried to resist the urge to put some on. *Don't wear makeup, don't dress nicely*. As she put the makeup case into the drawer, the rules echoed in her head. Clara brushed her hair without adding any bows or hair clips and adjusted her gray dress, the only one she owned. Back into civilization.

Clara drove her tan Chevy two-door station wagon down the dirt hill, reaching a narrow road that twisted and turned. She jerked the wheel to stay on track as the car bounced over the exposed tree roots. The thirty-two minute ride was scenic, as her eyes wandered back and forth from the road to the beautiful foliage. The hills, the fresh, crisp air, the warm sunlight. Fall used to be her favorite time of year, but there was nothing to look forward to anymore.

Your Best Meal Grocery Store and Pharmacy was a shabby place. The triangular sign had rust around the edges, and the lightbulb above the door flickered. But it had all the essentials: a produce section, a deli, and a butcher. There were only a few cars in the parking lot, perfect for Clara to slip in and out without being recognized. A man's voice in her head repeated the rules.

Now, don't look anyone in the eye! Be quick and don't attract any attention to yourself. Don't ask any questions.

She grabbed a cart and stocked up. Two weeks' worth of groceries. In and out. She kept her head down, staring at the glossy floor as she selected each item on her list: bread, eggs, milk, bacon, coffee, tea, chicken, apples, and other ingredients for the simple recipes she had memorized. After picking up some napkins, Clara tossed her wavy hair over her shoulder and stopped. *What was that?* she thought, standing in the produce section. She tightened her grip on the cart.

Out of the corner of her eye, a tall man wearing a black suit and tie faced her direction. He stared at her. Why would anyone stare at her? No one in this town should recognize her. Or, more importantly, know what she did. Clara couldn't look at him; making eye contact was against the rules, but it was difficult to resist the urge. *Don't do it. Don't do it.* She had to know if she was about to be caught. *You can't, you can't. Keep shopping and ignore him.* Her mind couldn't let it go. She must know, she must know now. She gave in, turning and holding her breath, bracing for the worst.

No one was there. The man had vanished.

How could that be? Her mind wasn't playing tricks on her; she saw him clear as day. Did he leave the store to alert the authorities? She must check out and leave. Clara would glance in the cashier's direction so as not to appear rude but not make eye contact, as she placed her groceries on the counter. Her body froze.

DETECTIVE HOWARD CLOSING IN ON MULTIPLE MURDERER

The newspaper headline stared at her, this time from the *New York Daily News*. Clara had to leave.

"How are you doing?" said the cashier, emotionless.

Clara flinched, stuttering. "I'm doing well, how are you?"

"Good, thanks." The woman said this as though she were nearing the end of her shift. Clara kept her eyes on the groceries, fidgeting with her hands. The woman ringed up each item slowly, put them into bags, and loaded them into the cart. *Faster please. I have to leave. I have to go back to the cabin.*

The police could barge in at any moment and take her away.

"Seventeen dollars and twenty-three cents," she said, holding out her hand. Clara paid her, and the worker handed her a receipt in exchange.

Clara couldn't race out of the store, instead walking at a normal pace to her car. How badly she wanted to search the parking lot for the man in the suit, but she knew better. She threw her groceries in the backseat and headed back to the cabin.

It began to drizzle as her car pulled up the hill. Clara kept checking the rearview mirror to ensure no one followed her. No man in a black suit was driving behind her. He was probably the one who left the newspaper on her doorstep. Maybe he was also ruining her cabin whenever she went on her daily hike. Clara needed to put it out of mind now. The cabin stayed in one piece. No police waiting to take her away.

Making a few trips back and forth to unload the groceries, Clara organized them in the kitchen cabinets and refrigerator. She put the apples aside before arranging them in a wooden bowl, picking one out to have as a snack. Thunder boomed as she walked to the window. The rain harshly clashed with the ground, and the sound of it soothed her. The window was beginning to fog up, so she took her hand and gently wiped the condensation with her hand to have a clearer view. The only movement was the leaves being blown off the trees by the wind. No man in a suit as far as she could see.

She made coffee and sat on the covered porch with one of her favorite novels, *The Great Gatsby*. The temperature plummeted as Clara laid a blanket on her lap, staring out into the woods. A thick fog appeared just off the ground, oozing toward the cabin. Clara took a bite of the apple and furrowed her eyebrows as she stopped chewing. It was too sweet. She pulled it away and drops of a red liquid dripped off the apple onto her dress. Was her mouth bleeding? She wiped her lips with her hand but nothing materialized on it. The apple showed a normal bite mark, and the blood drops disappeared from her dress. Clara covered her mouth with her hand as the metallic taste lingered on her tongue. She stood and threw the apple into the woods.

Something made a noise behind her, and Clara flinched. She shook her head as her ceramic teacup shattered on the wooden porch. She grabbed a broom and dustpan from the front closet and carefully picked up several broken pieces of her teacup. Luckily, it wasn't her favorite, only a plain white one. Being put too close to the edge, it must have slipped off the end table.

She fixed her posture, returning to the front porch and sitting with her journal. She began sketching the man in the black suit, a thin and lanky man without a face. She drew a floating hammer, ready to strike the man's head. Clara stopped drawing, her hand freezing up. An earthy aroma came from the woods. It almost smelled like a cup of coffee, but Clara knew the scent well. It was a cigar. Someone stood near the cabin, smoking a cigar, but no matter how hard Clara searched the woods, not a soul could be found.

Clara walked into the cabin and closed the door for the night. When she entered the bathroom to wash her face, her makeup case stared at her, opened. She swore she put it into the drawer before leaving for the grocery store. She ran her fingers across the various red and coral shades of lipstick. *No.* No more makeup.

No. More. Makeup. No more.

Clara closed her large makeup case and put it in the bottom drawer, finishing her evening routine. Once the night fell, Clara found herself sitting on the small sofa in her cozy family room, unwilling to go to bed. A chill filled the air, passing through her skin. The cabin was dark except for the lamp on the end table, but she couldn't bring herself to turn it off.

As she stared at the front window, a cold breath touched the back of her neck. She sat absolutely still as someone felt the back of her head, grooming her long hair. A decision had to be made: whether to reach her hand back there or turn quickly. She sat as frozen as a statue, as her heart pounded hard and fast. She had to turn to face whatever it was.

Clara braced herself and stood, jumping backward, her legs hitting the wooden coffee table. She clutched her chest, trying to slow her breathing. Nobody was in front of her. Everything was fine. She would survive another night and have another ordinary day tomorrow. She wouldn't allow her victims to keep torturing her and entering her mind. They deserved to die after what they had done. Except the one... why did she kill him? She didn't mean to; her emotions got the best of her. If she could be given the chance to go back, she would. How badly she wished she could. Clara covered her eyes, feeling like bricks were piling on top of her head and crushing it to pieces. No, Brooklyn was a better place without those men around. She shouldn't be feeling this way. Except for him... But the plan worked, and she escaped.

Clara crossed her arms. It was time for bed.

After turning on a lamp, she closed and locked her bedroom door. The cramped room had one small window with the curtains drawn and an empty closet. The window was locked, and Clara checked under the bed to make sure that man wasn't hiding under it. She climbed into bed and put the white sheets and quilt over her. No distractions at night. Her thoughts could keep her company, but she didn't want them. Crickets chirped and bullfrogs croaked outside. Clara learned to tune them out. The house creaked with the wind. Nothing to worry about. Branches hitting against the walls wasn't a big deal. Deer and other wildlife walked around the cabin at night. But then there were footsteps inside.

Back and forth.

Back and forth.

Walking between the living room and kitchen. Their feet

pounded against the wood floors, causing them to creak. This couldn't be real; she was imagining things. She should close her eyes and fall asleep, and the footsteps would stop. But what if someone hid out there, inside her home, waiting for her to fall asleep? Did he pace with a knife in his hand? Was it the man in the suit from the grocery store who was stalking her?

Back and forth.

Back and forth.

Clara clutched the quilt, sitting up straighter, her body shaking.

And then the pacing stopped.

8

Marcus lay on the tile flooring, his blood spreading like wings on either side of him, as Oliver approached him; his feet planted behind Marcus's torn head. Oliver closed his eyes, hoping Marcus would disappear when he reopened them. Fingers wrapped around his ankles. Oliver jumped backward as Marcus crawled toward him, his brain hanging out of the back of the skull. The blood smeared against the floor, as Marcus's nails scraped against the tiles, clawing himself closer to Oliver. Oliver backed away with wide eyes, his hands shaking as he held them out defensively. He pressed his back against the wall as Marcus pulled on his leg.

"You should have saved me!" Marcus yelled breathlessly while blood poured out of his mouth. The tears in his shirt revealed his open chest with a struggling heart and punctured lung.

Oliver's mouth was wide open, but he couldn't make a sound, no matter how hard he tried. Marcus's nails tore into Oliver's pant leg.

"You didn't save me!" Marcus screamed.

Oliver jumped, catching himself before falling off the couch in Nancy's living room. George ran to Oliver, playfully hitting him on his chest and stomach. Nancy stood across from him, staring at him.

"You were screaming," Nancy said with her arms crossed.

"Oh." Oliver yawned and sat up straight. "I didn't think I did that, but I guess I wouldn't know."

Oliver gave her a small smile for reassurance, while she continued to stare at him with concern. She wiped her hands on her apron.

"Breakfast is ready," she said, walking into the kitchen.

Oliver picked up George and carried him to the kitchen table. Nancy had already set the table for the three of them, and she brought over eggs and bacon. George sat in between Oliver and Nancy, as she put food on George's plate and patted his head. Oliver ate, but Nancy sat back in her chair, staring into space. She barely touched her dinner plate last evening either.

"You should eat, Nance."

Her eyes locked with his for a minute. Nancy nodded and ate a forkful of eggs. She took a sip of coffee. "Ollie?"

Oliver turned to her. "Yes?"

"Detective Howard didn't say a thing about the investigation. Do you think they'll find who did this?"

"A police officer told me he's one of the best; that if anyone can solve this, he can."

Nancy rested her head on her hand, eating some more eggs. "Is there anything else?"

Oliver avoided looking at her.

"Tell me," she said. She knew him too well. "I can handle it."

"Are you sure?" he asked.

"Yes."

"I'm done!" George yelled, so Nancy wiped his mouth and hands with a napkin. He ran into the living room to play with his toys.

Oliver took a deep breath, wondering how he could tell her everything. "Well, as you know, Marcus was seen at Grayson's Pub Friday night with a woman." He stopped, as she signaled to him to continue. "They talked for about an hour before leaving together.

There was also a man who approached him at the bar, asking for his money back."

"Where did they find Marcus?" she whispered.

He shook his head. "Nance—"

"Tell me, Ollie," she interrupted. "I'm not a child, I can take it..."

"I know you're not."

She put her hand over his. "I'm sorry, Ollie, I don't mean to snap at you. I just need to know where he was found."

"Your old apartment, he didn't sell it."

Nancy sighed, running her hands through her hair. "We got into a terrible, terrible argument before you came over on Friday, and I... I felt like I was going crazy. He insisted he was going back to work... I knew he was lying...I should've stayed home."

"You did the right thing by telling Detective Howard. You're another witness who saw Marcus leave with a young woman, and hopefully the description will help track her down." A question burned in the back of his throat. "They didn't see you?"

"The girl looked right at me, but there's no way she knew who I was. It made me feel sick, especially when they got into the Corvette. Then, Marcus never came home." Nancy teared up again. That wasn't the answer Oliver wanted to hear, but he tried not to show it.

Nancy made eye contact with Marcus's possible killer.

He couldn't think about that right now.

"Do you want to take a walk with me to my apartment?" Oliver asked. "Get a breath of fresh air? It might feel good."

"I'd rather stay here for now. I'm going to take a shower." She turned toward him. "Can you stay another night? I know the couch isn't very comfortable, but I can't be alone at night."

"I'll come back in a few hours. I'll run some errands, too."

"Thank you, Ollie." Nancy choked up, pressing her hand against her mouth.

"Of course." He gave her a small smile. George played with his toy cars and airplanes, making sound effects and giggling in the corner, unaware that he would never see his father again. Oliver wanted to stay and watch over Nancy, especially if the killer might have seen her. He finished eating his breakfast, collected their plates and set them by the kitchen sink. As he began to wash them, George ran to him, waving his car in the air.

"Uncle Ollie, my car broke!" he said, tearing up.

Oliver took it from him, but one of the wheels fell off and wouldn't go back on no matter how hard he tried to push it back into place. "I'm sorry, buddy. Looks like the wheel popped off. It still drives okay, though."

Oliver rolled it over the counter to show George and handed it back to him. George ran back into the living room while Oliver finished washing and drying the dishes and silverware. He picked up his keys and wallet and closed the door behind him, letting out a deep breath. The air around the apartment weighed down his lungs as he stepped down the stairs and left the building. The constricting feeling of grief had attached itself to Nancy and wouldn't loosen its grip. Having to sit and watch Nancy struggle without having any agency to make the situation better shattered his heart into pieces.

How would Nancy grapple with telling George about his father's death? George would start asking for his father sooner or later. Nancy not only worried about her son but also dealt with the own loss of her husband. The way she couldn't eat and cried when thanking Oliver... he couldn't think about it now. He couldn't show it; he had to remain stoic and strong for Nancy. *The only way out was through.*

Oliver kept his head down, walking around crowds of people laughing and having a typical Sunday morning of attending Mass followed by spending time with family and friends. Not trying to navigate the murder of their brother and the crumbling of everything they knew. The ladies wore nice sundresses, the gentlemen wore dapper suits, and the children walked by their parents' side.

Oliver didn't want to be around any of them. No wonder why Nancy wanted to avoid the crowds.

Climbing down the stairs into the subway, Oliver sat in the car, staring at his reflection in the window. His eyes had bags, and he slouched. He was on his way to Queens to visit Dr. Ed Taylor, one of Marcus's closest friends. If anyone knew about Marcus's gambling, it would be him. Oliver straightened his posture, checking his watch as the car stopped and doors opened. Dr. Taylor's apartment was around the corner, a grand white brick building. Oliver greeted the doorman and entered into a lobby with marble floors and a chandelier hanging above a round table holding a vase of daisies. Beautiful carved wood surrounded the gold elevators as Oliver stepped inside, taking it to the third floor.

352, he noted the label on every door. *Here it was.* He knocked on it. The door swung open with a dark-haired man standing there dressed in a gray suit.

"Hello, Dr. Taylor. I'm Oliver, Marcus's brother."

"Hello, Oliver." His voice was deep.

"Well, um, my..." He stuttered, not wanting to go through this again. Nothing could be worse than telling Nancy, but he couldn't keep repeating this news. "Marcus is dead."

"I'm so sorry about your brother, we were good friends."

"Thank you. Has Detective Howard visited you?"

"He has." He nodded. Dr. Taylor gestured Oliver into his apartment. Oliver walked through the modern kitchen with a glossy white round table and blue leather chairs, matching the blue fridge. White cabinets hung over the wooden countertops, and the floors were patterned black and white. It opened to the living room featuring white leather couches and a large window that offered the view of the East River overlooking Manhattan.

"Please take a seat, would you like coffee or tea?" he asked.

"No, thanks."

Dr. Taylor joined him. Oliver stared at Dr. Taylor's folded hands, thinking about the questions clouding his mind about his brother, affairs, gambling, and finances. The questions swarmed, not giving him a chance to sort through them. He needed to focus.

"Dr. Taylor—"

"Please call me Ed."

"Ed, Marcus might have been threatened by a man an hour or so before he was killed, demanding his money back. I wanted to know if you knew anything about this man, or if Marcus mentioned to you anything about his gambling."

Ed cleared his throat. "Marcus belonged to a club where he played poker and craps. The kind of people involved... I told him to stay away, but he loved the rush, winning lots of money in the beginning. Then, the debt began racking up. It is possible that man is responsible for your brother's death."

"Did Marcus tell you how much debt he was in?"

"No, he complained about it, but he never gave me any details. I didn't want any details about that club. Knowing anything made me a liability for my family."

Ed wore a wedding ring. Marcus didn't give his family the same courtesy.

No, Oliver shouldn't be thinking like that. It was inappropriate.

"Did Marcus seem stressed about the debt?" Oliver asked.

"His behavior grew more erratic, but he hid his feelings well. I didn't ask him about it. To be honest, I didn't want to know."

Oliver folded his hands on the table. "Marcus never told me about any of this. I had my suspicions. I thought it was strange for him to be in debt with his amount of income, but I never thought he would put himself in this kind of danger."

"It started about a couple of years ago, but the last year it's certainly gotten worse. Same thing with his affairs. They were sporadic at first, but then they became a pastime for him."

Oliver shook his head at the thought of infidelity as a 'pastime'. "Did he always see a different woman, or were there any he saw more than once?"

"I'm not sure. I didn't want to know about that behavior either.

I loved your brother, we had some great times together, and I will miss him dearly. But he had his faults."

That was a nice way of putting it.

"One way Marcus inspired me was his love for his work. He would work with patients day and night, testing out new medications and therapies. Yes, it would inflate his ego when they improved, but I could tell it genuinely made him happy. It can be a rewarding career, and he always pushed me to work harder."

"Yeah, he loved his job," Oliver agreed. "He always pushed me too to work hard and advance in my career. He would help me with applications and job interviews. I recently got promoted at the *Flatbush Times*, and it was because of him. He pushed me to ask for better pay and inquire about open positions. I'll miss asking him for advice on that sort of thing."

"He did have a heart, your brother. Once he gave out too large of a loan to a patient's family to help keep their son in Sinclair's to continue receiving treatment. I found out when I overheard the father thanking him in another room."

Oliver nodded. "That's nice to hear. Thanks, Ed. I better get back to Nancy."

"Of course. Anything you or Nancy need, please let me know." They stood, and Ed held out his hand for Oliver to shake. "Oliver, I would stay away from looking into what happened to Marcus. He was involved with dangerous people. Maybe it didn't have anything to do with his gambling, but this road won't lead to anything good. Nancy has already lost her husband, she doesn't need to lose you, too."

Oliver shook his hand. Ed led him out of his apartment and paused. "You, Nancy, and George are welcome here anytime."

Oliver thanked him again and left the building, giving a nod to the doorman. He stepped aside to avoid a manhole on the sidewalk, stepping down the stairs to the subway to return to Brooklyn. As the car moved through the darkness of the tunnel, he dwelled on the possibility of Marcus's death being money-related. Detective Howard must think it was a valid road to go down.

Once he arrived in Brooklyn, Oliver had a couple more errands to run. He first stopped at St. Catherine of Siena Cathedral. Steps led to three sets of doors, the steeples pointed above the rooftop, and bells rang. It must be one o'clock already. The three doors opened at once as churchgoers filed out of the noon Mass. Oliver stepped to the side and waited for a path to clear before climbing the stairs. A priest, wearing a green chasuble, shook hands with parishioners as they exited the church. After the last person left, Oliver approached him and shook his hand.

"Hi, Father. I need to make funeral arrangements for my brother."

"Marcus?" Father Richard asked.

"Yes."

"I'm so sorry, Oliver." He did the Sign of the Cross. "My goodness, he was so young. What terrible news, I'm sorry to hear that. I will add his name to our intentions this week."

"Thank you." Oliver lost count of the number of times he had said that lately. Hopefully he wouldn't need to break this news to anyone else. "Are you available to make the arrangements?"

"Not right now, I need to go to the hospital for a parishioner who's having surgery tonight, but I can meet with you tomorrow morning. Does eleven o'clock work for you?"

"Yes."

"You'll be in my prayers, Oliver. Tell Nancy that she and George will be in my prayers, as well." He shook Oliver's hand again.

"I will." Oliver left St. Catherine of Siena, climbing down the steps and returning to his apartment to collect his things to stay overnight with Nancy and George. A mother and her two children walked out of a toy store, holding hands. Oliver stopped in front of the shop window. A young boy played with a toy car painted with vibrant red, white, and blue, and it was double the size of George's broken one. George would love a new car, so Oliver went inside to purchase one for him. *George is going to be excited when he sees this.* He held tightly onto the car as he left the store and returned to his apartment building, passing by Fluffy lying on the doormat of his neighbor's apartment. As he unlocked the door, he picked up a large tote bag to fill with fresh pajamas and an additional outfit. He set the toy car inside and headed out, returning to Nancy's apartment building down the street.

Oliver stood outside of her apartment building, feeling the heavy air on his lungs once again. *Stay stoic. Stay strong.* This would be the hardest thing Nancy would have to go through. He surveyed the brick exterior top to bottom and took a deep breath. Oliver entered and climbed the creaky stairs. Once arrived, he knocked on the door, and Nancy let him in.

"You don't have to knock, Ollie," she said as he followed her into the living room. She had on a casual sundress with turquoise flowery details on the skirt and capped sleeves. Her brown hair was long and groomed, curled around her finger.

"I brought you a surprise, George!" Oliver said, trying to gather the tiny amount of excitement left inside him.

George's mouth made the shape of an o. "What? What?"

Oliver removed the car from the bag and held it in front of him, as George took it from his hands and grinned.

"That's really sweet of you, Ollie. What do you say, George?"

"Thank you, Uncle Ollie!"

"You're welcome. Be careful with it, all right?"

George ran into the corner and kneeling on the floor, moving the car over the hardwood floors. He hit it against the radiator, but Oliver didn't say a word. He remembered breaking an apartment window when he and Marcus were growing up. Besides, George deserved to have some fun.

"Can we speak in the bedroom for a moment?" Nancy asked, pointing to it.

Oliver nodded, following her inside and closing the door. Nancy leaned against the wall, holding her chin and staring at the floors like she was trying to collect her thoughts. The room was still as the sun beat down onto the bed, making the white quilt sparkle and exposing a small amount of dust floating in the air. Silence consumed the room, even George's sound effects couldn't permeate through the cracks in the door. Oliver couldn't guess what she wanted to say.

Nancy crossed her arms, locking eyes with Oliver. "Did the police find anything? Any clues?"

Oliver cleared his throat, needing a glass of water to soothe it. "No, I haven't heard of any clues."

"I've been thinking about what you said, about how some guy from a gambling club might have killed Marcus, but I don't think that's the case."

"Why?" Oliver asked, squinting.

"I couldn't quite place it at first, but something doesn't feel right about it. Of course I may be wrong and perhaps, Detective Howard will find that. But I think it's the young woman who left with him. Marcus was stumbling a little; he was drunk. He doesn't handle alcohol well, and it wouldn't be impossible for her to take him down."

"Marcus had his wallet on him, and the detective sorted through the cash," Oliver said. "He wasn't robbed. Whoever killed him wasn't interested in his money."

Nancy nodded. "And the manner he was killed... I think she wanted revenge against Marcus, but I have no idea why."

9

Thunder boomed in the streets of Brooklyn, NY. Flashes of lightning broke through the cracks in the curtains in Nancy's family room, and rain crashed against the windows. The apartment door creaked open slowly, trying not to make noise, and closed with a quiet click. Footsteps approached the couch Oliver slept on, light but enough weight for the floors to creak. Oliver sat up slightly, rubbing his eyes to get a look. A shadowy figure stood beside the couch, holding an object. His vision still wasn't clear, so he rubbed his eyes and looked again. A flash of lightning revealed a young woman, wearing a black dress and gloves and clutching a knife in her hand. Oliver turned on the lamp on the end table, and a young woman with long brown hair stood before him with bloodshot eyes, smeared red lipstick, and blood covering her dress and hands. Oliver backed himself against the back of the couch, the back of his head hitting the wall.

"Ollie!" Someone whispered, shaking him awake. "Ollie!"

Nancy leaned toward him in her nightgown and held onto his arm. "You must have been having a nightmare."

"Yeah, I guess I was." It felt as real as the bruise forming on the back of his head. Nancy looked concerned at him, finally letting go of his arm. "You can go back to sleep, I'm fine."

"Are you sure?"

"I'm fine, Nance, I am." He assured her.

"All right." She didn't seem to believe him, but she returned to her bedroom anyway and closed the door. It was almost seven o'clock, and Oliver was too shaken to go back to sleep. He broke out in a sweat in an already hot apartment. He sat, slouching. What if that young woman tries to go after Nancy next? Nancy said they made eye contact outside of Grayson's Pub. What if the young woman recognized her?

Oliver went into the kitchen and drank a glass of water, trying to remove these thoughts from his mind. The police would get to the bottom of Marcus's death. He had no evidence that the young woman knew who Nancy was. But the young woman probably researched Marcus and his family prior to killing him. Even if she did know about Nancy, the chances were probably low that Nancy would be the next target. But it didn't matter how low the chances were. A chance was too much of a risk. Oliver must find out where the police were in their investigation.

A thump came from outside the door, and the door didn't have a peephole. Oliver set the glass on the counter, slowly approaching the door and holding his breath. He envisioned the young woman standing on the other side of it, holding a knife to murder him and Nancy. He wouldn't let that happen. He grabbed a knife from the drawer, clutching it in one hand and grasping the doorknob with the other. After he whipped it open and held the knife higher, no one was there but a newspaper on the doormat.

After putting the knife away, Oliver picked up the newspaper, closing the door with his foot and turning the pages until he reached the obituaries. He sat at his kitchen table, setting the newspaper down and tracing his finger down each page. His brother's name would be there after the arrangements were made. Oliver closed the paper, burying his head in his hands. He waited for when it would finally hit him that he would never see his brother again. At least in this life. The apartment door would burst open with his brother pounding his feet on the floor and laughing about getting into a fight at a local bar. He would hold open his arms wide for George who would be most pleased to see his father again. Nancy would be furious at how late he came home but happy he came home at all. The scene unfolded in Oliver's mind so clearly that it could be real. But the front door remained closed, and Marcus would never step through it again.

A photo of Marcus, Nancy, and George sat on the end table. George sat in a highchair at the kitchen table, blowing out candles on his birthday cake while Marcus and Nancy stood behind him, smiling. Oliver took that picture, excited to celebrate George's second birthday with them. Nancy's dress was the same one she wore the first time he met her.

* * *

Six years ago, Marcus dragged Oliver along to a work party at a local bar. Oliver walked alongside him to Grayson's Pub, putting his hands in his pockets as the chilly breeze picked up.

"Why are you walking so slow?" Marcus asked.

"Why do you think?"

"Oh, come on!" Marcus hit Oliver across his back. "Listen, Oliver. You need to get out more and socialize and make connections. It's not good for you to sit around the apartment every weekend alone. Someone here might have a friend who has a cousin who works at the *New York Times*. How do you think I ended up at Sinclair's? Connections. This will be good for you, and I promise to buy you a couple drinks, all right?"

"Fine, but don't leave me alone while you talk with everyone."

Marcus opened the door for him as the heat hit against his cheeks, and he rubbed his hands together. A couple of dozen men packed into the back of the bar. Some hovered around the pool table, while a couple of others played darts. The rest drank and smoked at the bar. The chatter echoed to the front as Marcus placed his hand on Oliver's shoulder, pushing him toward the group. A guy raised his hands in the air, approaching Marcus and shaking his hand.

"This is my brother, Oliver. Oliver, this is... should I introduce you as Dr. Taylor?"

"No, I'm not one of those guys!" Ed said, shaking his hand. "I'm Ed."

"Of course you are! What are you talking about?" Marcus exclaimed.

"Nice to meet you," Oliver said.

Ed turned to Oliver. "Likewise. Your brother can be a real jackass, you know."

"I'm aware." Oliver laughed, as they walked to the bar to order drinks. After he took a seat, a couple more men walked in, shouting Marcus's and Ed's names. So Oliver sat alone at the bar while Marcus laughed with his friends near the entrance. He took a sip of his beer. *Of course.* This was a mistake; he should've known better. Marcus always left him alone at these things, and Oliver would spend the rest of the evening with no one to talk to. *After this beer, I'm sneaking out.* Marcus wouldn't notice if he was gone.

That's when a girl in an olive green dress sat beside him. She cradled a cup of tea and put a matching sweater over her shoulders. She tucked her long brown hair behind her ear, as she rubbed her lips together.

"What are you doing here?" she asked before taking a sip of her tea. "I'm dreadfully bored."

"My brother asked me to come." Oliver pointed to him. "He's Marcus, the guy talking to the gray-haired man over there."

"Oh, that's my dad, Francis. He's the reason why I'm here." She put her fist under her chin and gave Oliver her full attention. "He always wants me to come to these things for some reason. I don't know anyone, and I'm not looking to become a nurse."

"Maybe he doesn't like going out alone?" Oliver asked.

She shrugged. "Maybe."

"Yeah, I'm not sure why I'm here either."

"Are you looking to be a doctor or something?"

Oliver shook his head. "No, my brother's almost done with medical school, and he's interning at Sinclair's. He loves psychiatry and all things medical, but I don't find it interesting."

"I don't either! Medical talk is so boring to me; I can't stand it."

"My brother can go on for hours about it."

"Same with my father!"

They both laughed, locking eyes with each other.

"I don't know your name," she said, taking another sip of tea.

"I'm Oliver. What's yours?"

"Nancy. So if you're not interested in medicine, what are you interested in?"

"I want to be a writer, a journalist. I'm interning at the *Flatbush Times*."

"Oh, my! That's so exciting!" Nancy leaned toward him as Oliver cracked a smile. "I love writing. Tell me what you're working on!"

No one had ever asked him that question before. "Well, I just started and my job mainly consists of getting coffee and taking notes at meetings."

"Well, you have to start somewhere, right?" She put her hand on his arm briefly.

Her smile was warm and beautiful. No one found Oliver remotely this interesting. Ever. Marcus would wave him off if he went on too long about his work, but he had no problem talking for days about his work with his patients.

"Hello?" The bartender asked, as Oliver flinched and Nancy laughed. "I said, would you like anything else?"

"No, I'm all set. Thank you."

As the bartender walked away, Nancy turned to him. "I have an idea."

"What's that?"

"My friends are at a dance a few blocks down."

Oliver's eyes widened. This had to be a hint. "Would you like to go together?"

She nodded. "I would. I'm going to tell my dad."

Nancy left her stool and approached her father. Her father introduced her to Marcus, and she shook his hand. As she was explaining her plans, her father and Marcus turned and looked at Oliver. Nancy's father grimaced but softened his face after Marcus said a few words. Oliver's hands became clammy as he rubbed them against his pant legs. Thankfully it was cold out, and that should take care of it. Maybe drinking some more beer would help.

After a few more minutes, Nancy returned. "Are you ready?"

"Yes." Oliver said shyly. They left the bar together.

Leaves fell off the branches of trees as the streetlights began to turn on. They walked side by side. He stuck his hands in his pockets as Nancy held onto her purse with her gloved hands. The skirt of her dress swung with each step she took.

"I have to confess something," Oliver said quietly as they continued walking. "I've never really danced before."

Nancy turned to him with a look of amazement, trying to conceal a smile. She was unsuccessful. "Really?"

"Intern hours are a killer, and that's why I was with my brother tonight. He's always telling me to get out more. I don't like being around a lot of people, but I know it's good for me."

She giggled, wrapping her arm around his. "I also have a confession to make."

He listened intently.

"I'm a lousy dancer."

He chuckled. They stepped into the dance hall where a band played on stage with couples crowding the shiny wooden floor. Large luminescent lights were mounted in the ceiling. At least it was a fast-paced song. Nancy waved to a couple of girls dancing with their partners, as she guided him to the dance floor, holding his hand tightly. The song changed to a slow one as Oliver took her hand in his and wrapped his arm around her waist. Her hand held onto his while the other lay on his shoulder. Nancy's feet moved and her body swayed to the rhythm without having to think about it. This must be a place where she and her friends hung out often. Nancy's eyes locked with his.

"You're not too bad," she said. "See? It's not complicated."

"You lied to me. You are good at dancing."

Her eyes twinkled, as she moved closer to him. "Thank you for saving me from having an awful evening. This is much better."

"Yes, it is," he agreed.

* * *

Oliver brought himself back, staring at the photograph of his brother's family. He went to make a cup of coffee and returned to the table to pass the time while the sun rose. About a couple of hours later, Nancy stepped into the kitchen, putting on an apron and starting to make breakfast. She cracked a few eggs, whisked them together, and threw them into a frying pan. Her hands were shaky and her dress had a small tear in its sleeve. She shouldn't have to concern herself with making breakfast for him; she had enough on her mind already.

"It keeps me busy, Ollie," Nancy said, noticing him staring at her. "I don't mind making you breakfast."

"Are you sure?" he asked.

"Yes, I'm sure. I could go with you today to St. Catherine of Siena if you'd like."

"No, I have everything taken care of. You don't have to worry about it." Oliver paused nervously. "I was wondering if you'd like me to reach out to your father and tell him about Marcus and the arrangements."

Nancy met his gaze for a moment. "No."

"He loved Marcus, Nance."

"Believe me, I'm aware. I don't want him there, and I don't care to see him."

Oliver nodded as she turned to the stove again and added a few strips of bacon to the pan. He grabbed some plates, silverware, and napkins to set the table.

She sighed, looking over at Oliver. "I didn't mean to be rude, Ollie. It's kind that you thought about reaching out to my father, especially after..." Her voice trailed off. "I've had it with feeling guilty. He doesn't control me anymore. Look where his control has gotten me."

Nancy rolled her eyes and took a cleansing breath, turning her attention back to the stove.

Oliver sat back in his chair, not knowing how to respond.

"I'm going to take George to the park," she said. "I think you're right, it'll be good to get some fresh air."

"That's good."

"It was sweet of you to get George the toy car. He hasn't stopped playing with it."

"Oh, yeah. He's a good kid."

"Yeah," she whispered. Nancy slid the eggs and bacon onto a large plate and set them in the middle of the kitchen table. Oliver called George who ran over to him and sat on his lap, and Nancy sat in the chair next to him. George held the new car with one hand and ate with his other. Nancy picked up the paper to read it, flipping it open to the first page after eating a forkful of eggs.

"Are you going to the—"

"Don't say p-a-r-k yet, or he won't finish his breakfast." Nancy interrupted him without looking up from the paper.

"Oh, sorry."

"Don't be sorry."

Oliver took a few more bites of his breakfast and checked the clock. It was only ten o'clock, but he had to make a stop before St. Catherine of Siena. George finished eating, jumping down from Oliver's lap and returning to the corner to play with his other toys.

Oliver left to get ready in the bathroom and returned to the kitchen.

"I better get going. I'll see you two later." Oliver picked up his and George's plates, but Nancy held her hand out.

"I'll get those, Ollie. What time do you think you'll be back?"

"I'll be back by dinner at the latest," he said, buttoning his suit jacket.

"Okay. Please be safe."

"I will."

Nancy nodded and continued to eat, as he collected his keys and wallet before leaving the apartment. Clouds hovered over the earth, but the heat persisted. Oliver returned to his apartment building to visit a friend and neighbor who happened to work for the New York Police Department. The small object found in Marcus's pocket consumed his thoughts. The way Detective Howard stared at it meant it was a valuable lead.

Oliver passed by Fluffy and his apartment and knocked on the police officer's door. He cracked his knuckles. The officer might not be home; his shifts changed every week. No answer. He knocked twice more. No answer. Oliver sighed, giving up and heading to his own apartment when the door swung open.

"Oliver!" Benny said, hitting Oliver on his shoulder and shaking his hand. A towel was wrapped around his waist. "Come on in! I haven't seen you in a while."

"Hey, Benny."

Benny gestured to his small couch. Oliver collected the pile of old newspapers and placed them on the floor, so he could sit. "Do you want something to drink?"

"No thanks." Oliver sat as Benny looked around his kitchen. The hinges of a couple cabinets needed to be tightened, and drops of water dripped into the dishes in the sink.

"That's good. I'm basically out of everything," Benny said, opening his refrigerator and scanning the shelves. "I have to run to the store, I guess."

"Yeah, I've got to do that too." Oliver chuckled. Benny went into the bedroom to hopefully get dressed. Dust collected on the end tables and coffee table, causing Oliver's nose to become stuffy. The blue rug could be vacuumed, too. Oliver wouldn't touch anything as the couch looked sticky. *What a mess.* He couldn't wait to leave.

Benny joined him in the family room, fully dressed, and sat on a loveseat. "I'm sorry to hear about your brother. How have you been holding up?"

"I'm doing all right. I haven't thought about it." He didn't want to think about it.

"The crime in this city is getting out of hand," Benny said.

"Do you think they'll be able to solve my brother's case?"

"Detective Howard is one of the best, if not *the* best. My money's on him solving it."

Oliver had heard that before. "I've heard good things about him."

"No one likes to work with him, but he's very smart and makes connections other people overlook."

"That's good to hear, I want it to be solved quickly. I did want to ask you about something to do with the case."

"Go ahead, Oliver," he said, signaling for Oliver to continue.

"Have any clues been found?"

"Rumor has it, they recovered a black hair clip from Marcus's jacket."

Oliver's squinted. "A hair clip? That's it?"

"They're keeping it under wraps for the most part, so that's all I've heard."

"I understand. Sorry to have to leave so quickly, but I've got to get going."

"No problem! I'll see you around." They both stood and shook hands. "Sorry again about your brother. I'm sure we'll find who did this."

"Thanks Benny." Oliver let himself out, passing by his apartment and Fluffy to leave his building. It was 10:35 a.m. Time to head down the street toward St. Catherine of Siena Cathedral to make the final arrangements for Marcus's funeral.

He stopped at a red light on a street corner, glancing at a newsstand and giving it his full attention. Every newspaper front cover discussed his brother's murder. On one hand, maybe someone could provide information if they saw Marcus after leaving Grayson's Pub with some woman. On the other hand, he didn't like his brother's death being broadcasted for all to see. The newspaper talked about privacy, but they had reached out to Nancy for comment. Of course, she wouldn't give them anything.

The light turned green, but Oliver couldn't leave. A young woman stood in front of him with long brown hair, staring at Marcus's portrait. She picked up a copy and read through the story. She set it back, continuing to stare at it with rapt attention. She couldn't look away. And neither could Oliver. She might have known Marcus.

Oliver approached her. "Miss?"

She flinched at the sound of his voice.

"Didn't mean to scare you, sorry," he said.

The young woman turned to him, holding her chest, but she didn't seem scared. "No, it's fine."

"Do you know Marcus?"

She hesitated. "I don't think so. He looked familiar, that's all. I can't believe someone would do something so evil to another human being. It's horrible. Do you know him?"

Oliver nodded. "I'm his brother."

Her jaw dropped. "I'm so sorry, I can't imagine what you're going through. I'm heading to church now, I'll say a prayer for him and your family. My thoughts are with his wife."

My thoughts are with his wife.

"Thank you, that's very kind of you." Oliver squinted. "What's your name?"

"Eliza." She responded quickly.

"Eliza?"

"Yes, and you?"

Oliver wanted a last name, but she didn't give him one. He didn't even trust that she gave him her real first name. "Oliver."

"Nice to meet you, Oliver. Again, I'm sorry for your loss." She straightened her posture and left him, crossing the street. Oliver waited to see if she would actually walk into the church. And she did, stepping up the cement steps and opening the wooden door triple her height. *Liar.* She knew Marcus. Something felt off about her.

10

As Clara walked down the streets of Brooklyn to St. Catherine of Siena Cathedral, she passed by groups of businessmen, tourists, students, and women with their children. The heat became suffocating as the air felt heavy and thick.

There was a clothing store where women bought fashionable dresses and skirts of every color of the rainbow. The young ladies smiled, picking out their favorite ones to try on. Clara continued, staring through the window at the pretty clothes. She next passed a bookshop with men and women browsing the shelves, reading the blurbs and chatting about which ones they should buy. A young woman in a blue skirt and white shirt held hands with a young man in a tan suit as they walked down the aisle. Clara paused before remembering she was already late to her weekly meeting with Father Benedict. She didn't have the time.

Since the traffic light turned red, she stopped at a street corner, clutching her purse. A woman leaned against a flagpole, while her boyfriend placed one hand above her head and looked into her eyes. A child held hands with their father, asking for ice cream over and over again.

The light turned green again, so she continued on. A couple

more blocks until she would reach her destination. Clara glanced at a newsstand against the side of a building and jolted backward.

MARCUS ANDERSON MURDERED

MARCUS ANDERSON FOUND DEAD IN HIS APARTMENT

MARCUS ANDERSON STABBED TO DEATH

* * *

Clara brought herself back to three nights ago, the night of Marcus's murder. She watched her bloody dress and Marcus's trench coat burn to ash in her backyard. She exhaled. Yes, Marcus must have ripped her hair clip out of her hair to trap her, but this city was large. Her father and mother hadn't caught her. That was what mattered most.

Another man down, one more to go.

"What are you doing?" her father asked. "It's nearly eighty degrees out."

Clara turned. The heat from the raging fire felt like it was burning through her dress and melting the skin and muscle in her back. Her father's eyes, on the other hand, burned through hers. "I was smoking and dropped my cigarette."

"Aren't you hot?"

Yes, she was burning. Clara shook her head. "I'm fine. I just got back from a dance hall with Betty and Kate."

Her father walked closer to her. "Have you been crying?"

Her eyes must still be swollen and red, no amount of smiling would make that go away. "Well, it took an embarrassingly long time for a guy to ask me to dance. Hurt my confidence a bit."

"Men can be assholes. You can't take it personally." He went to grab a bucket from the shed and proceeded to fill it with water from the hose before handing it to her. "Put the fire out and get some sleep, all right? You'll feel better in the morning."

Clara nodded.

"Goodnight."

"Goodnight," she repeated.

Clara waited for him to go back inside. Her father slammed the door, turning off the lights in the kitchen. She turned again to face the fire, waiting to ensure Marcus's trench coat was destroyed inside.

* * *

The newsstand stood before Clara again and the headlines continued to stare at her. The trench coat had been destroyed three nights ago. No need to worry about a hair clip.

"Need help with anything?" the worker asked, making Clara flinch.

"No, thank you."

He continued reading a magazine.

The portrait of Marcus stared at her with his groomed mustache resting on his thin lips, smirking at her. She picked up one of the papers. A stark contrast to the man lying on the floor with his head bashed in and a stab wound in his chest, the life leaving his eyes. What did Marcus think about while taking his last breath? Clara would bet it wasn't his family.

Detective Howard is leading the case to solve the vicious murder of Marcus Anderson, a man who loved his family and dedicated his career to the science of psychiatry.

They're describing Marcus as a family man? Clara rolled her eyes.

Detective Howard is following leads and is determined to hunt down the person responsible for such a heinous crime. When asked about potential clues, Detective Howard declined to reveal any information at this time. He said the investigation is ongoing and will give updates when appropriate. He also requests the public to give privacy to Marcus Anderson's family during this difficult time. If you have any

information about Anderson or this case, do not hesitate to contact the New York Police Department.

She set the paper down. The article said a lot without saying anything at all. No new information.

Shit, I'm late. She was supposed to meet with Father Benedict at 10:30, not 10:45.

"Miss?" a man said behind her. Clara jumped and turned around, holding her chest for dramatic effect. He put his hands in his pockets. "Didn't mean to scare you. Sorry."

"No, it's fine." He was Oliver Anderson, Marcus's brother. He had the same height and stature as Marcus, but carried himself differently and looked to be a few years younger. Clara needed to say as little as possible and leave. No need to read into this.

He tilted his head. "Do you know Marcus?"

Oliver spoke about his brother in the present tense. The loss must not have hit him yet. Why was he looking at her quizzically? Almost as though he had a picture in his head he was trying to match her to. Had he seen her before? Why did he approach her in the first place? She was hesitating too much.

"I don't think so. He looked familiar, that's all. I can't believe someone would do something so evil to another human being. It's horrible. Do you know him?"

Oliver sighed. "I'm his brother."

"I'm so sorry, I can't imagine what you're going through," Clara said. "I'm heading to church now, I'll say a prayer for him and your family. My thoughts are with his wife." She stopped herself before saying Nancy.

"Thank you, that's very kind of you." Oliver looked to be deep in thought, not paying attention to the words coming out of his mouth. Another question had to be coming. "What's your name?"

There it was. "Eliza."

"Eliza?" He gave her a look of disbelief.

"Yes, and you?"

"Oliver."

Yes, she knew that. She needed to leave.

"Nice to meet you, Oliver. Again, I'm sorry for your loss." Clara left him, crossed the street, and arrived at St. Catherine of Siena Cathedral, a Roman Catholic Church, putting a black veil on her head. She opened the large, dark brown stained door and stepped inside, wondering if Oliver watched her. The door shut behind her, and she took a deep breath.

The air was no better in here; it was still and reeked of incense. She passed by an array of lit candles, making her feel hotter. She stepped into the church, a long aisle leading to the altar with five large columns holding the 130-foot-tall ceiling. Four people kneeled in the pews separately, one of them staring into their folded hands, while the others stared above the altar at the crucifix. White marble covered the extravagant altar, with a gold-encrusted tabernacle standing between two stone angels facing each other with their palms pressed together.

The stained-glass windows on the sides of the church explained different biblical scenes, ranging from the Garden of Eden to Moses parting the Red Sea to Jesus's appearance to his disciples after His resurrection. The windows had bright colors that became enhanced by sunshine. The left side of the altar featured a statue of the Blessed Mother with a few roses at her feet, while the right side displayed St. Joseph with a child Jesus.

Clara checked the front doors a few times. No sign of Oliver. If he were to follow her, he would be in the church by now.

In the front right-hand corner of the church was the confessional. A man walked out and passed her by, heading to the pew to do his penance. Clara walked in next, asking for the divider to be removed. She didn't come for confession.

"Hello, Clara," said Father Benedict, setting a book beside him and taking off his reading glasses. "You're a little late. I was starting to get worried."

"Sorry."

"It's no problem. How has your day been so far?" He scratched his bald head.

Terrible, but Oliver couldn't find her in here. "It's going well, I did some window shopping before coming here. Nothing exciting."

"What kind of shops?"

"A clothing store and a bookstore."

"I love a good bookstore." He smiled. Clara returned one, crossing one leg over the other. "Have you been reading anything?"

Clara shook her head. "No, I've been too busy lately, but I want to."

"Yeah, you must have a lot on your plate. How is your family doing?"

"Everything's been all right lately," she said, crossing her arms.

He tilted his head downward and arched his brow. "Has there been any arguing?"

"I would call it fighting, rather than arguing."

"You're arguing with me about whether it's arguing."

"Sorry." She gazed at the floor. This confessional was too hot. "I'm trying to have more patience with my father."

"Glad to hear. He means well, Clara. He has made some mistakes, as we all have, but I can tell he cares about you very much."

"Mistakes" included, but were not limited to, committing adultery and never putting his family first.

"Do you think he's making an effort with you?"

"Yes," Clara lied, pulling out a cigarette from her purse.

"No smoking in this vestibule, Clara."

She sighed and placed it back.

"Now, tell me how you cope with this. Cigarettes?"

If only he knew. "Yes, cigarettes. They calm me."

"I'm glad you're continuing to visit each week. It's good to release your anger and frustrations through communication."

"Yeah." She shrugged. "Thanks for listening every week."

"Of course," he said with a smile. "Continue to pray for

patience. If you're seeing your father making an effort with you, you should make an effort with him. Not forgiving someone hurts yourself. It's the only way to truly move on."

The muscles in Clara's neck tensed up, but she managed to nod anyway.

"Is there anything else you would like to talk about today?"

Clara gazed at the ceiling quizzically, pretending to search her thoughts. Afterwards, she shook her head.

"Remember what I told you last week? Say it, Clara."

Clara took a deep breath.

The priest made a mistake. He hadn't told her anything important last week.

"Thank you again, Father," she said.

"Of course," he repeated. "If you need anything, I'm always here."

"See you next week."

"See you next week," he repeated, picking up his book and reading glasses.

Clara collected her purse and left the confessional, walking toward the front doors when Oliver entered, speaking to another priest. Clara hid behind a wall, craning her neck and holding her breath. *Please don't come this way. Please don't come this way.*

"I'm so sorry again to hear about your brother's death, Oliver," Father Richard said, walking alongside him.

"Thank you, Father."

They stepped into an office, Father Richard gesturing to Oliver to go inside and closing the door. Clara knew better. She should leave the church and get on with her day. Nothing good could come from eavesdropping. A force pulled at her ankles. There might have been updates in the investigation. Against her better judgment, she crossed the room. She looked around. No one paid any attention to her. She leaned toward the door and squinted.

"Have you seen the papers?"

"I have."

"We're going to need a closed-casket service."

"The poor wife and boy," someone sighed. It didn't sound like Oliver's voice, it must be the priest's. "Have the police any clue who did such a dreadful thing?"

"No, but they did find a clue."

The hair clip.

"And all the police found was a hair clip."

The fucking hair clip.

"We'll keep the investigation in our prayers, and I've added Marcus to our daily intentions."

"Thank you, Father."

They moved on to discussing funeral arrangements. Clara gazed toward the confessionals, and Father Benedict stared at her with his eyebrows raised. She held her breath and straightened her posture as he waved her over. Of course a priest caught her eavesdropping. It was a terrible idea, and now she would have to explain why she was trying to overhear a conversation between a priest and the brother of a murder victim.

"Maybe say some prayers, Clara. They can help clear your mind and relieve stress."

She didn't have time. Oliver Anderson could leave the office and see her. He let her walk away last time, but that wouldn't be the case again. She glanced at the side door at the front of the church.

"Is something wrong?" he asked.

"No, you're right. I'm going to say a prayer." Clara said as she kneeled in a pew. He smiled at her in approval and returned into the confessional, putting up the divider and closing the door. An elderly man walked into the other side for confession. Clara turned. Father Richard's office was still closed. She couldn't risk running into Oliver again. This prayer had to be quick.

Dear Lord, please stop the burning. I try to extinguish the flames, but I can't, no matter how hard I try. I always feel like I'm on fire. Please stop the burning, Lord. Sometimes I can't take it anymore.

Clara turned again to check the door. Closed. The meeting

would be over soon. How long did it take to make funeral arrangements? She couldn't imagine it taking very long.

I promise I'll be good again. I promise I'll put this life behind me soon. Please take this pain away. I know you can.

Clare checked one more time. Closed.

Amen.

She made the Sign of the Cross and walked up to the front of the church just as a door creaked open. *Shit,* she thought, sprinting around the corner, her shoes tapping against the marble floor. Clara looked around the corner as Oliver left the office. She backed into the wall as Oliver stepped closer, gazing around the church, probably searching for her. He must be onto her. Clara looked in the opposite direction, her muscles tightening, before footsteps faded away. Oliver left the church with his hands in his pockets. She waited a few minutes, staring at the lit candles on either side of a statue of St. Catherine of Siena. The flames flickered as the statue stared at the ground, holding a cross and flowers in her arms and wearing a crown of thorns. A couple of elderly women left their pew, walking out of the church. Clara followed them.

The cars swarmed in the streets, but all Clara could think about was how to stay in the clear. The police found her hair clip in Marcus's pocket. It was a big city: that fact she would cling onto for dear life. Besides, Marcus having one of her hair clips in his pocket didn't incriminate her of murder. *Stop obsessing over the damn hair clip. You're being paranoid.*

Clara needed to lie low for a little while and put her plans on hold. Standing on a street corner and waiting for the light to change, she took a cigarette out of her purse and lit it. One more man left on her list, but it wouldn't be wise to act right away. The investigation needed to simmer down first. They would establish the connection with her victims too easily if she continued right away. Her goal was so close to her grasp that she could reach out, the tips of her fingers touching it before her arms would give out, causing her to fall short.

No need to ever see Oliver. It wasn't like she would ever cross paths with him again. Both of them being in church was a wild coincidence. God was funny, He really made her face one of her greatest sins today. Clara smirked, crossing the street and walking a few blocks. Everything would be fine. The police would run out of leads, if they hadn't already, and the case would turn cold in no time.

She returned home as footsteps creaked down the stairs. Her father held the railing with one hand while rubbing his eyes with the other. He must have come home for lunch. Her mother's purse was gone from the front closet, so she must have gone out. Clara tried to keep her expression blank, but her mouth wanted to frown. The house was never empty.

"Clara, would you make me some lunch?" her father asked, reaching the last step.

"Yes, because I have to make some for myself."

"That's my girl." He smiled, as she fought the urge to roll her eyes.

Clara followed him through the family room into the kitchen, and her father sat, continuing where he had left off in the newspaper from this morning. "Can you make me a pot of coffee as well, please?"

"Yes." Clara poured cold water into their machine, followed by coffee grounds into the basket, and assembled it to brew. The water washed over the grounds, dripping into the pot, and the smell overtook the air. Clara couldn't drink coffee often. It made her nervous.

"Do you have any plans tonight with Kate and Betty?"

"No, I don't have any plans. Maybe I'll take a walk."

"I'm sorry about working so late. I have a couple patients who are on the cusp of a complete recovery, and I'm doing everything I can to make that happen."

"I understand." She collected the ingredients to make turkey sandwiches, laying them out on the counter. The pages of the newspaper turned as she took out four pieces of bread, two per plate.

"It shouldn't be too much longer, and I'll be home a lot more. Maybe we could go to the show for your birthday like we used to."

"That would be nice." Her father used to let her choose a movie and get a large popcorn on her birthday. Sometimes he would take her to Richardson's Candy Store to pick out a chocolate bar afterward. She always looked forward to her birthday. Times had changed.

"Yeah, it would." He agreed as he flipped the newspaper page again. "Do you remember Dr. Anderson?"

Clara stopped for a second before unwrapping the turkey. "I do. What about him?"

"He was murdered a couple days ago."

"Really?"

"Yeah, I feel terrible for his family. They shouldn't give these gruesome details about his death in the paper like this; it's inappropriate."

"The paper's probably hoping to sell more copies, that's all they care about."

"Yes, I agree. I'm going to have to go to the funeral."

"Oh." She added turkey on two pieces of bread.

"There's no date yet, but I'm sure it'll be this week or next. I would really appreciate it if you would join me."

Clara froze for a split second and took the mayo out of the fridge. It took everything in her power not to slam the jar against the countertop. "I don't want to go to a funeral—I won't know anyone there. I didn't know Dr. Anderson well at all."

"Well, I'll be there, and it's just a Mass. We'll pay our respects and move on. You won't make me go all alone, will you?"

Her mother must have turned him down. Clara knew her father too well to believe he would let her out of this one. No excuse would be good enough.

"I'm guessing I have no choice."

"You would be right." He chuckled, flipping a newspaper page again.

Clara took out a knife and stared at it, spreading the mayo on the two pieces of bread. She finished making the sandwiches, giving one plate to her father along with a cup of coffee.

"Thank you, Clara," he said, setting the newspaper aside and taking a sip from his mug.

"You're welcome." Clara sat across from him with her plate and a glass of water. They started eating in silence before her father left to check the mail. She continued eating as the grandfather clock ticked in the corner. A few minutes had passed, but he hadn't returned. Clara took another bite before leaving the table and approaching the front window. Her father was talking with a neighbor. As turned her head, she froze. He'd left his medical bag next to the front door. Since he looked to be in deep conversation outside, Clara raced up the stairs to the bathroom to grab a small glass jar she kept her bobby pins in. She dumped the bobby pins onto the counter and returned downstairs. After checking on her father again, she knelt beside the bag and searched for the Secobarbital, a white powdery substance. She dug through the pens, notepads, mints, and other medications.

Come on. Come on.

The clock kept ticking. Her father would be returning inside any moment.

"Got it!" she whispered, holding the vial. She poured some into her jar, but not enough for her father to notice. Clara shoved the vial into the bag as she ran to her bedroom. She opened her floral jewelry box sitting on her dresser and removed a compartment to hide the glass jar inside. After putting the compartment back and closing the box, Clara returned to the kitchen table and took another bite of her sandwich. Her father walked in through the front door and joined her once again. She drew in a deep breath, she needed to calm down. He looked at her, tilting his head.

"That took a little bit," Clara said.

"Yeah, I was talking to Kevin next door. He's been having issues with his refrigerator. He asked his son to fix it, but he couldn't. He'll have to hire someone."

"Or he might have to buy a new one."

"Yeah, that's what I told him." Her father checked his watch and finished his sandwich. "Well, I better be getting back to work. I'll see you later."

Clara smiled at him as he patted her shoulder. "Bye, Dad!"

He collected his medical bag and headed out the door. Perfect timing. Clara was left alone to think about how she had to attend the funeral of the man she had killed. And avoid Oliver Anderson in the process.

11

Oliver climbed the steps of St. Catherine of Siena to plan the details of Marcus's funeral. The young woman from the newsstand entered a few minutes ago and should still be inside. One of the three large wooden doors opened with an elderly lady with a white veil walking out, holding a Rosary. Oliver held the door open for her as she thanked him. He gazed around the entrance, searching for the young woman, but Father Richard came out of his office and approached him. He was one of the five priests who served at this parish.

"Hi, Father Richard." Oliver shook his hand.

"Hello, my friend. I'm so sorry again to hear about your brother, Oliver," the priest said, walking alongside him.

"Thank you."

Father Richard led him into his office. It had a painting of the Blessed Mother on the wall and a cross and a small statue of St. Catherine of Siena standing on his desk. One of the three windows was stained glass, the colors reflecting onto the marble flooring. While Father Richard sat behind the desk, Oliver sat in a chair opposite him.

"Have you seen the papers?" Oliver asked.

"I have." He nodded.

Oliver's body shuttered, thinking about the state of Marcus when he found him. Nancy didn't want a wake, nor did he. "We're going to need a closed-casket service."

"The poor wife and boy." Father Richard sighed, making the Sign of the Cross.

"And all the police found was a hair clip."

"We'll keep the investigation in our prayers, and I've added Marcus to our daily intentions."

"Thank you, Father." Oliver folded his hands in his lap.

"Are you in need of counseling?"

Oliver shook his head. "Not now, I would like to just make the arrangements today."

"All right, I'll give you a few readings to choose from for the first and second readings." He handed pages of them to Oliver to look over. "Are there any songs you would like to be played?"

That young woman matched the description: long brown hair, about the right height, looked to be no more than twenty years old.

"Oliver?"

Oliver glanced up distractedly and shook his head. "Whatever is usually played will do."

"Uh-huh," Father Richard said, putting his hand under his chin. "It's very kind of you to take care of this for Nancy."

Oliver kept his eyes on the paper. "It's the least I can do."

Father Richard jotted down notes as Oliver looked over the readings.

He will swallow up death in victory; and the Lord God will wipe away tears from all faces.

If God is for us, who is against us?

The sting of death is sin.

After several minutes, Oliver chose the ones that spoke to him, ones he hoped would bring the most comfort to Nancy. Father Richard took them back and wrote down Oliver's choices. He sat back in his chair with his hands folded, elbows resting on the armrests. "How are you doing, Oliver?"

He had already told Father Richard that this meeting was for funeral arrangements, not counseling. Still, no one had asked him this question yet (well, besides Benny). Not that he would blame Nancy, of course. She had enough to deal with.

"I haven't fully processed everything."

"That's normal; it's a huge shock." Father Richard said. "I'm available anytime to talk, Oliver. It would be good to get some things off your chest, release the tension you've been holding in."

"I'll keep that in mind."

"Please do," he said. "You're always welcome here. Nothing you say will ever leave these walls. Now, tell me more about Marcus. I need more material for my homily."

Oliver explained everything he could about Marcus, mainly discussing Marcus's love of psychiatry and the breakthroughs he had made with his patients. That was what he truly lived for. Afterwards, Oliver spoke about Marcus being a husband and father. He didn't want to lie and say Marcus was the greatest family man to have ever existed, but Marcus did love George and his health issues did tear him apart at times. Marcus pretended it had no effect on him, but Oliver knew better.

"Thank you, Oliver," he said, jotting down a few more notes before setting his pen down.

"Thank you. Have a good day."

"You too, Oliver."

Oliver and Father Richard stood, shaking hands again. He left Father Richard's office and stepped into the main church, searching the pews. The young woman he ran into at the newsstand was nowhere to be found. Did she actually come inside or pray, or did she pretend and leave through the side exit? Oliver let out a sigh, leaving the church. He should have followed her; he let her get away again.

My thoughts are with his wife. Why did she single out Nancy?

She went to St. Catherine of Siena, so she must live close by. She didn't give the impression that she knew who Oliver was, but she knew who he was now.

Oliver had no way of tracking her, nothing to go on. He may never run into her again. Granted, she might not have been the correct young woman.

The streets were bustling that Monday afternoon with wives interlocking arms with their husbands, children running around playing ball, and elderly men walking and smoking. He was about to return to Nancy's apartment, but maybe surprising Nancy and George at the park would be better. As he walked a few blocks, he passed by the apartment where Nancy had lived with her parents. He stopped, staring at a lamppost out front.

* * *

Six years ago, Nancy waited under the lamppost the second time they met, leaning against it and holding onto her purse with gloved hands. Oliver locked eyes with her as he made his way down the street, and she met him halfway. Her cheeks were rosy, and she kept fixing her curled hair after the wind disturbed it.

"Hi, Ollie!" she said, shivering. "What would you like to do?"

"There's a new soda fountain that opened a few blocks down. Would you like to get one?"

"I'd love to." Her lips matched her red dresscoat. They interlocked arms and made their way to Walter's Soda Shop, full of teens and twenty-somethings, sitting on stools and sipping soda pops and milkshakes. Black-and-white tiles covered the floor, the jukebox played "Rock Around the Clock" by Bill Haley and His Comets, and turquoise paint covered the walls. The stools had fire-engine red leather cushions by the counter. Oliver led her to an open booth by the opposite wall with bright blue leather seats and a shiny white table.

"I'll grab us some soda pops," he offered.

Nancy nodded and sat in a booth, setting her purse beside her. Oliver approached the worker wearing a white apron, a matching hat, and a red bowtie. The man tapped the counter along with the music.

"Two Coca-Colas please," Oliver said, as the guy behind the counter nodded and took his money. As he filled the glasses, Oliver looked at Nancy. She sat with her legs crossed, staring at the traffic outside, resting her head on her hand. Oliver smiled before the worker returned.

"Here you are, sir."

Oliver took the pops, added straws, and joined Nancy.

"Here you go." Oliver gestured toward the glass and her eyes followed.

"Thanks!" Nancy and Oliver leaned in toward their glasses and took a sip. "Oh, that's sweet."

"Really good but very sugary."

Nancy giggled then took another sip. She crossed her arms on the table. "Well, I have some news."

"What?"

"I've started a new job!"

"That's great, Nance! Congratulations! Where?"

"Starr's Dress Shop. I help ladies coming in find the perfect dress. One lady came in today and bought one for over one hundred dollars! Can you imagine?"

"I can't!" He shook his head.

"They're so beautiful with only the best fabrics and designs. When I'm bored, I stare at them."

"Is it hard to sell dresses sometimes?"

"Sometimes. My boss implores me to be pushier, which of course is my job, but it's something to get used to." She shrugged.

"Yeah, I understand."

"And for such an expensive store, you'd think they have a better register. It's stressful when the line keeps getting longer and longer, with customers losing their patience." She stopped for a moment.

"It's a good place to work, and I like the girls I work with. Enough about me. Tell me about your job!"

"Well, I may be getting an assistant position to this journalist I've been interning with. The work is much of the same, taking notes and getting coffee, but I get to shadow him when interviewing people which will help me learn the ropes. He also said I could help with editing his stories."

"That's great, Ollie!" Nancy clapped. Heat rushed to Oliver's cheeks. "You have a lot of talent, I'm sure. You'll move up the ranks in no time."

"Thanks, Nance. I hope so."

"You'll be making the big bucks!"

"Yeah, I wish." Oliver waved dismissively.

"You'll have to tell me all about the stories you'll be working on! I want to hear every detail, especially about any murder cases."

"Murder cases?" Oliver asked surprisingly, staring at her with fascination.

Nancy smiled. "Yes, they're interesting! Why are you looking at me strangely?"

She playfully hit the top of Oliver's hand.

"I promise to tell you all the graphic details, nothing will be spared."

"That's all I ask."

Oliver laughed as Nancy took the last sip of her soda pop. Nancy was funny, charming, and chatty with beautiful long hair and dark brown eyes. Every time they locked eyes, he never wanted her to look away again. Thank God Marcus had dragged him to that work get-together. Marcus was a good big brother at times, caring about him and watching out for him. This evening couldn't be over already.

"Would you like to go for a walk?" he asked.

"Not really."

He furrowed his eyebrows.

"It's freezing out."

"Oh! Yeah, you're right. What do you like to do when you're not working?" Oliver asked.

"My friends and I go to dances and shop. I also like to go to the show."

"Let's go see the show!"

Nancy smiled wider as Oliver stood, extending his hand to hold hers. The heat from her gloves radiated to his hand. They left the soda shop, walking quickly to the theater as Nancy shivered again. *Oklahoma!* played in a few minutes, so Oliver bought their tickets and they grabbed a couple seats toward the back row. As Oliver wrapped his arm around her, Nancy leaned her head on his shoulder.

"Thanks for the tickets, Ollie," she whispered in his ear.

"Of course."

Nancy kissed him on the cheek, resting her head on his shoulder again and watching the movie. Oliver leaned his head against hers, her silky hair pressed against his cheek, and he couldn't stop himself from smiling. Date ideas ran through his mind about what they could do for fun next. Maybe they could go ice skating in Rockefeller Plaza or to a Broadway show. He needed to start planning their next adventure together. It didn't matter, though. Being with Nancy was time well spent. It was finally something to be excited about.

* * *

"Ollie!" Nancy yelled.

Oliver returned to the present, turning around. Nancy waved at him at the street corner, holding George's hand with the other. He waved back to her, crossing the street and joining them. Nancy's white dress was dingy and old, and her matching gloves had stains on them that couldn't be removed. George looked dashing in tan shorts and a blue collared shirt, jumping when he realized Oliver was walking toward him. Nancy held him back from running into the street.

"Uncle Ollie!" he said as Oliver picked him up and hugged him.

"We were going for some ice cream, do you want to join us?" Nancy said.

"Of course I would."

They walked together to Walter's Soda Shop. Her hair kept getting disturbed by the wind, but she didn't bother to fix it. Oliver held George as she gazed dead ahead. Oliver wished he could reverse time.

As they stepped inside, Oliver handed George to Nancy and offered to order for them. Nancy sat with George in a booth, as George picked up the salt and pepper shakers and banged them against the table.

"What can I get for you?" the worker asked.

"I'll have two Coca-Colas, a glass of water, and a small bowl of vanilla ice cream."

"Coming right up."

Oliver leaned against the counter, staring at Nancy who had her chin resting on her hand as she stared out the window. George played with his new car, rolling it on the table.

"Here you are, sir."

Oliver paid, carrying the tray to the table.

"Thanks, Ollie," Nancy said, taking a sip. "It's really sweet of you."

"Of course." Oliver sat across from her and George as Nancy handed the ice cream and a spoon to him. She squinted and tilted her head at Oliver as if she were studying him.

"What?" he asked.

"Is there something going on?"

Oliver didn't respond, taking a sip of his soda pop.

"Ollie, I think I know your mannerisms by now." The corner of Nancy's lips curled. "It has something to do with Marcus, doesn't it?"

Nancy's eyes weren't the same as when he first met her. They were glossy and wide, losing the innocence and optimism they once had. Life had betrayed her and mistreated her, her joy robbed from her. The difference six years could make. And Oliver couldn't do anything about it.

"Yes," Oliver conceded. He wouldn't mention possibly running into the same young woman Nancy saw leaving Grayson's Pub with Marcus. There was no evidence she was the correct person; it was only a gut feeling he had. "I met with a neighbor who's a police officer. He said they found a hair clip in Marcus's pocket, but that's all he's heard so far."

"That's not much," she said, unimpressed. "A hair clip could belong to anyone."

"He also said Detective Howard will solve this."

"That's what I keep hearing."

My thoughts are with his wife.

Why did she say that?

Nancy took a sip of her pop. "Are you sure there isn't anything else?"

Oliver shook his head, though Nancy wouldn't buy it. She didn't press it at least, continuing to sip her soda pop, and George continued eating his ice cream.

"When's the funeral?" she asked.

"Next Monday, the 21st."

"I've thought about it some more." Nancy sighed. "You were right. It would be wrong not to tell my father. I called his nurse and told her about Marcus's death and the funeral. She said he would probably forget the news anyway. She's going to bring him, but I'm going to keep my distance. We won't be sitting near him."

Oliver nodded.

As they drank their soda pops, not another word was spoken about Marcus, the funeral, or the investigation. After they left the soda shop, Oliver turned toward Nancy. "I'm going to pack a few things from my apartment. I'll be back before dinner."

"All right, I'll see you then," she said, holding onto George's hand.

They walked in separate directions. First, Oliver stopped at Todd's Hardware Store to buy materials to fix the wallboard he put his fist through in his apartment. He couldn't stand to look at the mess anymore. It was a painful reminder of his outburst. Hopefully fixing it wouldn't be too difficult.

After paying for his items, he left for his apartment building, taking the elevator alone to the seventh floor, and unlocking his door. Oliver set the materials on the kitchen counter, sighing at the hole in the wall. He cut out a new drywall piece to match the size of the hole, then nailed it in place, spackled it, sanded it, and painted the new wallboard. Oliver took a step back, unable to tell that there had ever been a hole there. After cleaning the mess and putting the materials away in free space in his bedroom closet, Oliver collapsed on his bed, unable to keep his eyes open. Before he knew it, he was sound asleep.

* * *

Oliver woke up, the sun pouring into his bedroom. All was still and silent. Glasses clinked together in the other room, and he furrowed his eyebrows. He should be all alone in his apartment, and he made sure to lock the door. Leaving his bedroom, his footsteps were light and cautious. The living room was blurry as none of the furniture could come into focus. The floors became uneven as he held onto the wall to help him balance. Marcus stood in the kitchen, reaching out toward Oliver. Oliver backed away as Marcus lifted his foot to take a step before falling flat on his face, colliding with the tile flooring. Blood splattered over the cabinets and a pool began to form around his head. A knife stuck out of his back.

Out of the corner of his eye, the young woman appeared beside Oliver and whispered into his ear, "Where's Nancy?"

Oliver shot up in bed, his body shaking. He looked at the clock on the wall. 10:55 p.m. *Shit*, he thought, jumping out of bed and rushing toward the phone. He was supposed to be at Nancy's apartment by dinner. He never expected to fall asleep so fast, let alone for seven hours. The phone rang and rang with no answer. Oliver hung up and dialed again. Waited and waited, but no answer. He hung it up, declining to pack any extra clothes and instead return to Nancy's apartment as quickly as possible. Hopefully she was asleep in bed and didn't worry about him being late. Oliver locked the door, ran to the elevator, and hit the button multiple times. He pressed the first floor and put his hands on his hips. The moment it opened, he rushed down the busy streets of Brooklyn, running to Nancy's apartment building, climbing the creaking stairs and walking to her apartment. Oliver opened the door, slowly closing it so as not to disturb anyone. He froze. What was that sound? No one was in the kitchen, and he continued into the living room. A single lamp was on, sitting on an end table. Nancy sat on the couch, sobbing into her hands. Did something happen to George?

"Nance?" he asked.

"Oh my God, Ollie!" She looked up at him, her eyes red and swollen with tears streaming down her cheeks. Oliver sat beside her as she wrapped her arms around him and held him tightly, resting her head on his shoulder. "I'm so glad you're okay!"

"I'm so sorry, I fell asleep in my apartment. Let me get you some tissues." Oliver went into the kitchen, grabbed some napkins, and returned to her side. She wiped her eyes dry.

"Where's George?" he asked.

"In my bed, asleep." She tried to catch her breath, but her lungs struggled. "I can't explain it. When I came out here and couldn't find you, I just lost it, Ollie. I thought I lost you, too."

Oliver held her as her chin rested on his shoulder.

"I'm sorry, Ollie, I probably look like I'm going mad."

"No, not at all, not at all. I'm here, and I'm not going anywhere. All right?"

Nancy let go.

"All right?" he repeated, putting his hand on her shoulder.

She sniffled. "Yes."

"I'll make you some tea, okay?" He stepped into the kitchen to boil water, grabbing a couple herbal tea bags and two mugs. Oliver leaned against the counter, taking deep breaths. Tearing up, he grabbed a napkin and wiped them off. He needed to be strong for Nancy. How could he have fallen asleep for so long? Nancy was kind and good. She shouldn't be suffering like this. If he could take away any of her pain, he would without thinking. *Be strong for Nance*. The water boiled, and he brought the two mugs into the family room, handing one to Nancy. Oliver turned on the other lamp and sat next to her as she cradled the cup.

"I'll go to bed soon," she said.

"No, I'll stay up all night if I have to."

Leaning her head on his shoulder, she closed her eyes for a moment, and her shoulder rose and fell. She opened her eyes as she took a sip of her tea. "I don't know what I would do if I lost you, Ollie."

"I'm not going anywhere," he repeated.

Cars drove down the street with police sirens here and there. As they sat in silence, Oliver wrapped his arm around her shoulder. Nancy's body trembled, and he did his best to remain still, trying to shake his nightmare. He felt the chilling breath of that young woman against the side of his neck as she whispered into his ear.

"Where's Nancy?"

12

Clara opened her closet, moving her hangers over one at a time. She studied each dress, taking in their vibrant colors, fitted waists, and full skirts. Some had polka dots. Some were light and flowy and loose, while others were heavy and elegant. She stopped. One of her dresses was missing, other than the one she burned in the backyard with Marcus's blood on it. Her red dress with a tight skirt and fitted bodice had vanished. Clara checked her watch; there was no time to spend on searching for it. She found her other black dress, slipping it on and zipping it. She put on a matching lace veil and gloves.

She stared at herself in the mirror, bracing herself for Marcus's funeral. *I look awful*, she thought, applying extra powder to cover up her eye bags. All she did was toss and turn last night.

Thanks to Oliver Anderson.

She never expected to cross paths with him again, let alone at his brother's funeral. The man she killed over a week ago. After surviving today, her stress would evaporate. All she needed to do was avoid Oliver. He should be busy enough; he was the lone brother of Marcus and would be comforting Marcus's wife and son. He wouldn't want to waste time talking to her. Besides, the church would be full. If she and her father stuck to the back of the church, Oliver wouldn't notice she was there.

Deep breaths. Deep breaths.

Everything would be fine.

Clara applied light pink lipstick and rubbed her lips together. She practiced her frown in the mirror. Not too much to be overdramatic and vying for attention, but not too subtle to seem emotionally vacant and cold. She needed to blend in with the sea of black. Black dresses, black veils, black suits. No one would notice her, and no one should recognize her.

Everything would be fine.

"Clara, are you ready?" her father yelled from downstairs.

"Yes, I'm coming!" she yelled back.

"All right, I'll be out front." The door opened and closed as footsteps approached her bedroom.

"You look beautiful, Clara," her mother said, leaning on her bedroom door frame. Her heart-shaped face smiled at Clara, her cheeks lightly powdered with blush. So youthful and kind.

"Thanks, Mom."

"You should add some pearls."

"No, thanks. I want to look plain today; I don't want to stand out. This day isn't about me."

"Since when?" Her mother laughed as Clara cracked a smile.

"Have you seen my red velvet dress?" she asked.

"No, I haven't. Have you washed it lately?"

No, she hadn't. "Yeah, it might be in the cellar."

"It's nice you're going with your father. I'm sorry I can't go for you."

"No, don't be sorry. Dad is the one forcing me to go."

Her mother said nothing in response, glancing at the floor.

"Well, I better get going. He's waiting for me."

"I'll see you later, honey." Her mother gave Clara a hug and returned to her bedroom.

Collecting herself and taking a few more deep breaths, Clara left her room and stood behind the closed front door. Oliver could not see her today. He couldn't. She braced herself before joining her father outside. He waited by the iron gate, resting his hands on top of it.

"Ready?" he asked.

Clara glanced back at the house as she left it and walked beside her father. The fabric of her veil and dress could melt as the sun's rays permeated them. People strolled on the sidewalk, going about an ordinary day undifferentiated from any other. They wouldn't remember today; it would simply blur together with the days surrounding it. Today should be a regular day for Clara; her father never should have made this request of her. Little did he know about the possible consequences.

"I do appreciate you coming with me, Clara," her father said.

"It's not a big deal." Oh, how she wished that were true.

"How about we go out for a soda after? We haven't done that in a long time."

"Sure." She would have to escape this funeral without being seen by Oliver first. Nothing would make her happier than to celebrate escaping the fate of an arrest and possible death penalty. A few people walking in front of them also wore black. They must also be attending the funeral.

"Do you think the funeral will be busy?" she asked.

"Oh, yes. Marcus was a popular guy. He got along well with everyone."

That was good to hear. Made it easier for Clara to blend in with the sea of black. "Did you like him?"

Her father tilted his head and seemed to think about it. "Not very much, no. But I don't like to speak ill of the dead."

Clara wanted to say she agreed, but kept her mouth shut. *No need to respond.* The light turned red as they stopped by the same newsstand where Oliver asked her if she knew Marcus. She shouldn't have stopped and read it. It wasn't like she hadn't seen a newspaper headline about one of her victims before. Something about this one was different, though. She couldn't quite place it.

They crossed the street and up the steps into the cathedral. The crowd poured inside with every man wearing a black suit and every woman wearing a matching dress and veil. Clara held onto her father so as not to lose him, suggesting they find a seat toward the back. A coworker of his waved to them, putting them closer to the altar than Clara would've liked, but they were seated around twenty rows back, off to the right side with enough distance. They kneeled and said their prayers as people continued filing in and packing into the pews.

Clara closed her eyes for a moment. It was best to avoid eye contact with anyone, so she could claim ignorance. If she and Oliver made eye contact and she fled the church, it would appear she was avoiding him. She couldn't look any more suspicious to him than she already did. He asked for her name for a reason; he was not stupid. He had a look of distrust in his eyes. *I can't believe my father dragged me here.* She could've come up with an excuse. Even if her coming pleased her father, it wasn't worth the possibility of Oliver seeing her again.

However, Clara was grateful her father didn't pry further into why she lit a fire in the fire pit the other night. The lie that she dropped a cigarette was shit. She was a better liar than that.

Everyone stood and turned their attention to the aisle where pallbearers carried in a glossy wooden coffin, followed by Oliver, Nancy, and George. Nancy's eyes were glazed over, and the son, George, held his head down in distress. Oliver walked beside Nancy, glancing subtly on each side of the church as if searching for someone. Was he searching for her? Clara folded her hands, keeping her head down, and turned toward the opposite direction as he passed by her. After a few minutes, Clara checked the aisle and he and his family were close to the altar. Oliver didn't turn in her direction.

Clara gripped the pew in front of her. She shouldn't have come to this. Everyone stared at the coffin as they followed it in unison.

The organ filled the church with "Amazing Grace", almost covering up the noise of a child who accidentally dropped a kneeler.

The Mass started. Thankfully, Oliver didn't read either of the readings, remaining in the front pew next to Marcus's wife. Clara studied her. Nancy didn't seem as sad as a wife who had lost her husband to a killer. Clara had done her a favor. Maybe she knew that already, and that was why she wasn't as upset as a grieving wife should be. Marcus didn't deserve a grieving wife after what he had done.

"No one studied harder than Marcus." The priest rested his hands on the pulpit as everyone sat. "Those were the first words Marcus's brother, Oliver, shared with me. He dedicated his whole life to the science of psychiatry and helping patients treat their mental illnesses and give them a better life than the one they knew. Marcus answered God's call to use his intellect and curiosity to help those in need. It is what we all strive to do in our daily lives."

Oliver looked at Marcus's wife many times in a span of a few minutes, studying her and moving closer to her. He clearly seemed to care about her. Good to know.

"Oliver said he admired his older brother and looked up to him his entire life, setting a good example of who he should be and how he should act. Marcus has a wonderful wife, Nancy, and son, George, putting their faith in him as the father and leader of their household. He loved them and put them first in all his decision-making and actions."

He didn't think of them when he wanted to sleep with me. This was all bullshit. If Clara didn't get caught this time, maybe the homily at her funeral would highlight her as an outstanding citizen.

"He lived a great life, though he did not deserve to live a short one. God has a plan for us all, and we pray today that Marcus is being reunited with his parents and other relatives he dearly missed here on earth. Dying is not the end, but the beginning for us. We believe in Heaven, the next life awaiting us all. We pray Marcus is in the comfort of our Lord, and we pray for his soul."

Clara yawned as the priest finished his homily and moved onto the Nicene Creed. Everyone stood, saying the prayer in unison. The Mass carried on and on, and people began rising to receive Holy Communion. *Oh, God.* It struck her. She had to walk up to the altar. Oliver would surely see her. She could sneak to the bathroom, but her father wouldn't approve of her missing Communion. There was nothing she could do. Her best bet was keeping her head down and staring at the floor. It was in God's hands now.

Clara folded her hands before her and walked across the pew, following the people in front of her to the center aisle. Her heart pounded louder than the organ being played; the ringing in her ears couldn't distract her. Every step she took closer to the altar, her temperature rose. Oliver kneeled at the end of the first pew, looking up periodically from his folded hands. She was only a few feet away from him now. Taking a few more steps, she stood beside his pew. He could be looking at her for all she knew, but she couldn't glance in his direction. Any eye contact would cost her.

He might have been staring at her. *Keep looking down. No eye contact.* She knelt before the priest at the altar and received the Host on her tongue. She stood and returned to her pew. The music stopped. Oliver's pew creaked a couple times. Did he move to get a better look at her?

Clara couldn't help herself. *Don't look at him, don't look at him.* She had to look. Turning, Clara got her answer. And it wasn't the one she had hoped for. She returned to her pew and kneeled in prayer, desperately needing one. She glanced up from her folded hands toward the front. Oliver turned briefly again to stare at her. Her stomach dropped. He was onto her. She needed to leave, but several people remained in line to receive Communion, and the priest needed to give the closing prayer. Trapped.

Once the prayer began, everyone stood for the last time. The music chimed in again with the chorus singing "Salve Regina". The pallbearers once again picked up the casket, carrying it back down the aisle and returning it to the hearse. *Shit.* Oliver would be walking past her again, this time seeing her face. He would recognize her as the person he spoke to in front of the newsstand; the person whom he seemed to distrust.

Oliver kept glancing at her, his eyes moving back and forth between the casket and her. He tried to be subtle, and others probably didn't notice. Clara bowed her head, pretending to pray as the casket was carried past her. Once she looked up again, people began filing out of their pews and walking down the aisle to leave Mass. The singing stopped, but the organ continued playing as they departed the church. Oliver had already left, driving behind the hearse to the cemetery. The goosebumps on her skin wouldn't subside as the sun beamed on her.

Clara removed her veil, tucking it in her purse as she and her father made their way to Sandy's, a soda fountain a couple of blocks away from the church. The floors had subway tiles, and a bar was lined with a steel countertop. The stools against the bar were cemented into the ground, with red leather cushions on top. Teens surrounded the jukebox, and they selected "Hard Headed Woman" by Elvis. Clara and her father approached the counter to order.

"I'll have a Coke and a hot pretzel, please," Clara said.

"I'll have coffee," her father added, taking out his wallet.

Another worker handed Clara her Coke and pretzel, and she found a round table by the window while her father paid. She took a bite, staring at the people walking by. They were all a blur to her. She took a sip from her straw and swirled it in her drink. Oliver made eye contact with her several times during Mass; he must be onto her. He wouldn't be seeking her out if he didn't suspect her. Clara gave her father a small smile as he joined her, as if there was nothing on her mind.

"The culture is going to hell with all this Elvis nonsense," her father said.

"I like his music," she said. "He's very popular."

"I'm aware. I guess I'm becoming an old man."

"Thanks for the pretzel and Coke."

"You're welcome. Remember when we used to come here once a week after you got out of school? We should start something like that again. Maybe I could meet you on my lunch break once a week."

"Yeah, we should." Clara agreed.

"I remember bringing you home a Coca-Cola when you had a nasty cold. I found you lying on your bed with a red nose and used tissues all over the place, and you've never been happier to see me. And when I say me, I mean the Coca-Cola." Clara laughed absent-mindedly. He took a sip of his coffee and hesitated. "How have you been doing, Clara?"

"Fine."

"I only ask because you seem to be on edge lately."

She squinted. "Really?"

"Yes," he said matter-of-factly. "Are you?"

Clara shrugged. "No, I'm enjoying summer, that's all."

"I haven't mentioned the fire outside, but I don't believe you dropped a cigarette. You smoke all the time, which is fine, it's good for the nerves. However, you didn't drop it into the barrel, starting a fire. You stood there, staring at the fire, instead of running to get some water. You were trying to burn something, Clara. What was it?"

Clara loved crafting lies. Lies gave her a glimmer of hope in such a miserable world. She lived and breathed the stories she told herself. It didn't matter whether they were real. She would cling to them until her last breath.

"I wore one of mom's dresses around the house, and I got a terrible stain on it. I know I shouldn't be trying on her clothes, and I was worried the stain would upset you—"

"So, you destroyed the evidence," he said, interrupting.

"Yes." She nodded. "I'm so sorry, Dad."

"I would rather have a stained dress than you burning one of your mother's dresses. Just don't take any of her clothes again, they're not yours."

"I won't, I promise," Clara assured him before taking another sip of her Coke.

"All right." He took another sip of his coffee. "Did I tell you I was interviewed by a detective about Marcus's murder a couple days ago?"

Clara's body tensed up, and she shook her head.

"Yes, a man named Detective Howard came in and questioned everyone. He's a no-nonsense kind of fellow."

"How did it go?" she asked, holding her Coke so tightly the glass might shatter. "What kind of questions did he ask?"

"The usual. He asked me how well I knew Marcus, what I was doing on the night of his death, if I knew of anyone on the staff that didn't get along with him. You know, those kinds of questions. I couldn't believe the nerve of him, though, asking for a list of Marcus's patients. We would never hand them over."

"Wouldn't that violate their privacy?"

"Exactly what I told him."

"Are they getting close to solving who killed Marcus?"

"I have no idea, he didn't give any details. He asked the questions, I answered, he wrote them down, and that was it."

Clara took another bite of her pretzel. Detective Howard. They wrote about him in all the newspapers, and he seemed to be taking the case seriously. Her father was questioned two days ago; the case was far from turning cold. And she had one more man on her list. She couldn't lie low; it must be done. The teens returned to the jukebox, crowding around it and putting on "Trouble" by Elvis. Clara wondered what it was like to be one of them. Her father shook his head and sighed.

"You really like this garbage?" he asked her.

"Yeah."

"Get out of here!" He waved.

Clara giggled, trying to act like she didn't have any worries. She finished her pretzel and pop, so they left the soda fountain and headed home. They stopped at a street corner where the light turned red. They passed by another newsstand on the corner, but Clara didn't dare look at it this time.

"Must be difficult for Marcus's family to see his face all over those newspapers and having people discussing his death," her father said, as Clara focused on the light ahead.

"Yeah, it must be."

Thank God. The light changed and they moved away from the newsstand. *Enough with talking about Marcus.* A couple more blocks to hit another red light.

A couple was having a screaming match in one of the apartments. The open window had floral kitchen curtains waving in the hot breeze. The husband screamed about how his wife never asked about his job, and the wife screamed about how he was never around to help with the kids. Something being thrown against the wall. Clara flinched, staring at the light and waiting for it to change.

July 15th, 1955, Brooklyn, NY

Three years ago, she could still hear the screams from her own house. The shivers coursed down her spine, and adrenaline rushed through her veins. Clara sat on the steps leading out the back door of their townhome. Her body shook uncontrollably, and thick smoke came out of her mouth. She inhaled her cigarette again for relief. How much more of this could she take? The summer would never end; at least another month remained until she would start her sophomore year of high school.

"You slept with her, didn't you?" her mother screamed, as her father read the morning newspaper. "You didn't come home last night."

"I did come home last night," he said calmly. "I did not cheat."

Her father remained unfazed. He repeatedly cheated on her and could look her in the eye and lie. He would lie over and over again.

No problem. This had become a morning ritual. Clara would have to cover her ears and close her eyes, pretending to be somewhere else. Today, she pictured being at Coney Island, sitting on the beach with the roaring waves and the chatter of other people around her. The seagulls flew above her, chirping, and she could feel the sun shining on her skin.

"You are a goddamn liar!" Her mother slammed her hand against the kitchen table in front of him.

Clara turned and was brought back to reality again.

"I am not a liar, and this conversation is over." He turned the page in the newspaper.

"This conversation is not over!" Her mother struck her father across the face. He took a sip of his coffee. Clara turned back around, pressing her knees to her chest and continuing to smoke.

Her mother left the house, slamming the door so hard the coat rack tipped over.

"Clara, come in and clean in here," he said.

Clara climbed the steps and walked into the kitchen. As always, he had to pick up her father's mess. Two white cabinet doors were left ajar, and glass was shattered onto the black-and-white tile floors. It had been much worse before; this was nothing. She grabbed the broom and dustpan and swept the glass, then picked up a tipped-over chair. She held the broom tightly, causing her palms pain.

"You want to say something?"

Clara slammed the two cabinets shut.

"You should be the one cleaning this mess!" Clara yelled, as she went to the coat rack and lifted it off the floor, picked up the coats one by one, and hung them up again. "You're the one going around and cheating behind her back! How can you live with yourself? Aren't you disgusted by what you see in the mirror?"

"I live with myself just fine. I would never cheat on your mother, Clara, and you know that." He took money out of his wallet. "Here's some money for lunch. Don't get yourself into any trouble today."

"Out of the two of us, you're the one that's going to get into trouble today."

What the hell was he talking about? She never got into trouble. He held out his hand with a five-dollar bill, and she took it. Clara needed to get the hell out of this house.

* * *

Clara returned to the present, standing beside her father and staring at the red light that refused to change. The couple continued screaming obscenities at each other in that brick apartment building. Once the fighting started, it never stopped. Until death.

As they continued home and climbed the steps to the front door of their townhouse, her father took his keys out to unlock the door. Her mother's purse was gone from the front closet. The house was empty. Clara started climbing the stairs to go to her bedroom, but her father called her name. She turned with one hand gripping the railing, ready to explain to him how she needed to get out of this dress to make him lunch.

"Someday you'll have to tell me what you were burning, Clara."

A jolt rushed through her body as her eyes widened. Of course her lie didn't work. Her dad was the only one she could never convince. His head lowered with disappointment as he left the foot of the stairs for the kitchen table. Her father pulled out a chair, sat, and flipped through a newspaper. Clara took a deep breath and went to her bedroom to lie on her bed with her hands folded over her stomach. She closed her eyes.

Oliver Anderson recognized her from the newsstand.

A man named Detective Howard was hunting down the person who killed Marcus, interviewing her father.

Her father didn't believe that she burned her mother's dress. And the timing didn't work in her favor. Her father must have known she was burning something the night of Marcus's death. Did the ashes give away what it was? Why did her father use the phrase "destroyed the evidence?"

Burning.

The walls of her bedroom closed in around her, the ceiling dropping and pressing against her face and chest, her lungs unable to expand. The ceiling crushed her nose and broke through her forehead, the bones in her face cracking into small pieces. Her ribs broke into jagged shards, puncturing her heart, but its thumping grew louder. *Please make it stop. Please make it stop.* She couldn't raise her arms to try to push the ceiling upward. She would die lying on her bed, smothered by her own walls.

"Clara, are you coming down?" her father yelled.

Clara gasped, sitting up, holding her chest. The walls returned to their proper place, and the ceiling stood eight feet tall as usual.

She tried to catch her breath. "Yes, I'm coming!"

No time to waste. Her next victim, Dean Caraway, called her.

13

Oliver stood at Nancy's side, waiting for the pallbearers to carry Marcus's casket down the aisle. Nancy said few words this morning, keeping to herself. She kept her eyes on George as she held his hand. George looked adorable in his black suit. Nancy told him his father was in Heaven now and wouldn't be coming back, but Oliver doubted George understood the permanence of it. Clashing with the gothic church, the sun was unrelenting. Father Richard wore a white chasuble and gestured for them to follow the casket. The organ began playing and the smell of incense filled the air. Guests of the packed church all stared at them, so Oliver tried to focus on the altar. *They shouldn't all be staring at Nancy like that.* She wasn't an exhibit at the zoo; this was one of the hardest days of her life. Maybe they shouldn't have given the details of this funeral in the obituary, not with all the press the case had been getting. But it probably would've been leaked, anyway. There might have been people present who wanted to gossip, not support Nancy.

The organ rang in Oliver's ear as the choir sang "Amazing Grace." The walk lasted an eternity to the first pew. Nancy didn't take her eyes off the casket, and Oliver kept his gaze straight ahead. Oliver entered the pew last, standing next to Nancy. The priest continued, stepping up the stairs to the altar with two altar boys standing on either side of him. The casket sat in front of him. His brother, Marcus, lay inside. Marcus was not out drinking and having a good time, and Oliver would never see him again. For all his faults, Marcus didn't deserve to die the way he did. No one did.

Nancy sniffled as she wrapped her arm around George. Her father sat on the opposite side of the church with his nurse. His eyes were glossed over with a lost look on his face. He slouched over in the pew. Nancy didn't look at him once.

The readings came and went, followed by the gospel, and Father Richard began his homily.

"No one studied harder than Marcus." The priest placed his hands on the pulpit. Father Richard went on and on about Marcus's life and his love of family and psychiatry.

Oliver wished he could look up to Marcus as most little brothers want to look up to their older brothers. He did, in some aspects. Marcus taught him how to work hard and advance in his career. He tried to push Oliver outside of his comfort zone to meet new people. But Oliver deserved better when he was fifteen, his age when his parents passed away. His brother inherited their father's brilliance, but he also inherited his gambling addiction. After their parents died, Oliver had to guard their parents' money with his life to prevent them from being thrown onto the street. But Oliver would never forget how Marcus comforted him.

* * *

Oliver sat as a fifteen-year-old boy on the floor of his parent's bedroom, crying about having to live the rest of his life without his parents. The cherry wood grand bed, the matching dresser, and nightstands with green stained lamps hovering over intelligent books kept him company. Moving his hand over the thick red carpet, he sighed. They wouldn't want him wasting time when he could be studying or working. The door cracked open, eighteen-year-old Marcus peeked his head through it before letting himself in and sitting beside Oliver on the floor. He put his arm around Oliver.

"It's going to be okay, Oliver," Marcus said quietly. "We'll get through this together."

* * *

Oliver snapped out of it as the organ played "Ave Maria" sung by a brilliant vocalist who volunteered his time. Oliver bowed his head and folded his hands as Mass continued, and it was time for Holy Communion. Though his feelings toward his brother flooded his mind and made him question whether he deserved it, he was first to kneel at the altar and receive. Oliver should be engulfed in grief. He did miss his brother at times and loved him despite his faults, but he told himself that wasn't good enough.

Oliver returned to the pew, along with Nancy, kneeling and praying for Marcus's soul, while glancing up every so often to see if he recognized anyone. Most of the guests were from Marcus's work. Dr. Ed Taylor stepped up next to receive. The woman standing a couple of people behind him looked familiar. A veil covered her hair and forehead and she kept her head down, but he had definitely spoken to her before. She might have been the young woman he approached at the newsstand.

Sure enough, it was the same young woman approaching the altar for Communion. What did she know? Was she the young woman with Marcus the night he died? Oliver had to find out. He kept staring at her as she kneeled at the altar and stood again, returning to her pew. She gazed in his direction, making eye contact with him. She sat toward the back of the church among Marcus's coworkers. She either worked for the hospital or was related to someone who did.

Father Richard said the final prayer, and the pallbearers picked up the coffin and carried it down the aisle. Oliver, Nancy, and

George followed it again. Before leaving the church, he had to catch one more glimpse of that young woman to ensure it was her. She kept her head down, but it was her. How was she involved with Marcus?

They left the ceremony, with Oliver driving and Nancy sitting in the passenger's seat and George in the back to St. John's Cemetery, following the hearse. Once they arrived, Oliver opened the door for Nancy and helped George get out. They stood together in front of Marcus's burial plot. His casket was lowered into the ground, and the priest said a final prayer for his soul. They threw dirt and flowers on top, then left the cemetery for Nancy's apartment.

"Uncle Ollie, can we go to the playground?" George asked from the backseat.

"Sure," Oliver said. "Is that all right with you, Nance?"

"Yes," she whispered. Nancy had her hands folded in her lap and didn't say another word. Oliver glanced at her, wanting to comfort her somehow. She took off her black veil and set it in her lap, staring ahead at the road. They changed into casual clothes and had a silent lunch before walking to the local playground. They passed by Starr's Dress Shop, and Oliver remembered the last time he stopped by there.

* * *

Six years ago, Oliver stepped inside a small flower shop, bursting with roses, daisies, sunflowers, lilies, tulips, and more. The aroma was sweet, smelling like a fresh meadow. One worker watered pots, while another wrapped bouquets. Oliver put his hand to his chin, wondering what Nancy would prefer. Roses seemed like a good bet. He selected fully bloomed ones, bringing them to his nose and smelling them. They were wrapped in red tissue paper, and Oliver waited in line at the register. He pulled the four quarters he scraped together, hoping that would be enough.

"Next, please!" the cashier called.

Oliver set the bouquet on the counter covered with water drops, leaves, and flower petals.

"$1, sir."

He handed him the four quarters. *That worked out well.* "Thank you!"

Next stop was Starr's Dress Shop, a couple more blocks down. Nancy should be heading out on her lunch break any moment. *She will love these flowers*. Nancy stepped out of the shop and walked in the opposite direction. Oliver quickened his pace, trying to catch her. She stopped at the street corner, and Oliver called out for her.

"Oh, hi!" Nancy beamed, turning to face him.

"For you," he said, handing her the flowers.

"Thank you!"

"You're welcome."

"Ollie, you're the sweetest!" They kissed, and Nancy pulled the roses to her nose. As she pulled them away, her smile faded.

"Ollie, I-I have to tell you something."

"What is it?" Oliver asked.

She hesitated. "Do you want to go to the park across the street?"

He nodded, concerned. They crossed the street to a local park and found an open bench next to a bike path. People riding bikes, runners, and walkers passed by them. Children played in a playground nearby, shouting, swinging on the swings, and sliding on the slide. Nancy tried starting her sentence multiple times but kept pausing like the words were sharp pieces of glass in her throat. Oliver waited, fidgeting with his hands. This must be something serious, and he couldn't take this anymore.

"My father wants me to marry Marcus," she blurted. Oliver opened his mouth, but no words came out of it, as Nancy moved her free hand through her hair. *Marcus?* This didn't make any sense; this had to be a mistake. Oliver had hung out with Marcus many times over the past five months, and Marcus had never brought up Nancy once. He furrowed his eyebrows, staring into Nancy's eyes.

This had to be a joke, or something. But Nancy wouldn't joke about something like this. "No matter what I say to him, he won't budge. I told him how I love you—"

"You love me?" he asked, interrupting her. A smile briefly crossed his face.

"Of course I do, Ollie," she said matter-of-factly, tearing up. "I told him over and over again that I don't love Marcus; that I could never love him. But Marcus has become his protégé, and they've grown close. My father trusts him."

"I could meet with your father." Oliver offered. "We could have a nice dinner."

"He loves Marcus; Marcus has become the son he never had. And it won't solve what he thinks is the problem."

"What is the problem?"

Nancy sighed, rolling her eyes. She clutched the flower stems tighter. "I don't care how much money I have. I never did, and I never will. My father does."

"I love you, Nance, and I will do whatever it takes to stop this," Oliver said. Why was Nancy giving up so easily? Oliver could convince her father, explaining his affection for Nancy and ensuring he would take great care of her. This wasn't over.

Nancy gave him a sympathetic smile and looked defeated, placing her hand on his cheek. "My father would disown me, and I could never do that to my mother. It would break her heart to never see me again. I can't do it."

No. No, this wasn't happening. If her father wouldn't budge, Oliver could convince Marcus not to marry her. Marcus wouldn't marry a girl Oliver loved; he would never do that to him. "I'll talk to Marcus about this. He's never expressed any interest in dating you."

"I know." She wiped the tears off her face.

Oliver took her hand. "I'm going to talk to Marcus, and everything will work out. I will not lose you."

* * *

Oliver snapped back to the present as he hadn't been in this park since that conversation. Nancy let George walk to the playground as she and Oliver sat next to each other on the same bench. The gray clouds began to roll in as Oliver tried to come up with something to say. Since Nancy left the flowers on Marcus's grave, her hands were folded this time. She hadn't said as much as a sentence the whole day.

"How have you been doing?" Oliver said, turning to her.

"What is there to say?" Nancy shrugged, rubbing her lips together. "I've been alone my whole marriage. I don't think it'll be too hard of a transition."

Oliver wasn't expecting that response.

"I knew about the apartment, the car, the gambling, and the string of affairs. The money didn't add up. We should've had a lot in the bank, but we were buried in debt. Marcus hid it from me, saying he was taking care of it. He came home drunk one night, so I went through his briefcase and found the bank statements. I started putting away some money every week to make sure we didn't run out."

"I'm so sorry," Oliver said.

"Marcus did love George, though. That was genuine for sure."

"Yes, he did love George very much." Oliver agreed as that was true.

Closing her eyes, Nancy leaned her head back. She leaned forward again, and her eyes reopened. She let out a cleansing breath. "If I hadn't obeyed my father, my life would've been a lot easier."

Oliver didn't say anything in response. It was true.

"Ollie, I feel like a terrible person, a terrible wife," Nancy admitted as Oliver locked eyes with her. "I'm not as sad as I should be. I should be inconsolable, but I'm not."

"Everyone deals differently with grief."

"That's the problem." She sighed. "I'm not grieving like I should be. I feel like I haven't lost him because he wasn't ever mine at the start. I'm angry at Marcus. Angry, he's put me in this position. And then I feel terrible for thinking that, especially with how he died."

Oliver's eyes widened as Nancy crossed her arms and watched George swinging on a swing.

"When I'm sad, I feel foolish because of the way he treated me. When I'm not sad enough, I feel like I'm a terrible wife and guilt overcomes me."

"My relationship with Marcus was complicated," Oliver said. "It's something I have to work through and process. I think it's something that'll take time."

Nancy nodded in agreement, staring at Oliver before watching George climb a slide. "There's only so long I can resent my father for my own decision. I did what I thought was right, and I made the best of it. It's easier to just blame him; he could be a bastard. But seeing him today, he's not the person he once was. It probably won't be too much longer until he forgets who I am. I wish I could ask my mother for advice; I wish she were here."

"Your mother was lovely."

"She was. I miss her terribly." Nancy looked at Oliver again. "I am sorry, Ollie."

"Sorry for what?"

"For breaking your heart."

He shook his head. "You could never break my heart."

Nancy teared up. "I did, and I should have said sorry a long time ago. If it's any consolation, mine was broken too."

Nancy focused on George again after there was silence between them. "I talked to George about moving into your place for a while, and he seemed happy with that. He really loves you; you've been a great uncle to him."

"Well, George is my favorite nephew."

Nancy cracked a smile for the first time since Marcus died. Oliver missed her smile; missed seeing her happy. "Thank you, Ollie, for offering. And thank you for making all the arrangements. My mind hasn't been in a good place."

"Nance, I would do anything for you."

She held his hand. "I know," she whispered.

It was good Nancy wanted to move into his apartment. He could continue to watch over her, and no one would know her new address. Especially in case that young woman tried to find her.

"Mommy!" George yelled, crying on the ground and holding his leg.

"I got it, Ollie," Nancy said, running to George and rubbing his leg. She smiled at him, wiping the tears off his cheeks and probably giving him words of encouragement. It was wonderful to watch her as a mother. Nancy pointed to the playground, and George shook his head. He must be done playing. Nancy took his hand and returned with him to the bench.

"How's George?" Oliver asked.

"Fine, he tripped. He's tired; it's been a long day."

Oliver should be more tired, but he wasn't at all. His eyes felt heavy, but he couldn't rest. One question plagued his mind: Who was that young woman? She sat with Marcus's coworkers; there must be a connection to Sinclair's. Oliver, Nancy, and George walked back to the apartment, and Nancy checked the mail to find a couple of letters.

"I'm tired!" George complained, so Oliver picked him up and George rested his head on his shoulder.

"Dean Caraway sent me a letter," Nancy said. "That's nice."

"Who's that?"

"He was close with Marcus; they worked together. Dean's still a doctor at Sinclair's. He'd pop into our apartment from time to time before he got married. He's a good man."

"Huh." Oliver stared blankly ahead as they climbed the stairs.

"What?" Nancy asked.

"Where does he live?"

"I'm not sure, but Marcus probably had it written down somewhere. Why?"

"I would like to ask him some questions about who worked with Marcus at Sinclair's."

Nancy leaned against the wall in the hallway, and Oliver unlocked the door and swung it open. Nancy grabbed a blanket as Oliver laid George on the couch. Sitting at the kitchen table, Nancy tore open the envelope and read the card. Oliver filled a couple of glasses of water and brought one for Nancy.

"This is a nice card." She handed it to him, and he sat down next to her. It had a gold cross on the front with the word "Peace" written in cursive. The inside had a bible verse, followed by a handwritten note.

Dear Nancy,

We miss Marcus dearly, and you and your family will be in our thoughts and prayers. God Bless.

Sincerely,

Dean and Marie Caraway

"Was Dean at the funeral?" Oliver asked, setting the card on the table.

Nancy took a sip of water. "Yeah, I saw him sitting by Ed."

Oliver's eyes widened. Dean would've been sitting near that young woman.

"Lots of Marcus's coworkers came; Marcus would've been so happy," she said.

"Yeah, he had a good group of friends who cared about him."

"Yeah," Nancy said, nodding. "I'm going to make some coffee. Would you like some?"

"Yes, thank you."

Nancy went into the kitchen as Oliver read the card. Dean Caraway. It was difficult to believe he knew more about Marcus's personal life than Ed, but it was worth a shot. He must ask him questions about the young woman who sat near him at Marcus's funeral. Ed hadn't worked at that hospital for a year, but Dean was currently employed there. He would be able to tell him about the current going-ons at Sinclair Hospital Psychiatric Ward.

14

July 28th, 1956, Brooklyn, NY

Clara was reading *The Great Gatsby*, lying on her side on her bed during the summer break of 1956, two years ago. A glass shattered. A loud bang spread through the house like something heavy had been dropped on the floor. A door slammed downstairs. Clara sat up, staring at her closed bedroom door. The banging didn't stop. More glass shattered. Furniture must have been thrown. Her father was at work, so Clara had to deal with this all on her own. *I don't want to go through this again*. But she had no choice. The noises refused to stop. Ignoring it wouldn't make it go away.

Clara opened the door and stepped down the stairs. Each step burned her feet as her nails scraped along the railing. She craned her neck around the corner. The end tables and bookshelf were tipped over; a teacup lay shattered on the floor; their blankets were scattered over the room, one draping over their fireplace.

No one in the living room.

Clara continued into the kitchen where a carton of milk was

tipped over on the counter, milk dripping onto the floor. She froze and held her breath.

Her mother frantically tried to wash the broken dishes in the sink, her violet dress becoming soaked in water. Almost spilling over, the water rose in the sink. Clara remained calm. Her mother never responded well to a raised voice.

Clara first turned the faucet off. "Mom, leave the dishes to me. You need to lie down."

Her mother shook her head, focusing on the damaged plates. "No, I need to clean up."

"Mom, please," Clara pleaded, resting her hand on her mother's shoulder. "Put the plates down and go take a nap. I'll clean the house before Dad comes home. You're just tired."

"You're right, dear. I'm exhausted." Her mother wiped her brow, blood spilling from her hand.

"Mom, you cut yourself." Clara took a kitchen towel and pressed it against her hand. "Go upstairs, and I'll grab a bandage."

"All right, honey."

Her mother held the towel against her hand and walked through the living room. Her footsteps traveled up the stairs. Broken plates filled the sink, along with sliced apples and a couple of knives. What a mess. Clara felt the urge to start cleaning right away, but she had to focus on her mother first. She picked up the first-aid kit from a kitchen cabinet and passed through the living room, avoiding looking at it.

Clara stood outside the bedroom and took a deep breath before opening the door. Her mother lay in her bed with a wet washcloth on her forehead and held the kitchen towel against her bleeding hand. She liked putting a washcloth on her head while closing her eyes; she said it made her feel calmer. Clara sat on the bed beside her, and her mother opened her eyes and sat up slightly. As Clara wiped the cut with alcohol, her mother recoiled and gave her hand back. Clara covered it with a bandage and stood, ready to leave the room, but her mother called her over again, holding out her bony hand. Clara took it, standing next to the bed.

"Oh, Clara," she said, staring at her and holding her hand tightly. "You're the one thing I got right in this world. You're such a good daughter. You'll never leave me, right dear?"

She shook her head without hesitation. "Of course not, Mom."

Her mother smiled at her response. "You're such a good girl, Clara."

"I'm sorry about Dad."

"Your dad's not as bad as you think. He means well."

Clara wasn't so sure.

"Clara, promise me you won't ever leave me," her mother said, her eyes sunken.

"I won't, Mom. Never."

"I love you."

"I love you, too." Clara took the first-aid kit and left her bedroom, closing the door. Her mother needed some sleep, she had been exhausted after getting little sleep last night. Some nights, her footsteps wandered up and down the hallway upstairs and back and forth between the living room and kitchen. Clara would put a second pillow over her head to try to drown out the noise, to no avail.

Clara stepped into the living room and gazed around at the mess. It was for the best that her father wasn't home. He didn't need to witness the destruction her mother left behind. Everything would be in order and neat for him. She had until her father came home to make it so.

Her favorite tea cup was shattered next to the tipped-over end table. Clara picked up a large piece, holding it. She loved using it for tea when reading on chilly evenings. No time to dwell on it. It was merely an object. Another object to be discarded. Grabbing a broom and dustpan from the front hall closet, she swept the broken glass in the living room and kitchen and gathered the pieces into a garbage can. She folded the blankets, putting them beside the fireplace. Books lay on the floor next to the bookshelf, so she picked them up one by one and returned them to their proper place. One of the book's pages fell out of its spine, *The Clue in the Diary* by Carolyn Keene. Clara sandwiched it between two books, and it appeared brand new from that view. She loved that book, too. But that didn't matter, anyway. Her feelings weren't important.

Moving onto the kitchen, she cleaned the splattered milk, threw out the empty carton, and wiped off the drops of blood on the counter. She threw away the blood-covered apple slices. The left kitchen curtain over the sink was ripped. When her mother felt better, she would have to sew it up. Clara was never interested in learning how to sew; she was better at tearing things apart. She picked the kitchen chair upright and scrubbed the table clean. After everything was back in order again, she placed her hands on her waist and let out a deep sigh. Hopefully, her mother would take a long nap and feel better.

The doorbell rang. Clara grunted, not in the mood to talk to anyone. Whoever was at the door kept ringing the bell, so Clara rushed to open it before the ringing could awaken her mother.

Her friends Kate and Betty stood on the doorstep with smiles, wearing large skirts and pretty, brightly colored blouses with bows. Their hair was curled under their hats, and their teeth sparkled against their red lipstick.

"Clara, you look like a mess!" Kate said, fixing the collar on Clara's shirt. Clara looked at her clothes. Yes, she did look like a mess. Her white shirt was stained and her olive green skirt had dirt and dust all over it. She tried to shake it off, but it was no use.

"We're going to Walter's Soda Shop and then to the dance hall to meet some men!" Betty said as Kate giggled.

Clara shook her head. "I can't—"

"We heard Sam's going to be there." Kate interjected.

"Sam?" Clara asked. Sam was her crush from school. He had brown eyes, sandy hair, and cute dimples on his cheeks.

"See, I knew that would get her attention!" Kate said to Betty, elbowing her.

"Come on, Clara! What do you have to do?" Betty said as she lit a cigarette.

Clara turned and glanced up the stairs. She forced a smile while on the verge of tears. "I can't. I'm not feeling well."

"You're such a bummer sometimes, Clara!" Kate laughed as she and Betty walked away.

Clara closed the door and leaned her back against it, tearing up.

No time to go out with friends.

No time for youth.

July 23rd, 1958, Brooklyn, NY

Clara suppressed those memories, but sometimes they rose to the surface like the body of a person who had drowned. She thought of this while staring at her ceiling Wednesday morning, two days after Marcus's funeral. Another unbearably hot summer day with her father already leaving for work. She had five months left of being a teenager. But she never had much of a youth to begin with.

Her friends, Kate and Betty, had given up on her, though she couldn't say she blamed them. Other teenagers went to the movies, the beach, or the soda fountain to spend their summer days. Clara had other plans. One man was left on her list, Dean Caraway. What time was it? She checked her watch. 11:30 a.m. She jumped out of bed, walked into her bathroom, and closed the door. Clara had been watching Dean for the last couple of days, tracking his movements. He clocked into work at Sinclair's at 7 a.m., left the building for lunch at 11:55 a.m., and went to eat at The Donahue at 11:59 a.m. Dean, then, sat at the same booth in the front right-hand corner of the restaurant.

No time to lose.

Clara removed the tile covering the spot she hid her makeup case, setting it on the counter and returning the tile back in its place. After applying her eyeliner, light eyeshadow, and mascara, she stared at herself in the mirror. She took out a light shade of pink lipstick and applied it.

She dressed in a mint green skirt and white shirt, placing her feet in black heels. Her hair was curled. After returning her makeup case under the tile, it was time to lay a trap.

This was the pre-meeting. She would dress innocently and wear her makeup naturally. She wouldn't come on too strong so as not to scare him away. He was making the choice of having an affair. He needed to be comfortable, so Clara couldn't be pushy. He had to be the one to suggest it. And lastly, she had to make him wait for it.

As Clara walked downstairs, she closed her eyes and braced herself. When she looked at the living room, everything was neat and in its proper place.

"Honey, you look so nice!" her mother said, dusting the bookshelves. Her hair was curled and pristine, and her makeup was minimal and natural.

"Thanks, Mom." Clara teared up as her mother approached her and gave her a tight hug. Her mother rubbed Clara's back, and Clara rested her head on her shoulder.

"Make sure to be back before dinner, all right?"

Clara let go of her and promised. Everything would be peaceful and quiet until her father came home. She left the house and headed toward The Donahue, entering the bar at 11:55. She chose the corner booth Dean loved to sit in, as this would force him to notice her. Clara took a newspaper lying on the table and read it. *The Flatbush Times.*

NEW QUESTIONS IN THE MURDER OF MARCUS ANDERSON

Detective Howard is continuing to pursue leads related to the horrific stabbing of Marcus Anderson, the well-liked doctor who worked for many years at Sinclair Hospital

Psychiatric Ward. The inspector is looking at a possible connection to another victim, Bernhard Altenhofen. Altenhofen was also a practicing physician at Sinclair's and murdered with a knife. The investigation is ongoing, and the New York Police Department requests that anyone with any tips to call or visit one...

The newspaper slipped from Clara's fingertips. She was running out of time. The police were already pursuing the connection between her victims. Dean had to go before it was too late. Her palms were sweaty as she gazed around the bar. A few men sat at the bar, talking about their wives or complaining about their jobs. The other tables were taken with groups of men on their work breaks, laughing and having a good time.

"Anything for you, miss?" the bartender yelled.

"I'll have a Coca-Cola, please!"

He nodded and continued pouring more beer for a man rocking back and forth on his feet. The bartender stepped from around the counter and handed her a glass bottle with a straw. Dean would step in at any moment and walk to the booth, only to notice Clara sat there. He would be forced to look at her. Then, he would take a place somewhere else in the bar, hopefully at a spot where she would be in his view. Clara checked the clock on the wall. 11:58 a.m. One minute to go.

Dean stepped inside at 11:59 a.m. He looked at Clara as planned. Clara curled her hair around her finger and gave him a charming smile. Her man. Her special someone. Her darling. He glanced at her and sat at the bar instead, choosing a spot with Clara in front of him. Perfect.

Once every few minutes, their eyes locked. His face flushed red as he finished his beer and ordered another one. Clara pushed her hair behind her bare shoulder, sipping from her straw. He would need some help to make the leap. Dean hesitated, so Clara gave him a subtle wave to move him along. She looked away toward the wallpaper, giving him enough time to remove his wedding ring and put it in his pocket. It worked. He approached her, asking if he could have a seat.

"Yes, you can," Clara said sweetly, folding the newspaper and setting it aside. No need to discuss her last victim's murder. That would ruin the fun.

He sat across from her and took another sip of his drink. "You're very beautiful."

"Oh, thank you! What's your name?"

"Dean."

None of them ever gave the idea of lying about their name any thought.

"I'm Alice."

"Nice to meet you, Alice. Have I seen you before? You look a little familiar to me."

That damn funeral.

"No, definitely not. I would've remembered those gorgeous eyes."

Dean blushed. His eyes were as blue as the face of a man who was suffocated to death.

Clara took his beer and drank some, setting it in front of him. She made sure to imprint her pink lipstick on the glass.

"Do you want to head to my place?"

He cut right to the chase, making things easier. His wife and children must be out of the house.

No, you have to make him wait for it, Clara reminded herself. Besides, she had something else in mind.

"Oh!" She sighed. "How I wish I could today! I'm free tomorrow evening, though. I have just the place!"

His disappointment was washed over with lust and excitement. The last murder she needed to commit to ensure justice was done. So close to her grasp, she could almost touch it.

Clara tore off a portion of the weather page from the newspaper and took a pen out of her purse. She wrote down the address, sliding it over to Dean. The past three times, the man picked the place where they would die, but she couldn't take any chances.

"I can't wait for tomorrow night," Clara said, as Dean smiled and put the address inside his jacket pocket.

"I'll see you then."

"I better get going, bye!"

He waved at her, and she left him alone at the booth. Clara turned one last time before leaving the bar, flashing him another smile. She couldn't wait for tomorrow night, indeed.

* * *

Once the day turned to night, Clara had to make preparations for Dean's murder. A knife certainly wouldn't work this time. Yes, Dean worked at Sinclair's, so the connection remained. But she had to pick another weapon that would fade into its surroundings. That's why she chose an empty, abandoned building on the outskirts of Brooklyn.

Clara sorted through her closet, searching for the same black dress she wore to Marcus's funeral. Her red velvet dress still hadn't turned up, but the turquoise dress was also missing from her closet. Shifting through the rest of her closet, she furrowed her eyebrows. The dress had disappeared. She sighed, taking the black one off the hanger. There was no time to waste. Clara would have to figure out why her dresses were disappearing later.

She changed into a lacy black dress with a wide skirt, putting on matching gloves and a hat. No makeup was necessary for tonight. She walked lightly down the hallway and touched her ear lightly against the door. Her father snored, in the middle of deep sleep. She went downstairs, the grandfather clock ticking in the corner of the room, displaying it was a little after midnight. Not many people would be out and about at that time. No eyes could glare at her on the streets. They wouldn't be able to ask: Why was an innocent young woman walking the streets of Brooklyn holding a weapon?

Grabbing a large tote bag, Clara went into the shed in the backyard. Her father was no handyman, but there must be some tools she could use. His toolbox lay on a shelf with gardening tools and supplies, a couple shovels, and a lawnmower. She opened the toolbox to find nails, screws, and bolts. A couple hammers lay beside it. An ax leaned against the wall in the opposite corner with a rake and a hoe. She selected a hammer and an ax, putting them inside the tote bag and leaving the shed. Those should get the job done, and her tote bag wasn't too heavy to carry.

The streets were dead as the streetlights shined upon them. It would be easier to take the subway, but being stuck in a car with strangers would give them time to figure out what was in her bag. She straightened her posture as she walked several blocks. Her heels tapped on the cement as the breeze pressed hot air against her face. *Almost there.* She continued for a dozen blocks before reaching her destination. An old abandoned shack in the midst of a dying part of the city, badly in need of rebuilding. No one but druggies and prostitutes hung out around here. Clara must make this fast. The door creaked open, letting the streetlight pour into the small room.

She jolted backward and held her mouth with her hand as rats scattered. The two windows on the back wall were smashed to pieces, and the ceiling seeped, water dripping onto the cement floor. Graffiti was painted on the plywood walls. If Clara were to lean against one of the walls, the shack would collapse. It wasn't the most romantic place in the world. Hopefully Dean wouldn't mind.

She set the ax and hammer on the floor, concealing them in the front corner. Clara wouldn't play around this time. As soon as she laid eyes on him, her hammer would as well.

15

October 21st, 1958, Pocono Lake, Pennsylvania

Clara woke up, staring at the ceiling in her little cabin in the woods. Sunlight poured into her room through the window behind her bed. The closed door leading to the living room faced her on the opposite wall. Another night she survived. Getting out of bed wasn't easy, as troubling thoughts swarmed her mind like a buzz of a mosquito flying by her ear. No matter how she swatted it away, the buzzing only grew louder. One mosquito turned to a dozen, stinging her in her neck until she broke out in hives.

A ghastly man lay horizontally next to her, blood pouring out of his chest onto the bed and soaking the sheets. His eyes black and tired, his mouth open and dry. When she closed her eyes and reopened them, the man disappeared into thin air. Nothing was left but the intense beating of her heart. She could hold the top of her head and tear it in two.

That was enough. Clara wouldn't waste any time on the men who ruined her life. Except the one... No, she wasn't going to think about it.

She did the city a favor.

But what if it was all for nothing? *Stop thinking about it.* She peeled off her blanket, left her bedroom, and stepped into the kitchen to make coffee. Everything was how it should be, clean and organized. She picked up a pen and crossed off the day on the calendar before opening the window to let in a cool breeze. The birds chirped; they wouldn't stick around here much longer. They would fly to the south and embrace warm weather again, while Clara couldn't escape. Winter would be here soon, and she would be trapped in this cabin while a snowstorm raged outside. She could be stuck inside for weeks. With *him*. She opened the fridge to add milk to her tea.

Clara furrowed her eyebrows. She bought milk yesterday, yet the container was light, her arm lifted too easily. She opened it to find no milk inside. Holding it over the sink upside down, drops of milk fell from it one at a time. She slammed the carton in the garbage. Did she forget to buy milk yesterday at the store? She went through her purse, searching for the receipt. Eggs, bacon, napkins, toilet paper, milk. It didn't make any sense. She closed her eyes, trying to keep herself calm. It was time to make some eggs. Clara opened the egg carton, relieved to find a dozen inside. She cracked a couple, whisked them, and cooked them on the stove.

Clara sat on a stool at her kitchen counter and ate, staring out the window. The trees rustled, the leaves swinging, with the dying ones falling off. The Poconos was beautiful in the fall, especially when a mist rose from the warm ground in the morning. She felt the urge to walk through it and be transported somewhere else. A place where she had total control of her surroundings.

The waterfall in the distance made the soothing sound of the water crashing onto the ground. The water running over the stones, broken sticks, and dead leaves, down the hillside. It added to the ambience of living in the middle of nowhere, in what should be a peaceful environment. Clara set her fork down, furrowing her eyebrows. There wasn't a waterfall near her cabin. So why would she hear water splashing? She set her foot on the floor from the stool and jumped. Water poured from the bathroom into the kitchen, spreading across the wood flooring and touching the legs of the stool.

"Shit!" Clara whispered, running into the bathroom. The bathtub was overflowing. She didn't remember running a bath. It was possible she forgot. No, she couldn't have; she never took baths during the day. But what if she did take a bath during the day? Clara turned off the water, pulled up her sleeves, and unplugged the drain. Her socks and the hem of her gray dress were soaking wet. She gazed at the water level as it lowered.

She searched the cabin frantically, checking to make sure the front and back doors were locked; checking every closet, under the beds, and in any place where someone could conceal themselves. She was alone in the cabin. At least she was now.

No, that did not happen.

Clara left the bathroom and sat on a stool at her kitchen counter. She ate, staring out the window. The eggs were fluffy and tasty, and her coffee was earthy. Well, it tasted earthy and bitter since apparently she used the last of the milk.

She sighed. It wasn't worth getting worked up over small things. There were too many larger things to worry about instead.

After finishing her breakfast, she packed her backpack with a notepad, pen, and water. There was no sun shining today, so sunglasses weren't necessary. Clara tied her hair into a boring ponytail and wore her gray dress. Loading the backpack onto her shoulders, she left the cabin and began her daily walk up the side of the hill to the bare spot on top. A squirrel ran in front of her and climbed a tree. She used to wonder what it was like to be hunted, to be spotted in a crowd, lured to a secluded area, and murdered. Living every moment in fear that today would be your last; that someone was stalking you, waiting in the shadows. You might have been a good person, a complete stranger to the stalker, but were simply at the wrong place at the wrong time.

Clara didn't have to wonder anymore.

She had done that to those men. But they deserved it. She made a difference in helping the people of Brooklyn.

The thought had to be fleeting. Remembering it made her stomach turn.

She dropped her backpack onto the ground once she reached the top. She put her hands on her hips as she surveyed the land around her. The land seemed inviting and mysterious at first glance. Now it bored her. It was too quiet and empty.

Clara sat on the grass, crossing her legs and setting her notepad on the skirt of the dress. She readied her pen to write.

Dear Mom,

Every day I am reminded of the pain I caused so many people. Maybe that's the man's goal. To make me suffer, to live in fear; be stalked and murdered. He was spying on me in the grocery store the other day, I know it. He might be watching me right now, unless he's tearing apart my cabin. I'm being buried alive, being crushed by the weight of their dead bodies. My mind can't shut off.

One of my worst fears is that it was all for nothing. I hope that isn't true. I did this for a reason, I'm not a psychopath. I'm not sick. They all had it coming. Well, not all of them. I know I went too far... I never meant for it to go so far. You have to believe me, Mom. I didn't know I was capable of being so vicious. I was so angry, I lost control. I look back in disbelief and try to suppress the memories that haunt me. I know this is my purgatory, that I may never have peace again. The truth is, I've never had peace. The burning began when I was born and will continue until the day I die. But I need to know you're all right, Mom. I need to know you read my letters. That would make all of this worth it. Please write back to me! I'm begging you! Please, Mom. I love you very much. And I'm so sorry.

Love,

Clara

Clara folded the letter and tucked it in an envelope. She sealed it before placing it in her bag. Tears formed in her eyes as a chill raced down her spine. The weather was too cool to remain on the hill any longer, though the cabin was not an inviting place, either. The fog hovered over the ground as she walked on the dead leaves, crunching under her feet, along with fallen branches. A branch snapped in the distance. Clara halted, holding her breath. The fog was too thick to see through. Leaves crinkled.

Silence consumed the woods around her again. If there was someone out there, they would be able to hear every step she took. Clara paused for a few more seconds and walked again. It didn't matter how careful she was; the noise was the same. Clara stopped again. The mud covered her black flats. She turned to look behind her. On top of the noise of walking on dead leaves, her shoes left footprints.

As she continued walking, she stopped again as a second set of footprints walked down the same path toward the cabin. She placed her foot next to it. These were double the length of hers. Someone else was here. Making noise didn't matter, getting to the cabin unscathed did. So she ran like hell, her feet pounding the slippery ground. Clara slipped on a pile of leaves, sliding forward. Her back hit against the cold ground as the wind was taken out of her. She clawed the ground, dirt collecting under her fingernails. A cigar lay on the ground beside her. She gazed around the woods, and no one showed themselves. After standing, she ran into the cabin and slammed the door shut.

Clara leaned her back against the door as she tried to catch her breath. Her cabin seemed empty and in order. She drew the curtains and searched every inch. The bathroom, the two bedrooms, the kitchen, and living room. She searched every closet, corner, and under her furniture. No one inside but her.

Clara couldn't live this way for much longer.

Mud covered her calves, skirt, elbows, and hands. It was early, but she had to get cleaned up. Clara locked the door in the bathroom and ran a bath. She sat on the edge of the tub, swirling her hand in the hot water as steam filled the room. Clara stepped into the tub, her legs trying to get her body to escape due to the heat. Her skin stung at first contact, but adjusted. Lying her head back, she closed her eyes, resting her arms on each side. The heat soothed her aching muscles and calmed her mind. Her mind could drift away and leave the terror she felt in the woods behind her.

She opened her eyes, gasping and pushing her back against the wall of the bathtub. The water turned red, thick, and gooey. She pulled out her hand, feeling its viscosity as she rubbed her thumb against her fingertips. Was it blood?

The bathroom door creaked, but before Clara could turn her head to look at it, someone gripped the top of her head. Tried to scream. A bony hand pushed her head underwater, the nails digging into her skull. Lungs filled with water. Hands grasped the sides. Trying to pull upward. No use. Struggled. Hand's strength too great. Body weakened. Eyes closing. Giving up. Letting go. This would be the end. As Clara closed her eyes and drifted asleep, the hand loosened its grip, and she shot up from the water, gasping for air and coughing. Her head ached as the room spun around her. She rubbed her eyes to clear her vision. The water was once again clear.

The bathroom door, however, was unlocked and ajar.

16

Oliver stood across the street from *The Flatbush Times* with a briefcase in his left hand. His first day after bereavement leave. Back to the grind, and hearing "I'm sorry for your loss" over and over again today. His coworkers meant well, and he guessed that was the only thing one could say to a man whose brother had been murdered. Oliver never wanted to come across as impolite to other people's sympathies, but he resented hearing that phrase. He had heard it enough for a lifetime.

He pushed his shoulders back and returned for another day of typing obituaries. This job might have been tedious, but it carried more weight for him now. This time, he had Nancy and George to support. He couldn't afford to screw anything up.

"Hi, Oliver!" The receptionist waved at Oliver before pushing her wavy blonde hair over her shoulder. Dorothy was always in a positive mood. Oliver couldn't think of a time when she wasn't smiling. "I'm so sorry about your brother. You and your family have been in my prayers."

"Oh," Oliver said, leaning against the counter. "Thank you, Dorothy. I appreciate that."

"The service was beautiful. The office all chipped in for flowers for you and Marcus's family." She handed him a vase full of daisies and a card. "I picked them out myself."

Oliver took them, not remembering seeing anyone from his work at the funeral. "That's very nice of you, thank you!"

"Anytime." She smiled. "Welcome back, Oliver."

"I'll see you around." He waved goodbye, taking the elevator to the sixth floor and returning to his desk. The cards remained stacked from ones he completed on his last day of work, along with his empty mug and pens. He would never have guessed when he left work that day what had transpired that evening. His previous day of work felt like a lifetime ago. His life was divided into two: before Marcus's death and after.

Oliver set his briefcase down, grabbing his mug to fill with coffee for the morning. As he turned, a coworker almost ran into him, ignoring Oliver. Oddly, this made Oliver feel truly back at work. It was preferable to that man staring at him with his mouth wide open and offering his condolences. A fresh pot waited for him in the small kitchen. Once the coffee touched his lips, he felt ready to get started. He took his seat, waiting for Alex to barge in—like clockwork.

"More deaths!" Alex yelled, slamming a fresh pile on Oliver's desk. He grimaced and scratched his head in realization. "Oh, sorry, Oliver..."

"It's all right," he said, taking the first name off the pile.

"Good to have you back!" Alex patted Oliver's shoulder, putting a pen behind his ear.

"Thank you, glad to be back. Some more normalcy."

"Yeah, sometimes it's nice to get back into routine," he agreed. "Let me know if you need anything."

"Thanks, Alex."

"Anytime." Alex smiled, leaving Oliver at his desk toward the back of the large room. Oliver picked up the first name and got to work. He completed his first card of the day and placed it on the pile. He paused and frowned. The last card on his completed pile was Bernhard Altenhofen. A man who died from a stab wound to the chest. He picked up Bernie's card and sighed, placing it on the pile again. He couldn't think about his brother now. He readied his hands on the typewriter keys.

Alissa Peters—July 19th, 1958 from Brooklyn, NY. Loving wife to Paul Peters and mother to David. Services will be held at Flatbush-Tompkins Congregational Church on July 26th at 9 o'clock. Friends are invited.

Done.

Cause of death: leaned against an unsecured railing on a balcony, plummeting to her death on the cement sidewalk below.

"Oh my God," Oliver whispered, grimacing. *What a horrible way to die! That poor woman.* He wondered how often that occurred.

Oliver set the note aside and continued on to the next one. Thankfully, the next person died of old age and lived a long and fulfilling life. After Oliver finished typing the man's obituary, he moved onto the next one. Okay, this one didn't include the cause of death. It was nice when it wasn't included; it felt like a break.

Christopher Hoffmann—July 20th, 1958 from Brooklyn, NY. Devoted husband to Linda and father to Michael, Robert, and Leah. Services for family and friends will be at St. Francis of Assisi Church Roman Catholic Church on July 25th at 11 o'clock.

As Oliver kept typing throughout the day, he tried to stop himself from thinking about his brother and that young woman. Being distracted could lead him into trouble with his work. Typos would slow him down. He couldn't afford to make any mistakes. *Stop thinking about it. I shouldn't be thinking about personal matters at work. It's inappropriate.* Oliver shook his head, completing his final card of the day. He handed the completed obituaries to Alex on the way out, deciding to leave the flowers and card overnight. Too many errands to run. He took the stairs to the first floor to avoid the crowded elevator and walked past an empty receptionist's desk. *Perfect.* He didn't want to engage in any more chit-chat. *I shouldn't be thinking that way.* Oliver thought to himself, pushing the front door open. Dorothy was probably the one who collected signatures on the card in addition to buying him flowers.

Oliver walked toward Marcus's old apartment, the one he should have sold to help pay for George's medical bills. The place was sold after being on the market for three days, which brought Nancy relief. This should help them pay off most of Marcus's debt. Oliver wanted to walk through it one last time to make sure it was clean and nothing was overlooked. As he walked around the crowds of people, he stopped dead when he read the headline of the afternoon newspaper.

NEW QUESTIONS IN THE MURDER OF MARCUS ANDERSON

He moved closer to the newsstand and held a copy.

Detective Howard is still pursuing leads related to the horrific stabbing of Marcus Anderson, the well-liked doctor who worked for many years at Sinclair Hospital Psychiatric Ward. The inspector is looking at a possible connection to another victim, Bernhard Altenhofen. Altenhofen was also a practicing physician at Sinclair's and murdered with a knife.

Oliver gasped; he typed the obituary of that man. Was it possible that this man's murder and his brother's could be linked? Was that small-framed young woman capable of killing more than Marcus? He put the newspaper back, his hands unsteady, and turned the corner. It could make sense if the link was Sinclair Hospital Psychiatric Ward; that young woman sat with Marcus's coworkers at his funeral. But a small woman capable of going around Brooklyn, murdering men who worked for Sinclair's? It sounded outlandish. But he shouldn't rule it out either, anything was possible...

The apartment building gave him the chills. At least this would be the last time he would ever step inside it. He entered the elevator and pressed for the fifth floor and put his hands on his hips. His brother and Bernie were both stabbed in the chest; both worked at the mental hospital. What could this possibly mean? He stared at the carpeted floor.

"Excuse me, please."

Oliver flinched. A woman around thirty appeared in front of him. He moved aside so she could press the button for her floor. She got off at the third floor, while Oliver waited for the elevator to climb two more stories. The doors opened, revealing a long hallway no longer filled with police officers and ambulance attendants. There was no gurney, no camera flashing. All was quiet except for one of the light bulbs flickering on the ceiling and the hardwood floors creaking. His body trembled as he anticipated what waited for him inside. Marcus lying on the floor with the knife used to kill him beside him? A pool of dried blood on the kitchen floor? The young woman waiting in the closet, ready to plunge a knife into Oliver's chest next?

Oliver walked past Marilyn's door and stood in front of his brother's door. He unlocked it, holding the doorknob before turning it. He pressed the door as it swung open slowly. The apartment looked identical to that morning; the furniture was in the same spot as before. He looked around to make sure no one was there, hiding in the shadows. Oliver stepped into the kitchen. The floors were clean and shiny, the nick in the tile from the knife had been fixed. The knife set was taken from the apartment; the countertops were empty. Everything was clean and in order.

He stared at the wall by the kitchen window. His mind could picture Marcus standing there the night they had one of their worst arguments. Their relationship could never be the same.

* * *

Six years ago.

"Nancy never says much," Marcus said, standing by the window wearing a tan suit. "I like that about her."

"That's not my experience." Oliver bit his tongue. It wasn't the time to get defensive. He came to his brother's apartment for a reason. "Marcus, can I be honest with you?"

"Of course." Marcus turned to him, lighting a cigar. He blew out the match and tossed it in the garbage. Puffs of smoke filled the kitchen.

"Don't marry her."

Marcus chuckled. "Oliver, do you realize what this would do for my career? Nancy's father oversees the whole hospital. I'll climb the ladder so fast and replace him in no time. Most importantly, I can't risk the hospital falling into the wrong hands. All of my progress I've made with treatments could be jeopardized if some bastard gets in there and cleans house."

"I don't care, Marcus. I'm in love with Nancy!"

"Oliver, I know you too well." Marcus exhaled, a smoke cloud forming between them. "You'll move on to someone new. She's your first love, but she most certainly won't be your last. You'll find another girl in no time."

"I'm asking you as your brother."

"I'm going to marry Nancy, Oliver. I'm sorry. There's too much at stake."

"No, you're not!" Oliver snapped, grabbing Marcus by his shirt and shoving him against the wall. "Don't marry her!"

"What are you going to do?" Marcus laughed as Oliver released him.

"I'm going to marry Nancy, and you'll find some wonderful woman who loves you and marry her. You'll thank me someday. Marriage is a business, and emotions only blind you—"

"If you marry her, I will never forgive you, and I will hate you for the rest of my life." Oliver interrupted him.

Marcus grinned. "You'll see I'm right someday."

Oliver stormed out of Marcus's apartment, slamming the door behind him.

* * *

Oliver returned to the present, his stomach dropping when he turned to the floor where he found his brother lying dead. His wide and bloodshot eyes, his open mouth, the twitching of his fingers, his arms spread out, and his blood spread across the floor. Nancy stayed up the whole night, worried sick over Marcus. George would have to grow up without his father. When he returned to Nancy's apartment hours later than he had promised, Oliver found her broken down in tears. He had a nightmare where Marcus screamed at him, saying Oliver should've saved him.

Oliver rushed into the bathroom and gripped the sink tightly, staring at the drain.

I never should've left. I never should've left.

How could he abandon his brother? He could've done more than confront him at Grayson's Pub. He could've done more to bring Marcus home. His mind wanted to scrub this memory like the blood had been scrubbed off the tile floor.

Oliver looked into the mirror and the young woman appeared behind him, wearing a black dress stained with Marcus's blood and holding a knife, blood dripping from it onto the floor.

"Oliver?" she asked.

Oliver jumped, turning around. It was Marilyn, peeking her head through the apartment door. He put his hand over his chest as his heart beat out of control.

"I'm sorry, dear. I didn't mean to frighten you."

He cleared his throat. "No problem, Marilyn."

"I wanted to say I'm so sorry about Marcus. Tell Nancy my prayers are with her."

"Thank you, that's kind of you."

"If you need anything, my door is always open."

"Thank you."

After Marilyn left the apartment, he looked at himself in the mirror again, collecting himself. Time to leave and never return.

Oliver left the apartment, dropped off the keys, and walked the streets of Brooklyn once again, returning to his apartment after picking up a pizza from Leo's Pizzeria. Once he stepped into the apartment, there was total silence. He kicked off his shoes by the door, entered the kitchen and set the pizza box on the counter. There were only a couple stacks of boxes left, Nancy had made progress in unpacking their things. His cabinets now had stacks of plates and bowls, and his drawer was full of silverware, cooking accessories, pots, and pans.

Nancy put her finger over her lips, pointing to George, who had fallen asleep on the couch. The phone rang, making Nancy flinch. Oliver moved to pick it up.

"Hello?"

"Hi, Oliver!" said a man. "This is Dean Caraway, my wife told me you called."

"Hi, Dean. Yeah, I was wondering if you're interested in meeting up tonight or tomorrow. I would like to ask you about Marcus's work."

"You sound like that detective."

"Did Detective Howard interview you?" Oliver asked.

"Yeah, he came to Sinclair's and interviewed almost all the staff."

"Huh."

"He's a pretty intense man. I can't meet tonight, but how about tomorrow night?" he asked. "You can come to my house if you'd like. How about eight?"

"Yeah, that works for me."

"See you then, Oliver."

"See you." Oliver hung up the phone, turning to find Nancy getting out plates and napkins and setting them on the counter.

"How was your first day back?" she asked.

"It went well," he said. "The office got us flowers and a card."

"That's nice of them. Where are they?"

"I left them at work, but I'll bring them home tomorrow."

The newspaper sitting on the counter caught his eye. He moved his finger over the headline, ***NEW QUESTIONS IN THE MURDER OF MARCUS ANDERSON.***

"What do you think about that, Ollie?" Nancy asked. "Do you think this has to do with the hospital?"

"I'm not sure." He shrugged.

"Dean should know a lot about this. He worked closely with Marcus."

"That's what I'm hoping for."

Nancy leaned against the counter and crossed her arms. "Do you think they'll ever figure out who did this?"

"Whoever's responsible was good at not leaving a trace, but I think they will find them."

George ran into the kitchen, awake from his nap.

"Uncle Ollie's place is so nice, isn't it?" Nancy said, stroking his hair.

"Uh-huh," George said, gazing around the room. He still held the toy car Oliver bought him tightly in his hand. Nancy told him to sit on the couch, and she gave him a slice of pizza. George sat between Nancy and Oliver as they ate dinner together. Oliver had to invest in a kitchen table and chairs. His apartment was nice and spacious, but it could be made more homey by adding some finishing touches. Nancy and George deserved that.

As Oliver ate with Nancy and George, this new development raced through his mind. Dean sat near the young woman at Marcus's funeral. She was related to someone who worked at Sinclair Hospital Psychiatric Ward, sitting in the section of Marcus's coworkers and their families. Dean should be able to identify the staff who sat around him. Hopefully meeting with Dean tomorrow night would give him a lead. The path to finding who killed Marcus led to that young woman.

Oliver must find her.

17

October 21st, 1957, Brooklyn, NY

Nine months ago, Clara ran a bath for herself as she did every evening. It soothed her, the scalding hot water; the pain tingling through her skin upon first touch. She laid her head back and closed her eyes. The biology exam today was difficult, but at least it was over and done. Kate and Betty agreed it was challenging. She had a paper due next Monday on *Great Expectations.* She would have to find time this weekend for that. A siren blasted through her window as an ambulance drove down her street. If she had it her way, she would attend college and move away from the city and explore the endless wilderness alone. Yet, the quietness would bring her grief. The adjustment wouldn't be easy. Those were fantasies, anyway; things to get her through the day. Her father hadn't budged on allowing her to attend college. A dream too distant for her grasp.

As she rested, sharp nails dug into her scalp, pushing her head underwater. No matter how hard she struggled, no matter how she gripped the sides of the tub, no matter how she moved her legs to push herself upward, the gravity of the hand forcing her head under was too strong. The lack of oxygen made Clara too weak to resist. She opened her eyes underwater. A shadowy figure watched over her, but she couldn't make out who it was. Any longer and Clara would drown. Her flailing arms and legs stopped trying to save her, sinking into the water. Clara's eyes closed as water filled her lungs.

The hand was suddenly pulled off her head, and she jolted above water, gasping for air. She held her neck with one hand, steadying herself on the side of the bathtub with the other. Once her vision became clearer and she could breathe, she turned toward the bathroom door. Her father restrained her mother, wrapping his arms around her from behind, as her mother lashed out, tears streaming down her cheeks.

Her mother screamed. "Clara! I'm so sorry, Clara!"

Her father pulled her mother out of the bathroom and closed the door, leaving Clara alone. She rested her chin on the side of the bathtub and cried. Her mind couldn't process anything. She didn't want to move, but needed to get out of the water. Clara crawled out of the bathtub, wrapping herself in a towel. She locked the door, slipped onto the floor, rested her head on her knees, and cried. It kept getting worse. The lashing out was only getting more severe as time went on.

Someone knocked on the door, causing her to flinch.

"It's Dad, Clara. Come downstairs when you're ready. I'd like to talk to you about something."

"Okay," she whispered. Her legs forgot how to stand. She never wanted to leave the bathroom ever again. Clara put her hand on the counter, jolting her body upward. She grabbed a few tissues to wipe her red, swollen eyes. Her cheeks were puffy. She ran her fingers through her hair, and they came away bloody. Her mother's fingernails must have scratched her scalp, breaking the skin.

After drying herself off and getting dressed, she brushed her soaking wet, tangled hair. Every brushstroke hurt. She winced and swallowed her pain. It wasn't that bad; it could be worse. Clara tried smiling at herself in the mirror, but her lips twitched too much to hold it steady, so she gave up. The door waited for her through the reflection in the mirror. Reaching with a shaky hand, she opened it. Clara peeked down the hallway that led to their bedrooms. Her parent's bedroom door was closed, and the lights were off. Her father must have given her mother something to sleep.

Clara stepped down the stairs lightly as she held both railings to steady herself. Her mind was foggy, unable to process her surroundings. Her father never talked to her like this. It must be serious.

Her father sat alone at the kitchen table, smoking a cigar. Clara joined him, wiping the remaining tears off her face. She crossed her arms and hunched over, unable to bring herself to look her father in the eye. She needed to be alone.

"I'm so sorry that happened." Her father held a straight face, staring at her.

Clara didn't respond.

"Your mother is sick, Clara." Her father explained. "She can't be left alone anymore, being a danger to herself and others. I'm going to bring her to Sinclair Hospital Psychiatric Ward. She'll be in the best care. Since I work in the same hospital, I'll be able to watch over her. She'll be in good hands."

"What?" Clara asked, her mouth hanging open. "You're going to take her away from me?"

He put his hand on her shoulder, but she shook it off. Clara's mind couldn't accept it.

"Clara, she would've killed you if I hadn't come home. I got here just in time to save your life. She picked the lock to get into the bathroom. You're a senior in high school, and she can't be left alone six or seven hours a day."

No, this can't be. Clara promised her mother that she would never abandon her. This couldn't be happening. "Can you hire someone to keep an eye on her here?"

"I have done everything I can," he said. "I have tried giving your mother medication here at home. I do nothing when she rages at me, accuses me of adultery, and throws things at me. Things have changed. Now, it looks as though you're not safe to be alone with her. Your mother can get better if given the proper treatment. She's not a lost cause, far from it. Doctors have made great strides in psychiatry. Sinclair's has great care."

"I can take care of her," Clara pleaded. "I've heard of such horrible things going on in that hospital. They won't care about Mom!"

"Clara, I've made up my mind. This decision was already difficult; I don't need to hear it." Her father put out his cigar in an ashtray, standing from the table and heading for the stairs.

"Please, Dad! I need her!" Clara cried, tearing up again.

"Goodnight, Clara." He climbed the stairs to his bedroom.

Clara felt the urge to destroy the house. She imagined throwing the furniture, ramming the couch against the wall, throwing a dining room chair across the room, and breaking an end table against the pillar between the kitchen and living room. Breaking the windows with a broom. Slamming the dishes onto the floor. How good that would feel. The rage was building inside of her like steam in a covered pot. She wanted to scream, so she pressed her hand against her mouth to discourage the temptation. Clara plugged her nose with the other hand. She waited and waited until she began feeling lightheaded. Her body resisted, demanding that she breathe.

Clara obeyed, taking her hands off her face and gasping for air. She paced downstairs between the living room and the kitchen. One o'clock in the morning, two o'clock in the morning. When her legs were too tired, she settled into bed, exhausted. Clara stared at the ceiling as she made the Sign of the Cross. She teared up, and her hands shook as she pressed her palms together in prayer.

"Please, Lord. Please, Lord, don't take my mother away from me. I'll do anything, I promise. I'll be the best daughter. Please! Please, my mom can't go to that hospital. Please, God, don't let her live in such a horrible, dreadful place. She doesn't deserve it, it's not her fault. Please God, please don't take her away from me! I'm begging you; I'll do anything! Please, Lord, please!"

. . .

July 24th, 1958, Brooklyn, NY

Clara sat on the edge of the bathtub, watching water dripping from the faucet. She snapped out of that memory. She had work to do. Tonight, she would murder Dean Caraway. She took her makeup case out from under the tile floor and stood before the vanity, all dolled up for her special date tonight. Bright red blush, dark brown eyeshadow, and black eyeliner and mascara. She ran her fingers over the lipstick, her favorite. Clara smothered it on, bright red as blood. She wore a black skirt and collared shirt, sliding her feet into her heels.

Her father worked late tonight, so she should have no trouble sneaking into the house. Clara reached for the front door.

"Where are you going, honey?" her mother asked.

Clara froze with widened eyes as she turned around. Her mother smiled at her, wearing an olive green dress. Her makeup was done tastefully with pink lipstick and matching blush. She looked calm and peaceful, not in any mood to lash out. She looked normal. Her mother would be fine on her own; Clara shouldn't be gone long.

Clara relaxed her shoulders as she loosened her grip on her purse. "I'm going to meet Sam. We're going dancing together."

"That's nice, but why are you wearing all black? You look like you're going to a funeral."

Clara looked at her outfit. "Black is Sam's favorite color. Depressing, I know, but he says he likes the color on me."

"Well, have a good time, but make sure you're back before your father comes home."

"I will, Mom. Bye!"

"Goodbye, dear! Have fun!" Her mother waved her goodbye, and Clara left the house. This time, she could take the subway, getting there in half the time. She leaned against the wall, waiting for the train to arrive. All the planning, stalking, and killing led to this. One more man to go. Her life could return to normal, leaving her past in the rearview mirror and focusing on her future. If tonight was successful, the burning would stop.

The train arrived, so she stepped inside and took a seat. Girls sat in pretty dresses, giggling about the men they were going to meet. A couple of men debated whether the Yankees or the Dodgers were a better baseball team, and another man sat quietly in the car, reading the newspaper. That man looked familiar, but she couldn't make eye contact or draw any attention to herself. She clutched her purse on her lap, staring into the blackness of the tunnel, faintly seeing her reflection in the window. The train came to a stop.

Clara got off and climbed the stairs, heading to the abandoned shack. She looked behind the door, and the hammer and ax were there from last night. Dean should arrive at any moment, and she would strike him before his lips had a chance to meet hers. It went too far with Marcus. If she hadn't gotten lucky, he would have... Clara didn't need to think about it.

She picked up the hammer, wrapping her fingers around the grip. Leaning against the wall next to the door frame, Clara concealed herself behind the open door. Dean should be stepping inside any minute now. Every time her lungs expanded, nails that stuck out of the wall dug into her skin. She couldn't make a sound, though; she couldn't breathe too loudly. Her muscles had to remain still. When the time came, she would sneak out of the shadows. Footsteps approached the shack. Clara held her breath as Dean looked around, stepping further inside.

"Alice?" he asked with a shaky voice. Maybe he had been reading horrible stories in the newspaper.

She gripped the hammer tighter, holding it up unsteadily and taking light footsteps toward him. Before he had a chance to turn, she struck Dean on the back of his head. He screamed in agony, falling onto his knees and rolling over onto his back. Drops of blood splattered across her face as she dropped the hammer, and it crashed against the cement.

Clara picked up the ax, gripping it with both hands. She stood over him as his head gushed with blood, rushing onto the floor and spreading across it. Dean rocked on his back, holding the side of his head with his bloodied hand and moaning in pain. He stared at her as she readied the ax again.

Clara could leave him. She could turn and leave the shack, letting him die a slow, painful death, letting his head bleed out as life drained from his body like a battery. But if someone were to find him and save him, Dean would remember her physical characteristics. He said she looked familiar to him when they met at Donahue's. It was possible he could place her as being present at Marcus's funeral and the daughter of one of his colleagues. Detective Howard would put the pieces together that Marcus and Dean both met with a young woman before being murdered. Well, in Dean's case, attempted murder.

No, it was too big a risk. Dean must die. She raised the ax. Dean's mouth moved, but he couldn't speak. He was in too much pain to make a word. She imagined him begging, pleading with her to spare his life. *I have a family, you see? I have a beautiful wife and three wonderful children. Who will walk my daughter down the aisle on her wedding day? Who will take my son to his first baseball game?* No, he didn't think about them when he decided to sleep with another woman, but he sure as hell was thinking about them now. Only when his life was in danger. Pity it was too late.

Clara would put him out of his misery. The ax struck him in his chest, the blood splattering onto her. She backed away briefly as the moaning ceased and his muscles stopped twitching. Nothing but silence. Dean was dead. It was done.

Clara spread out her arms and took a bow.

Footsteps inched closer behind her as Clara jumped around and screamed. A man approached her, reaching out toward her. Clara squinted, unable to make out his face with the street light beaming behind him. Fog poured into the room, covering his calves and feet. He walked closer to Clara, as she ripped the ax out of Dean's body, gripping it tighter and raising it in self-defense. The man was Oliver Anderson, Marcus's brother. Clara held the ax, but the man turned into smoke after she blinked.

She dropped the ax; its collision with the pavement echoed. The man on the subway reading a newspaper looked awfully familiar, but she couldn't quite place her finger on it. His name was Oliver, Marcus's brother. Clara stepped on a broken piece of glass, and it broke through the sole of her shoe. She ignored the piercing pain ripping through her body. It wasn't important.

"Oh my God," Clara whispered, discovering something worse. Oliver was there the night she murdered Marcus. He witnessed what happened in that apartment. When she left the apartment, wearing Marcus's trench coat over her blood-soaked dress, a man at the other end of the hallway watched her. The man wasn't a neighbor fiddling with his keys and trying to open the door. That man was Oliver Anderson, following her. He saw her leave the apartment, leaving behind his dead brother lying on the floor with a stab wound. He was onto her. He was watching her. He was stalking her. Her work wasn't finished yet.

Oliver must be next.

18

Oliver left his apartment building and stood still. Brooklyn was empty. No cars were driving on the streets, and many were parked on the side of the road. The sun tried to break through the clouds but failed, casting a shadow over the city. Oliver kept walking down the empty sidewalk, stopping at an intersection and looking up and down the next street. Not a soul could be found. He frowned. The playground across the street was empty, swings creaking when pushed by the breeze. Where were Nancy and George?

Oliver turned and raced to his apartment, needing to check on them. He ran down the street and stopped. The young woman waved to him across the street, wearing a black dress, stained in blood, and carrying a shiny knife. She was beside the entrance to Oliver's apartment building as he walked closer to her. She opened the door as Oliver screamed and tried to run toward her. His feet wouldn't move, and he couldn't make a sound. The young woman smirked at him and entered the building.

* * *

Oliver's nightmare the previous night stuck with him the following day. No matter how hard he tried to stop thinking about that young woman, he could not. He couldn't think about anything except meeting with Dean tonight and asking him about Sinclair's. Dean had to know who that young woman was. After typing his last obituary for the day, he collected the flowers and card from his desk and headed to his apartment. As he walked down the street, a group of people surrounded the windows of a television store, pointing at the latest news. Oliver passed by them; it was probably about uninteresting gossip or politics.

"Another murder?" a man asked his friend. "I can't believe it."

"Well, we do live in New York City," his friend joked.

Oliver stopped, giving the shop window his full attention. He squinted, trying to make out the headline and moving his head back and forth behind the crowd of people gathered. Several televisions glowed through the glass, each showing a different channel. Only the one in the center showed the breaking news. Body found *something* restaurant *something* Donavan. Oliver sighed, looking around to see if there was another window nearby showing the same story. Finally, a couple of men moved away, giving Oliver a better view.

BODY FOUND IN ATTIC OF DANNY'S RESTAURANT IDENTIFIED AS PETER DONAVAN

What the man said was true; this was New York City. The murder of Peter Donavan might have no connection with his brother's death. It would all depend on where Peter Donavan worked. That's another question he could ask Dean Caraway tonight. Oliver prayed to God that Peter Donavan fellow wasn't an employee of Sinclair's. A potential third murder? Did that young woman kill three men? He shook his head, heading home. It was important to wait for all the facts before reaching a conclusion. No need to get worked up over something that might have had nothing to do with Marcus.

Oliver collected the mail from his mailbox before taking the elevator to his apartment. When opening his door, the smell of a blueberry pie welcomed him.

"Ollie!" Nancy said, turning after taking a pie out of the oven and setting it on the stove. "Did you hear the news?"

He put his briefcase beside the door, closing it shut. "About another murder?"

Nancy approached him, wiping her hands on her apron. "Yes, I can't believe it."

"Did he work at Sinclair's?"

"I don't know." She shrugged. "All they've released was his name, and I don't remember ever hearing it before."

"I'm going to ask Dean tonight and see."

"Can you imagine?" she asked with her mouth open as if she was at a loss for words. "I was just listening to the radio."

"I can't imagine it, but we don't have all the facts yet."

"You're right." She sighed and leaned against the counter. "Let's talk about something else; I can't think about it any longer."

Oliver handed her the flowers and the card. "How's George doing?"

"He's doing better today; he's had more energy. We resumed lessons, and they went well."

"Where is he now?"

"He's taking a nap on your bed. You don't mind, do you?"

"Of course not." Oliver picked up the mail and read through it, sitting on the couch.

"I made some chicken and potatoes for dinner. I have to stick them in." She pulled out a pan from the fridge and stuck it in the oven, setting a timer.

"That sounds good."

Nancy made tea for herself and sat next to Oliver on the couch. She cradled the mug, staring at the pile of records sitting on the table across the room. So many things must be swarming in her mind. So much worrying and fear under the surface. So many shouting voices. They must all sound the same, unable to be differentiated from one another. Nothing was worse than a mind that could never be turned off. Oliver knew the feeling.

"How are you doing?" Oliver asked, setting his bills aside.

"I worry about George, Ollie." Nancy teared up. "Today he asked me when Marcus was coming home from work. Then, he started crying when he remembered he's gone..."

"He's young. Death is hard to grapple with as adults, but George will understand as he ages and it will get better with time. He's a bright kid."

Nancy wiped off her tears and took a deep breath. The clock struck six, and Nancy went into the kitchen to check on dinner. Oliver turned the volume louder on the radio to the local news. A man spoke commandingly.

"The workers of Danny's Restaurant noticed a strange stench coming from somewhere in the establishment. They cleaned the kitchen, the dining area, and the bathrooms, but it refused to go away. Then, the owner heard rats scurrying above him, and he checked the attic. That's when he found Peter Donavan. Our sources say Mr. Donavan has been dead since late June and was a staff member of Sinclair Hospital Psychiatric Ward, revealing a possible connection to the murders of Bernhard Altenhofen and Marcus Anderson."

Oliver lowered the volume, placing his palm against the wall and leaning on it. He stared at the hardwood floor, trying to comprehend this news. Marcus was killed by a multiple murderer; someone hunting down staff members of Sinclair Hospital Psychiatric Ward. The only question Oliver could muster was why. What was the motive behind this? Why was that young woman so hellbent on killing these staff members? What did they ever do to her?

Oliver couldn't wait until after dinner to ask Dean his questions. This couldn't wait another moment; there was no time to waste. He needed to ask him now. Oliver took a deep breath and opened the door. George ran to him, smiling, and Oliver gave him a hug absentmindedly.

"Hey, buddy!" he said.

"Hi, Uncle Ollie!"

Nancy checked the ticking timer on the counter, turning toward him and staring into his eyes. "What's wrong? You seem distracted."

"They announced Peter Donavan worked at Sinclair's. There's someone hunting down workers at Sinclair's."

Nancy cupped her hand over her mouth for a moment.

"Three men who worked together died within a month of each other. It just can't be a coincidence." Oliver waved, and Nancy agreed. "I have to talk to Dean and find out if anything major happened there. Have the police given you any updates?"

"Nothing." She rolled her eyes. "I don't like talking to them, so I don't mind that they haven't been by."

Oliver held her hand gently. "I'm going to visit Dean now, I can't sit around and wait. He should be able to provide some answers."

"Be careful, Ollie, don't stay out too late."

"I won't, I promise I'll be back before it's dark."

"I'll heat up dinner for you when you come back."

"Thanks, Nance. See you later, George!"

George waved while holding onto the toy car as Oliver left his apartment once again to head to see Dean Caraway. Dean lived a few blocks away in a townhouse. Hopefully he wouldn't mind Oliver being early, but Dean would understand, given the new details about Peter Donavan's death. Dean could be the next target, considering he currently worked for Sinclair's. Oliver pulled the address from his pocket and read it then turned down the street.

1035... 1037... 1039... 1041

Oliver stood in front of Dean's brick townhouse, opening the iron gate and walking up the steps to the front door. He pounded on it a few times. A woman answered, her face going from excitement and hope to being washed over in disappointment. This must be Marie, Dean's wife.

"Who are you?" she asked, gripping the door so hard the bones in her fingers looked like they could snap.

"Oliver Anderson, Marcus's brother. I spoke to Dean yesterday afternoon, and he invited me over to talk."

Marie said nothing, staring at him with glossy eyes that didn't blink. She hunched over.

"I'm sorry," Oliver said, embarrassed. They were probably enjoying their family dinner; he shouldn't be interrupting like this. "I'm early, Dean told me eight. I'm a couple hours early. I can come back later if that's better."

Marie shook her head as if Oliver misinterpreted her stare. She cleared her throat, struggling to speak. "Dean isn't home."

"Oh, do you know when he'll be back?"

Her bottom lip quivered. "Dean hasn't come home since yesterday after work. He said he was—" She took a deep breath and wiped her tears. "He said he was going to see a patient, but he never came home. I called the hospital, and they said he wasn't in last night."

Oliver was going to be sick.

She drew in a deep breath as if trying to steady her voice. "I told the police, and they said they're looking for him."

"I'm so sorry to hear that. I'll keep your family in my prayers."

"Thank you," she whispered. Marie started closing the door. Oliver turned to return to his apartment, but Marie called out to him.

"I'm sorry about your brother, Oliver," she stuttered.

Oliver thanked her as she closed the door. That poor woman and the torment she must be feeling. He didn't have to imagine it—he had witnessed what Nancy had been going through since Marcus hadn't returned home. Dean and Marie had three young children, all of them asking when their father was coming home. Oliver collected himself, returning to the sidewalk.

The ground rocked back and forth like he stood on a boat during a hurricane. A fourth man. The bodies stacked up with no end in sight. The police must be onto that young woman. They must be hunting her down. She must have been a patient or had known someone who was one. She was sitting with Marcus's coworkers at his funeral. The nerve of her to attend his funeral! Oliver clenched his fists. Detective Howard was supposedly a brilliant detective. *If anyone could solve the case, he could*, Oliver was told this over and over again by police officers. What was taking him so long to find her? It shouldn't be this difficult, and he had already interviewed the staff at Sinclair's.

He said he was going to see a patient, Marie said. Marcus told him the same thing before leaving for Grayson's Pub. Both he and Nancy knew that was a dirty lie.

* * *

On the night of Marcus's murder after confronting Marcus behind the pub, Oliver walked to the end of the alley, crossing the street and standing on the street corner with the Grayson's Pub entrance in his view. He didn't smoke, but he could use a cigarette. His muscles couldn't stop tensing, and heat flushed to his face; it probably was as red as a police siren. He would stand there as long as it took to see where his brother would go next. Nancy sat at home caring for her son, trying to convince herself Marcus did go into work. But she knew better.

Almost an hour passed by as sweat dripped down Oliver's face. He wiped it off as he inhaled a deep breath. He checked his watch again and fixed his posture. Marcus left with a young lady, opening the door to a blue Corvette for her. The same Corvette he was supposed to sell to help pay for Marcus's treatment. Marcus didn't sell the car. Oliver clenched his jaw as his hands shook. He pursed his lips and narrowed his eyes at that shiny car as it passed him. Marcus stared straight ahead, oblivious, as the young woman wore sunglasses and smoked a cigarette. The car blasted "Jailhouse Rock" with the windows down.

Oliver continued the walk down the busy sidewalk and followed the car. It made a right where Marcus's and Nancy's old apartment used to be. This had to be some sort of sick joke. *Don't tell me*, Oliver thought, shaking his head and clenching his fists so hard his knuckles could snap. Marcus parked the car in front of the entrance, stepping out and opening the door for the woman.

Oliver stood across the street, staring at the apartment building looming over him, casting a shadow upon him. *I hope something terrible happens to him*. Marcus deserved to face consequences, but that would never happen. Marcus would gamble away money and sleep with other women expecting Oliver to help clean his mess for him. No more. His older brother was no longer Oliver's responsibility. He could go home. He should go home. Marcus was a grown man; he could take care of himself. Oliver should be able to have a typical Friday night and a normal brother who cared enough about his wife and son to spend time with them. Oliver should go home.

Instead, Oliver paced on the sidewalk. He wasn't going into the apartment building across the street. No, he would stay outside and wait for his brother to come out to confront him again. Oh, the words he wanted to say to Marcus. He wouldn't hold back as he did at Grayson's Pub. Maybe he should threaten Marcus that he would go to his apartment and tell Nancy. Marcus would only laugh, though, in response. Oliver needed to come up with a better threat. Maybe he would threaten to rat Marcus out to the police over his gambling. That could work.

Oliver tried to catch his breath as he stood still and stared at the apartment building again. Enough was enough. Seconds turned to minutes. Minutes turned to almost an hour. The young woman emerged from the building, wearing her sunglasses and Marcus's trench coat. Why was she wearing his trench coat? It was hot out. Maybe Marcus gave it to her as a little memento. Marcus was on his own, and Oliver needed sleep after a long work week.

So Oliver headed home.

* * *

Oliver snapped out of it, turning around since he mistakenly passed his apartment building. If only he had stopped his brother from entering the apartment building with that young woman... if only he hadn't let her, a multiple murderer, go...

What have I done?

19

October 1st, 1960, Pocono Lake, Pennsylvania

A clinking noise awakened Clara. She sat up straight on the sofa in the living room of the cabin. Clink. Clink. She approached the front window vigilantly. It was only a branch hitting against it as she let out a sigh of relief.

Though, the window had become filthy. She took a sheet from a newspaper and Windex from the kitchen. Clara paused in front of the door. It was unlocked. She checked to make sure it was locked every night before going to sleep. She couldn't have forgotten. *Did I forget? I know I didn't forget.* A bang came from the bedroom as Clara jumped and dropped the newspaper and Windex. The hand digging in her scalp, the bath water turning to blood... *No, don't think about it.* There was no use of dwelling on it. *Don't overanalyze it.* Her lungs filled up as she struggled to bring her head above water. It must have been the man. The man was making her pay for all the pain she caused. He waited for her in the bedroom and accidentally hit over a piece of furniture. She hadn't slept in her bedroom since the night she almost drowned... No, she couldn't think about it.

Grabbing a knife from the kitchen, Clara walked lightly toward the bedroom. She pushed the door, and it creaked open. The lamp on the nightstand fell onto the floor; the lightbulb shattered. He must be trying to take away her only source of light in the room. She couldn't go to the store to get more; she had another week until she could leave the cabin again. The closet door was closed as Clara held the knife in one hand and reached out the other. She swung open the door. No one inside. She let out a deep breath before turning and screaming, throwing the knife at a full-length mirror on the other side of the bed. The cracks spread to the edges; it could shatter at any moment.

No, it didn't, Clara thought, closing her eyes. The mirror looked fine. The knife never came into contact with the mirror; it looked as good as new. She opened her eyes again, but the mirror was still cracked. *No, it was fine. It was fine.* Clara returned to the kitchen, putting the knife into the drawer and slamming it shut.

Clara once again picked up the newspaper and Windex, going onto the porch. Layers of dirt and dust covered the window. She sprayed it, wiping it clean. Her reflection stared back at her as Clara turned away. Once she looked back at the window, it was filthy again. She furrowed her eyebrows as she wiped the window again. The dirt wouldn't go away. Why wouldn't it go away? The dirt stayed on the window, mocking her. The man was probably watching her from the woods, mocking her.

A tree branch snapped like a limb behind her. Clara turned around with widened eyes. No one could be found. But she knew better. She saw the cigar lying on the ground, as well as the man's footprints. He couldn't fool her anymore, no matter how hard he tried to remain hidden.

Clara ran inside. As she threw away the newspaper, the headline read ***CLARA HAGGARD'S TIME IS RUNNING*** with the rest of it being illegible. She put away the Windex, approaching the calendar on the wall beside the refrigerator. She flipped to the new page, a new month, October. The month when the leaves started to change, and the weather started to cool. She tilted her head as October 13th was circled on the calendar. What was October 13th? No birthdays she could think of. She didn't know why she had circled that date, nor remembered circling it in the first place. October was the last month on the calendar; the months November and December were torn out. Pieces of paper remained around the binding. No, she couldn't have possibly torn those out. Did she? No, she couldn't see herself doing that. Well, maybe... What was October 13th? Not her birthday, nor her parents, nor her friends. Not her parents' anniversary.

A hand began stroking the back of Clara's head as goosebumps spread on her arms like a rash. She turned around. No one was there. She kept feeling a hand touching the back of her head, fingers stroking her hair. Her touch was as real as whoever (or whatever) touched her head before she turned around. She placed her hand over her chest and slowed her breathing. She was alone in the cabin. There was no one else with her in the cabin.

"You must think I'm stupid, don't you?"

Clara jumped, turning around again to find no one. No Marcus Anderson. She rid the world of him and his arrogance. No, she wouldn't feel sorry for what she had done. Well, at least to him. But that was when everything began to unravel.

Don't think about it. It was time for her daily walk. She needed to stay within her routine, her structure. The only way she could feel in control. No time to waste making breakfast and having coffee. She packed her water and her pen and paper but couldn't keep her eyes off the window. The man must be watching her, waiting for her to leave the cabin. He must be thinking how foolish she was to leave again, so she grabbed a knife from the kitchen drawer as a precaution. She couldn't stand to be stuck inside any longer.

Clara took a step outside, staring out into the woods and clenching the knife in her hand. She locked the front door and stepped off the front porch. The sun beat down onto her. It was odd. Even though she had laid in the sun every day last summer on top of the hill, she was as pale as can be. After putting on her sunglasses, she headed up the hill for the 681st time.

No sightings of cigars or footprints as Clara stepped over fallen branches and large rocks. The ground had cracks in it; Clara couldn't remember the last time it had rained. Every few seconds, she looked behind herself to ensure no one followed as branches pressed against her shoulders. It seemed to have gotten narrower than yesterday. Leaves crunched under her feet as more fell every time the wind pushed against the branches. All was quiet except her footsteps.

After eleven minutes of walking, she reached her favorite spot. She gasped, stopping. Where was the bare spot on top of the hill? Only miles and miles of trees. *Did I walk the wrong way?* No, it couldn't be possible. She went the right way; she could make that walk in her sleep. There were lush patches of grass surrounding the tree trunks.

"No, this-this doesn't make sense!" she whispered, putting her hand around her neck. Her throat started closing up. She approached one of the trees, pushing up against it. Its bark rubbed against the palm of her hand. *I don't understand*. She pulled her hand away. This was the spot. She came here every day unless the weather prevented her. She was here yesterday. Those trees couldn't have just been planted; they looked as though they had been there for centuries. Clara leaned against the tree as the woods started spinning around her. She shakily sat on the ground, dropping her knife and covering her eyes. She took a few sips of water and tried to collect herself.

"I have to go back to the cabin." Clara decided, standing again and heading back. "I have to go back."

Tears streamed down her face as she wiped them off. It existed–the bare spot at the top of the hill. She knew it. She loved going there during the summer, lying down on the soft grass and feeling the sun on her skin. *None of this makes any sense.* She picked up her pace and ran down the hill. The cabin emerged before her as she ran up the front porch and unlocked the door. After setting her knife down on the counter, she rushed to the kitchen, pulling out her notepad and pen from her bag and sitting on a stool. Her hand shook too much to write. She held it steady with her other hand, but the writing couldn't come out legibly. Her mother would never be able to read this. Well, who knew if her mother read any of her letters, anyway. No, Clara needed to write to her; she had written to her every day. Her mother might be worried if Clara missed a day. She readied her pen, but her hand kept shaking.

Clara threw her pen. It bounced against the window and fell onto the floor behind her. She crossed her arms and stared out into the woods. Did the bare spot exist? Yes, it existed.

She jumped toward the living room as a telephone rang. Standing up slowly, it continued ringing as the handset shook on the cradle. She wasn't allowed to have calls. Even if she was, who was left who wanted to speak to her? Her own mother didn't even answer her letters. Who knew if she read the letters in the first place.

No, of course her mother read her letters. It was too painful to think otherwise.

The telephone stopped ringing as Clara stood in front of it on the narrow table by the side window. *Wait a minute.* The cabin didn't have a phone. When did this get here? And how? The man must be behind this. He must have broken into her cabin and left the phone here. Maybe he did so before almost drowning her in the bathtub. There was a sinking feeling in the pit of her stomach. *No, don't think about that evening. Please don't think about it.* She took a few deep breaths and relaxed her shoulders. As she stepped away, the telephone rang again. Clara stopped in her tracks, holding her breath. She turned around, debating whether it would be wise to answer it. If she answered it, the police would be on her doorstep in no time. The curiosity ate at her though. *You don't need to know who's calling. You don't need to know.* But she must. She must know.

The telephone stopped ringing again. Clara waited for it to ring again.

Four minutes went by. Nothing.

Clara made the right decision in not answering. After picking up her pen, she returned to her stool. Her hand still shook but not as bad as before; she should be able to write now. She pressed the pen to the page as the telephone rang again. Clara shrieked as she dropped the pen onto the counter, standing and facing it. She ran to the phone and picked it up. Silence.

"Hello?" she asked.

Silence.

The phone hung up on the other end. Clara hung up the phone, backing away from it. She shouldn't have said anything. They knew she lived here. They were closing in on her. Why did she speak? They knew a young woman lived alone in the middle of nowhere. It was over; they were onto her. How foolish she was to answer that.

Clara ripped the cord out of the outlet, slamming the phone against the floor. She approached the front window, crossing her arms. The car sat on the dirt driveway. Clara had always followed the rules. Never once had she left the cabin besides her biweekly trip to the grocery store. Just this once it would be fine to take a trip back into civilization. She needed one afternoon of normalcy after everything she's been through. She deserved it.

Clara grabbed the keys off the tray and left the cabin, climbing into the car and starting it.

20

November 8th, 1957, Brooklyn, NY

Clara woke up, staring at the ceiling. A November morning, eight months ago. She glanced at the clock on her nightstand, 9:30 a.m. She sat up in her bed. *I must have forgotten to set my alarm*, she thought, missing two of her morning classes. She tried to hear any movement downstairs. The townhouse had never been so silent. Her mother never let her sleep in so late. Clara jolted out of bed, throwing aside her sheets and running into her mother's bedroom. It was empty with the bed made and the curtains drawn. Everything was neat and clean, the matching dressers and nightstands dusted and their drawers closed. She ran down the stairs into the living room, relieved to find everything in order. The blankets were folded, and the furniture was in its proper place. The books were organized on the bookshelf. Clara continued onto the kitchen where once again nothing looked out of place with the exception of the torn curtain over the kitchen sink that hadn't been mended. The back door was closed and locked, so Clara moved to the front door. That too was closed and locked.

"Mom?" Clara yelled.

No response.

She peeked into the backyard. The fire pit stood in the center, covered with ashes and burn marks. The door of the shed swung open, revealing no one inside except for some tools. Clara ran down the stairs to the cellar which was used for storage. She bent over in the crawl space, nothing inside except for stacks of boxes, the washing machine, and boxes of powdered detergent.

"Mom?" she asked.

No response.

This can't be happening. Her mind spiraled. *No, please, no. This can't be happening!*

Clara climbed the stairs again into the kitchen. Her mother was gone.

"MOM!" she screamed. No response. She gripped the hair on her head and covered her mouth. Tears streamed down on her cheeks. *What have I done?* She shouldn't have slept in; she knew better. Her mother couldn't be left alone. Who knew how far her mother had traveled, who knew if she would return home. Clara had lost her mother.

The door opened, letting in the beaming sunlight and causing Clara to squint. Her father came home, holding his briefcase and closing the door. Her vision was too blurry, but he had her father's frame and wore the same hat. Her legs felt cemented into the floor when Clara tried to move them, but she dragged them anyway toward her father and admitted what she had done.

"Dad, I've lost mom! I'm so sorry. I slept in, and I don't know where she is! We have to go look for her. I doubt she would go far."

Her father didn't move, staring at her stoically.

"I'll get dressed and meet you in the car." Clara turned to climb the stairs, but her father grabbed her shoulders and turned her to face him again. She wiped off her tears, so she could see him clearly. He let go of her, stepping backward.

"Clara, I took your mother to Sinclair's this morning," he said.

Clara's heart sank as she backed away from him and shook her head. Her lip trembled, and her throat burned with every breath she took. She thought he had changed his mind; it had been a month since her mother almost drowned her in the bathtub.

"What?" she said, her lips trembling.

"This wasn't easy for me, but it's the correct decision. Your mother will get the care she needs."

"She won't get any care! This house is safe for her; she knows us. How could she do well in a sterile hospital surrounded by strangers?"

"Clara, it won't be forever. You deserve a mother who will take care of you; you deserve one who is well. We'll be able to visit her in due time. She's not dead—"

"She might as well be!" Clara yelled, pointing her finger at him. With no emotion and performative sympathy, he treated this like giving a patient a fatal diagnosis. Clara didn't want to speak to a doctor; she wanted her father. The patient wasn't some woman; the patient was her mother. "I will never forgive you for this! If she dies in there, it'll be your fault!"

Clara stormed up the stairs into her bedroom; the floor shook with every step. The door frame rattled when she slammed the door shut. She shoved her lamp, magazines, and ashtray off her nightstand then threw her nightstand against the wall. Clara lay on her bed. She covered her eyes as she mourned her mother. How confused and upset her mother must have been. She could envision her father with his arms around her, dragging her mother out the door, her mother begging and screaming to say goodbye to her daughter. Clara put a pillow over her face and screamed as loud as she could.

A car door slammed outside, so Clara approached her window facing the street. Her dad sat in his car about to return to work. He had an eventful morning of betraying his wife and checking her in against her will to a disgusting hospital. Clara felt the urge to break the glass and watch as a shard fell, cutting through the car roof and shaving her father's face off.

Oh, that wouldn't work. The glass piece wouldn't be sharp enough to go through a car roof. *Silly Clara.* After another moment, he drove away.

July 25th, 1958, Brooklyn, NY

Clara awakened the morning after murdering Dean, glancing at the clock. 10:30 a.m. She leaped out of bed, ran down the stairs and stopped when she spotted her mother making breakfast.

It wasn't eight months ago. Her mother wasn't gone; she was standing right in front of her in a turquoise dress; makeup well done. Her teeth sparkled. Healthy. Clara relaxed her jaw and shoulders.

"I finished making you breakfast, honey," she said.

"Thanks, Mom!" Clara sat at the set kitchen table as her mother made her a plate of eggs, bacon, and toast. As the food sat in front of her, it began to rot. The scrambled eggs shriveled before her, black spots spreading, giving off a rotten stench. Clara recoiled and gagged.

"What's the matter, Clara?" her mother asked, tilting her head.

Clara turned to the eggs again. Her unsteady fork moved through them, they were yellow, white, and fluffy. Not expired or moldy. Clara forced a smile and shook her head. "Nothing, these look good."

She hesitated, stared at her forkful of eggs, and took a bite. They tasted normal.

Her mother returned to washing the dishes. "Did you make it in time before your father came home last night?"

"Yeah, no problem."

"Did you have a good time with Sam?"

"Yes, it was a lot of fun. We went to the bookstore together and browsed the shelves, looking at the most interesting covers. We went to the bar afterward."

"That's great, honey! Sorry I didn't stay up, I was exhausted. Nothing exciting for me, except a man stopped by here last night asking for your father."

Clara nearly dropped her fork. "Who?"

"Oliver, I believe. I forget his last name. He was asking for your father, but he was out. Then, he asked me if I had a daughter, and I said yes."

Her mouth hung open. "And then, what happened?"

"He left."

"Did he say anything else? Ask any other questions?"

"No, he thanked me and left."

Clara sat back in her chair, staring at her breakfast, as her mother continued washing the dishes. She had lost her appetite. Her mother looked at her. Clara's hand shook as she picked up a piece of bacon and took a bite. She shuddered, wanting to go to her room, slam the door, and never leave. She kept eating for her mother, though, and finished her breakfast. Clara handed her mother the plate, almost dropping it. Thankfully, her mother didn't ask any questions as Clara ran upstairs and into the bathroom, hunching over the sink and trying to catch her breath. Her body shook uncontrollably.

* * *

Six months ago. She remembered the day her father took her to visit her mother in Sinclair's. The building loomed over her. The exterior looked like a church, but the inside was anything but. The intricate detail and gorgeous colors of the interiors of cathedrals were a complete contradiction to the sterile environment. Bright white lights, some of them flickering, in the ceiling and beaming on her, burning through her, burning inside her. White tile covered the floors, and the walls were painted white. No life inside those walls—only lives waiting to end. Clara didn't believe her father; her mother wouldn't be cured here. She would be made to suffer, but little did they know she was already suffering. The burning. The voices. It never stopped.

Her father placed his hand on Clara's back as they waited to meet with Dean Caraway. He was in charge of checking in patients. He might have come to their house that morning to help force her mother into the car. She crossed her arms as they stood in the lobby. A woman sat behind a desk, writing something as a doctor approached her with a smile.

"Marcus." Her father waved to him. Marcus approached them, beaming.

"Hello, Dr. Haggard," he said, shaking his hand. "Who might this be?"

"This is my daughter, Clara. Clara, this is your mother's psychiatrist, Dr. Anderson."

Clara didn't want to look him in the eye. Marcus held out his hand, and she reluctantly shook it. Her father stared at her sternly, expecting her to behave and be polite.

"Hi, Dr. Anderson," she whispered. What was Marcus Anderson doing to her mother? What kind of treatment was he giving her? He stood there arrogantly with a smile as if all of this was perfectly normal.

"Your mom is making tremendous progress," Marcus said. "We have her taking some new medication, as well as having her attend group and individual therapy. She is well taken care of here."

Clara nodded, avoiding looking at him.

"Where's Dean?" her father asked.

"He should be around shortly, but I can show you both to the visiting room. Follow me, Miss Haggard."

After Marcus turned, Clara rolled her eyes and followed him. Her father spoke with him about a new experimental treatment, but she didn't care enough to pay attention. She wanted to take her mother home. They walked through swinging doors and down a long hallway leading to a caged window. Marcus opened a door to the left and gestured inside. There was a long steel table with two matching chairs on each side, and a mirror on the right wall. The windows in this room were caged, too, and... a light flashed from the mirror. It disappeared as soon as it came. Clara turned around, but there was nothing behind her, just a white-tiled wall. Where did that light come from? Her father put his hand on her shoulder for a moment before Clara sat next to him, fixing the blue ribbon in her curled hair. The room absorbed any sound, any sign of life. Her father moved a chair... nothing. Clara moved... nothing. The room felt like it was getting smaller and smaller with each passing moment. Suffocating her. Stealing the oxygen out of her lungs. Robbing her of life.

The door creaked open as a man entered followed by her mother. She wore a white gown and no makeup. Clara stood and approached her, not knowing what to say. As her mother smiled at her, Clara broke down into tears. She held her tightly, stroking Clara's hair. Clara couldn't stop crying, no matter how hard she tried.

"It's all right, honey," her mother said. "I've missed you, too."

Clara let go, as her mother wiped her tears. "I'm so sorry, Mom!"

"Clara, please sit next to me," her father said. Clara returned to her seat, collecting herself, and her mother sat across from them.

"How are you doing, Mom?" Clara was afraid to hear the answer.

"I'm doing okay. I miss you both so much it hurts sometimes."

Another man barged into the room with two paper cups, one with a few pills and one with water. "Here's your afternoon meds, Mrs. Haggard."

She obeyed and took them, returning the empty cups to him. The man turned to her father. "Hi, Dr. Haggard, how are you today?"

"Very well, thank you."

The man left the room as fast as he came in.

"That was Peter Donavan," Her father explained to Clara. "He's one of our pharmacists and researchers."

"I don't want you to be sad, Clara," her mother said. "I do feel calmer than I ever have before, and I'm making progress. I'll be home in no time."

Clara knew her mother as she knew herself. She was lying. How could she tell the truth in front of Clara's father? Who knew what would happen to her if she spoke out of turn. Those pills they gave her were probably poisoning her mind and brainwashing her.

"I understand, Mom," she said carefully. "I'm glad you're feeling better."

"You look very well, Loraine," her father said proudly.

"Thank you, Chris."

"Don't you think she looks well?" He turned to Clara.

"Yes, you look well, Mom." She lied. Her father sounded like he was trying to convince himself.

"Oh, Clara, when this is all over, we're going on a nice vacation."

"That would be wonderful."

"Remember the cabin in the Poconos?" her father said. "It's been a few summers since we've been there."

"I love that cabin. So many happy memories there. We should go back as soon as you get out of here." Clara agreed, reminiscing to the days her mother would garden on one of the hills. Her father would take her on hikes, and they would have campfires with roasted marshmallows. Such peace and serenity at the cabin. No fights, no feeling trapped. Freedom that went the length of the endless woods.

"As soon as you're all better, we'll go there together as a family," her father said. Her mother gave Clara another smile.

There was silence for a moment.

"How are the other residents?" Clara asked her mother.

"Some are fine, but I mainly keep to myself."

"Are you able to go outside at all?"

Her father interrupted her mother. "There's a nice courtyard in the back where she can spend her free time. Right, Loraine?"

He must be hoping he would be able to gain Clara's approval of taking her mother to a mental hospital. She would never give it to him.

"Yes, it's quaint." Her mother nodded. "You don't need to worry about me, honey. I'm doing fine."

Clara tried to smile but her lips resisted. Her mother's hair was so unkept, in disarray, and her face was as pale as the walls. Clara glanced at the mirror and gasped. It showed her wearing a white nightgown with pale skin and white hair so dry it would snap with a brush. The hospital drained the color from its victims. When Clara looked at her clothes, her skirt was teal blue. She felt her hair, brown and curly.

"Is everything all right?" Her father turned to her, putting his hand on her shoulder.

"Yes." That was the last time she would ever stare into that mirror.

Clara focused on her mother instead. She looked like a zombie, a shell of her former self. Drugged out of her mind to mask any real feeling or emotion. If someone was inside, using her mother as a skin suit, it would have the same effect. Her personality had faded. The hospital, too, drained this from her.

"I still hear the voices…" Her mother's voice trailed off. Her father stood, ending their meeting.

"Can't we talk longer?" Clara pleaded.

"No, your mother needs to attend her daily therapy session. We'll be back soon, I promise."

She stood, running to her mother and hugging her. She teared up again. She would do anything, whatever it took, whatever laws she had to break, to get her out.

"I love you, Mom. I'll see you again soon."

"I love you, too."

Another man entered the visiting room, her father introduced him as Dean Caraway. He led her mother away by the arm. Clara clenched her fists. She wished one of the hanging lamps would drop and hit him in the head, causing him to fall over and cracking his skull open against the hard floor as his brains and blood would splatter everywhere. He needed to let her go. It was in his best interest to let her mother go. She had to watch him take her mother away down the long hallway, while her father put his hand against her back and guided her in the opposite direction.

* * *

Clara returned to the present, staring at herself in the bathroom mirror, breaking down and crying. She held her chest. Her face became red and puffy as the muscles twitched. Clara screamed, turning around. No one was there. She could've sworn Oliver was standing behind her. She checked outside the bathroom window to find kids playing in the street. She let out a shaky laugh. It was only the children. She ran to her bedroom and looked out the other window. Oliver was nowhere to be found, but she closed the curtains just in case.

"Clara, are you crying?" her mother asked on the other side of her bedroom door.

Clara cleared her throat. "No, I'm fine, Mom."

"All right, honey. You shouldn't be in your room all day. You should be going out with friends and having fun. Youth doesn't last forever."

"Yeah, you're right."

Clara couldn't sit around all day and hope Oliver stayed away. She needed to go on the offensive. She opened her closet and searched for a more understated dress. Her red velvet dress and turquoise dress remained missing, and it appeared another dress had disappeared. A light tan dress with a cinched waist and full skirt.

And it was gone. She sorted through the rest of her clothes. Where did those three dresses disappear to? Clara selected a navy blue dress instead with an hour-glass figure and a boat neckline. She grunted as she took the dress off the hanger and slammed her closet doors shut. There was only one person who kept taking her dresses away–her father. But Oliver was a more pressing issue.

After getting dressed and ready, Clara ran down the stairs and pulled out the phonebook, searching for his address. Oliver went to St. Catherine of Siena Cathedral, so he must live nearby. She tore it open and searched for the last name Anderson. There were three Oliver Andersons listed, three addresses. She would have to scope them out to find the right one.

"I'll start with the one closest to St. Catherine of Siena and go from there." She put on sunglasses, heels, and gloves, grabbed her box purse, and stormed out the door. Even with the sunglasses, she had to squint. The heat rose from the concrete as she crossed the street and walked a few blocks. Clara stood outside a run-down, brick apartment complex, crossing her arms as crowds of people walked by. She wiped the sweat off her forehead, and the glove had blood all over it. Her jaw dropped. Was her head bleeding? No one walking past her noticed as she tried to catch her breath, looking behind her. She closed her eyes then looked at her glove again and the blood had disappeared. Clara rubbed her fingers together, her glove was dry and clean. *Thank God.*

A woman and a young boy walked out of the apartment complex. She patted his head before holding his hand and crossing the street. The lavender dress had faded from too many washes; her son wore new clothes: tan shorts and a white collared shirt. They walked past Clara. Marcus's wife and son, Nancy and George. *That complicated things.* Were they visiting Oliver's apartment, or did they live there?

Oliver had to be at work, so now would be a good time to follow them and find out. Watching them go into a local market and shop, Clara followed them at a proper distance. She checked her watch. Fifteen minutes later they left for the post office. Twenty minutes after that they were in the library. One hour later they emerged and returned to Oliver's apartment. They emerged, and Clara followed them right back to Oliver's apartment. So, they did live there. Oliver was single, so she couldn't perform her usual routine. He carried himself differently from the men at Sinclair's, not having their arrogance. Clara would have to catch him by surprise in his apartment building to get him alone. She couldn't trick him into meeting her at a discreet location; Oliver would know what he was walking into. No, Oliver needed to be killed when he least expected it.

As she turned to head home, she collided with a man. Clara looked up, suspecting the worst, but it was Father Benedict.

"Hello, Clara," he said, chuckling as Clara stepped backward a couple of times. "Sorry I didn't see you there! Are you all right?"

"Hi, Father, I'm fine." Clara smiled so wide her cheeks hurt. "I'm sorry I missed our meeting yesterday."

"No problem at all, I wasn't going to bring it up."

Clara breathed a sigh of relief.

"I'm free now if you would like to talk."

Shit.

"Sure." Clara walked beside him to St. Catherine of Siena.

21

After Alex brought him a new stack of cards that morning, Oliver sat at his desk, typing away at his typewriter. One more day until the weekend. His fingers disconnected from his mind as he thought about the night Marcus was killed.

Name: Alexander Williams Sr.

Oliver stood outside of the apartment, across the street, watching the building as his brother was being murdered inside.

Description: Passed away on July 23rd.

Oliver went home instead of checking on his brother. Nancy called him the following morning. A sinking feeling in the pit of his stomach suggested something terrible had happened. What if the police didn't believe that Oliver had never stepped foot in the apartment that night? If they didn't believe him, Oliver would be considered a prime suspect in Marcus's death. Who would the police point their fingers at? A young, weak woman or the brother of the victim? The police would dig up his past with Nancy; it would be the perfect motive. A brother sought revenge against his brother for stealing his girlfriend and marrying her.

A devoted husband and father, Alexander leaves behind his wife, Sandy, daughter June, and son Alex Jr.

Where would that leave Nancy and George? Oliver was their only family, and he must protect them at all costs. So, he retraced his steps the next day, going into Grayson's Pub and asking the owner about Marcus's whereabouts. That should be enough for the police to never suspect him of being there. It seemed like it worked. Detective Howard hadn't been in contact with him for any further interviews, and the last time they spoke was when he interviewed Nancy in her apartment.

Funeral arrangements have been made for Flatbush Reformed Dutch Church on July 29th. All are welcome.

Oliver set the card on the completed pile, reading over the note again. The funeral was going to be on July 30th, not July 29th. *Damn it.* Oliver tore the card he typed and threw it in the small garbage bin next to his desk. He knew he couldn't think about his brother at work; he knew it would end in him making a mistake. Shaking his head, he picked up the card from the completed pile and typed it out again. He wanted to slam his fists onto his desk, but that would draw attention to himself. After redoing the card, he set it in the completed pile and grabbed his briefcase, leaving work for the Sinclair Hospital Psychiatric Ward.

Where could he go from here? It was too late to go to the police. Even if he told them what he witnessed, he would look suspicious. The mere fact a short, thin young woman would have the power to overtake a man with Marcus's stature was hard to believe. She was brutally killing men who worked at Sinclair Hospital Psychiatric Ward. He remembered her physical description from talking to her on the street corner a couple weeks ago.

Something did seem off about her when they spoke at the newsstand. He expected her to be on edge after what happened between her and Marcus, but she stood confident and unshaken. Why was she murdering the staff? There had to be a connection there. He would have to make a stop at the hospital and ask for their directory or the guest sign-in sheet. Maybe she knew a patient there. Or she was a patient herself, and the doctors believed they cured her and released her. No, they wouldn't provide him that information.

Oliver checked the clock, 5:00 p.m. He needed to keep an eye on the time; he didn't want to get home too late and keep Nancy and George waiting to have dinner.

He had to think of a good lie to explain why he would be interested in that information. The walk was coming to an end, and the lie hadn't materialized yet. The building towered over him, looking like it could've been a castle in the countryside of Ireland, not a mental institution. A lie had to come to him, but he couldn't stand outside staring at the place until it came. He needed to get in and out. The interior was an ordinary doctor's office, nothing grand like the outside showed. Everything seemed clean and orderly, and no one waited in the reception area. A young lady sat behind the front desk, jotting down notes and listening to the radio at a low volume.

He rested his hands on the front desk as the phone rang.

"Please excuse me, sir," she said to Oliver.

"No problem."

She answered the phone, pushing a strand of her blonde hair over her shoulder. She looked to be about thirty years old. "Sinclair's... I'm good, how are you?... Yes, you can visit tomorrow any time. Visit the front desk, and we'll get you signed in... Of course, thank you and see you tomorrow... Okay, bye-bye." She hung up the phone and turned to Oliver. "Hello, sorry about that. Are you here to visit someone?"

"No, I'm Oliver Anderson, Marcus's brother."

Her cheeks flushed red. *Oh, God. Please don't tell me she slept with him, too.*

"Hi, Oliver. I'm so sorry about Marcus. The funeral was beautiful. I'm Carol."

"Nice to meet you." She went to the funeral and was probably seated near that young woman. He needed to speak with her alone. *Come up with a lie, come up with a lie.* "Marcus had spoken about you often and how he enjoyed working with you. He said how organized you always are."

Carol fiddled with her pen. "That's so kind of him. He was a pleasure to work with as well. I do miss him."

"Would you like to grab a cup of coffee with me? I enjoy hearing stories about Marcus; it would really help."

"Of course! I would be happy to. My shift ends in a couple minutes, are you free now?"

"Sure, I'll wait for you outside."

"Great!"

Perfect.

22

Clara stepped into the gorgeous cathedral, staring at the statue of St. Catherine of Siena, wearing a white veil Father Benedict loaned her. The smell of incense filled the church. The only sounds were a kneeler being set down, shoes tapping on the marble floors, and the rattling of Rosary beads. A few parishioners were there for eucharistic adoration, but no one she recognized. Clara stared at the crown of thorns placed on the saint's head, and she cradled flowers and a cross in her arms. Holes in her hands. It must have been painful to have the stigmata; the nails sticking through her hands and feet and the thorns piercing her head. Maybe it felt like her head was on fire.

Burning.

"You like this statue of St. Catherine, huh?" Father Benedict asked, standing beside her.

"I do." Clara turned to him. "She's my confirmation saint."

He nodded in approval, leading her to the confessional. They sat inside, across from one another, and he removed the divider. "Oh, I apologize, Clara. I seem to have left my water in my office. I'll be right back."

He left the confessional, leaving her alone. Clara fidgeted with her hands and bounced her leg. She slid a cigarette out of her purse, but thought better of it and put it back. *Don't cry here.* She had to wait until she was alone in her bedroom. Her heart thumped in her chest as she took shallow breaths. The walls pressed against her body on both sides, squishing her between them. Her lungs strained against her ribs, working overtime to draw in deep breaths. She pushed against them, hoping to expand the space as it closed in on her.

No, I can't. I can't think about that day.

* * *

Her mind drifted to her last visit to Sinclair's. Four months ago.

Clara climbed the steps of that ungodly building with her father by her side. The palm of her father's hand pressed against her back as he opened the door for her. They stepped into the empty waiting room. The receptionist sat behind her desk, listening to the radio and smoking a cigarette. As the door slammed, she looked up and gasped, her face losing its color at the sight of them. She put out the cigarette and jumped out of her chair, approaching Clara's father.

"Dr. Haggard, we need to speak with you alone," she said, her voice trembling.

Her father remained unalarmed, nodding and turning to Clara. "Stay out here, I'll be right back."

Her father followed the receptionist through the swinging doors, down the sterile, cold hallway. Clara sat in the corner, fixing the hem of her mint green skirt. Her mother needed to see bright colors. She sure as hell wasn't getting that in here, and her mother always lit up at the sight of pretty clothes. Maybe that was where Clara got her love of fashion from. She adjusted the matching ribbon in her hair, tapping her foot against the floor. A clock ticked on the wall.

Seconds turned into minutes. Minutes turned into more than a half an hour. What was taking so long? She waited another ten minutes, but her father was nowhere to be seen. The clock continued ticking, so she turned toward the swinging doors. Her father told her to stay put, but there had to be a reason why it was taking so long. Clara stood, shuffling toward the door, pressing her palm against it and swinging it open slightly. No one in the long hallway. Everything was still and silent.

* * *

Father Benedict returned to the confessional as Clara flinched and opened her eyes. He was taken aback by her standing in the doorway. "Would you rather go into the office? Do you need more space, Clara?"

She shook her head. "No, I'm fine here."

He raised his eyebrows; he didn't believe her. Clara didn't believe herself, either. "Do you need some water?"

She wanted to say "no, let's get this over with" but replied with a simple no instead.

"All right," he said with hesitation, taking his seat across from her and folding his hands in his lap. "How has your family been doing lately?"

"The same," she said. "My father cheats on my mother, and they fight constantly. I don't even like it when they're in the same room together. They like to make each other miserable."

"Clara, I'm sorry to do this to you every week, I really am. But I need you to say it."

Clara held her breath. "Father, can I actually have some water?"

"Certainly." As he left, Clara took herself back again.

* * *

Clara walked through the swinging doors of Sinclair's, down the long hallway leading to the caged window. Dean Caraway dragged her mother this way the last time she visited. How good it would feel to slice off his hand after his fingers dug into her mother's arm. Maybe she should start by cutting off his fingers one by one before going for his wrist. No one should have been allowed to touch her mother like that.

The coolness of the tile flooring and walls kept the hospital cold. Or maybe it was that warmth wasn't allowed inside. Most of the patients' rooms were closed, but the ones left open revealed a small hospital bed, a sink, a desk, and a cabinet. The rooms were half the size of her own, the size of shoeboxes. No color. The beam of sunlight coming through the windows reflected off the shiny floors, the building rejecting it, sending it outside where life was welcome.

Clara stopped as a few men's whispers carried through the hallway. Taking light steps, she made her way in their direction, stopping short of a patient's room and leaning against the wall next to the door. One of the blinds in the window of the door was crooked. Standing on tippy-toes, Clara tried to see what went on inside. It sounded serious. One of the rooms had a group of three doctors whispering to each other and surrounding a bed. A limp, pale hand hung over the side. It appeared to be a woman in a white gown, a patient, but one of the doctors blocked Clara's view. She leaned, trying to catch a glimpse of who it was. The woman's eyes were closed, and her neck was bent in an unnatural manner. She was motionless and looked cold to the touch. The doctor moved to write something down, Dr. Anderson. Her father stood beside Dr. Anderson, his face looking grim, and the other man she had never seen before. Her father had mentioned a doctor whose name was difficult to pronounce. Perhaps that was him.

The patient must have died. Maybe they were waiting for a coroner to arrive. Still, Clara didn't understand why her father would leave her for so long in the waiting room. She should be allowed to visit with her mother while this went on. Why didn't her father stop in the waiting room to tell her what was going on?

Unless...

Oh, God...

Clara slapped her hand over her mouth as she backed away from the door until she ran into the opposite wall.

The patient was her mother.

Please, God, no! Clara stared at the door. She trembled as grief washed over her. It couldn't be true. She didn't have all the facts yet, but why would her father keep her waiting like this? Why did the receptionist look frightened the moment they stepped into the hospital? This must concern her mother. Clara cried. Her mother's poor, lifeless body was being studied. The doctors gazed at her like an object, trying to figure out what they should do with her. Her mother asked her to watch over her and protect her, and Clara allowed her father to take her away, commit her, and oversee her death. Her mother would never find treatment here; that was always a lie. Her father knew it, and Clara knew it. Now, she would never see her mother again, never see her smile, never hug her, never talk with her again. And she would be expected to move on with her life like nothing had happened. Like it was some kind of unfortunate event. Something that could happen to anyone.

Clara cried as the door swung open. Her father turned and ran to Clara, grabbing her and pulling her away, out of view of her mother. His fingers dug into her skin as her whole body shook in terror. His face drew closer to hers. It chilled her, never having seen her father behave this way before.

"Why did you come back here?" he pleaded with her, not in anger but in fear. "I told you to stay in the waiting room!"

Every muscle in her body froze as she sobbed. No words could come out of her.

* * *

The priest returned to the confessional with a cup of water, and Clara took a sip. He sat across from her. "Now, I'm sorry, but I need you to say it."

"My mom is dead," she admitted.

"It was absolutely tragic what happened to your mother, but it is important to accept reality. Only then can you heal. Your life is still worth living. You are so young, Clara. You have many exciting years coming your way. Don't give up on yourself. You can take all the time you need to process everything you've gone through, but you will make it through this. God has not abandoned you, and He never will."

"Thank you, Father. I have to get going. I'm making dinner for my dad tonight, and I haven't even gone grocery shopping yet."

"Anytime. If you need a listener, I'm here. I'll see you again next week?"

"Yes," she answered. Clara left the tight confines of the confessional and the church, desperately needing a breath of fresh air. She drank the rest of the water, crushed the paper cup in the palm of her hand, and threw it away. She took deep breaths as she rushed home, trying to get there, so she could break down and cry. Cars honked at her after she ran through a red light, and one of the cars slammed on its brakes to avoid running her over. Clara continued to look straight ahead. Her quiet, empty townhouse waited for her, and she needed to reach it before it was too late. The crowds of people made the sidewalks difficult to navigate, and Clara had to suppress the urge to shove them out of her way. The newsstand had racks of newspapers with the headline: ***FOUR MURDERS CONNECTED TO SINCLAIR HOSPITAL PSYCHIATRIC WARD***. Clara couldn't stop and read the story; she needed to press ahead. The townhouse was nearly in her grasp; it stood before her.

Unlocking her front door, she slammed it behind her and leaned against it. She covered her face as she cried. Why did Father Benedict have to make her say it? Why did he want her to suffer? Her mother didn't deserve to be remembered as she was, lying on a hospital bed with doctors surrounding her. Her mother had good days, and Clara had cherished memories of them shopping together, going for long walks in the park, and having conversations Clara couldn't have with anyone else. Her mother was not defined by her illness.

A plate was put on the kitchen table.

"I made you some brownies for a snack, honey." Clara uncovered her eyes, and her mother stood in front of her, pointing to a pile of freshly baked brownies, steam rising from them. "Don't eat too many, though. You won't have any room for dinner."

Clara approached her mother, wiping the tears off her face. "Thanks for making these, Mom."

She reached for one, but the brownies turned into ants crawling toward her, down the table legs and across the floor. Clara backed away and screamed, trying to stomp on them.

"Mom, help me!" Clara yelled.

"What's wrong, honey?"

Clara screamed again. Her mother's hair turned thin and gray, falling out of her scalp from the breeze coming through the front door. Her mother reached a hand which turned into ashes, falling onto the floor. The scar around her neck oozed with blood, and her mother's neck snapped.

Clara gasped, jumping backward and stumbling until she ran into a man behind her. Was it Oliver? She screamed, turning around. Her father stood before her, wearing a gray suit with a black tie.

"What's going on?" her father asked.

She had trouble catching her breath. The corpse of her mother disappeared, along with the plate on the table and the ants crawling on the floor. "I-I thought I saw ants running across the floor, but it was only a shadow."

"Are you all right?"

"Yes, I'm fine," she answered, as he squinted at her. "I was about to make dinner."

"Okay," he said carefully, raising his eyebrows.

"Give me a moment, I'll be right back." Clara climbed the stairs to her bedroom and closed the door. She approached the window and took in a deep breath, letting the sun penetrate her skin. Cars beeped, one driver giving the finger to the other. She glanced at the sidewalk, gripping the windowsill with unsteady hands. A shiver raced down her spine. Oliver and her father were engaged in a serious conversation. Her father's red tie sparkled in the sunlight. Oliver was onto her, she knew it! He knew about the murders she committed, and he revealed everything to her father. He put his hands on his hips, while her father crossed his arms and nodded. It was over. Her father would call the police, and she would be taken away. She tilted her head, unable to make out a word that was said.

"Clara, are you coming down?" her father yelled from downstairs.

Clara flinched, turning toward her closed bedroom door. "Yes, I'm coming!"

She turned toward the window again.

The sidewalk was empty, with her father and Oliver nowhere to be found.

Clara held her stomach, trying to pull herself together. She must act as though she knew nothing about her father meeting with Oliver, nothing of their plan to imprison her and convince the detective that she was the one responsible for the deaths of four men. She closed her eyes and slowed her breathing before putting on a smile. She could do this. It was like every other night. As newspaper pages flipped, Clara went downstairs. She relaxed her face and shoulders and joined him in the kitchen. He sat at the table, drinking coffee and reading. The headline once again shouted at Clara, ***FOUR MURDERS CONNECTED TO SINCLAIR HOSPITAL PSYCHIATRIC WARD***. She couldn't escape it.

Grabbing a frying pan, she took out some chicken from the fridge and spices from the cabinets. The butter sizzled in the pan as the fire from the stove heated it. The pages of the newspaper crinkled again.

"Have you heard about how someone is targeting the staff at Sinclair's?" her father asked.

Clara stuck a knife in one of the chicken breasts, flipping it over. Her back remained turned to him. "Yes, I feel terrible for their families."

Her father sighed. "Me too."

"Who could be behind something like this?" She turned, staring him in the eyes.

He glanced at the table and looked at her again. "I don't know."

Clara turned and gripped the handle of the frying pan, feeling the urge to throw it at his head. *Liar*; he was onto her and scheming with Marcus Anderson's brother to lock her away for life. She loosened her grip as she finished cooking the chicken.

"Make sure you stay safe, Dad. Be extra cautious. The killer's still out there."

There was silence for a moment.

"I plan to," he finally replied.

Clara heated up some potatoes in the toaster oven and added a chicken breast to a plate, setting it on the placemat in front of him. She fixed her own plate, joining him at the table. He continued reading the newspaper as they ate together in silence. The forks and knives tapped the ceramic plates, the newspaper pages continued to flip, and the grandfather clock ticked in the living room. Not one word was spoken. He didn't even look at Clara.

Her father ate a few bites from his plate, then set it on the counter.

"I'm tired, I'm going to bed." He continued to avoid looking at her, walking into the living room.

"Already? You didn't eat much. Are you feeling sick?" she asked, furrowing her eyebrows.

"No, I need rest."

Clara sat back in her chair and crossed her arms as her father's footsteps climbed the stairs to his bedroom. He had to go over how he was going to turn his own daughter into the police, crafting a story that would condemn her and exonerate him. So much so he went to bed four hours earlier than usual. She picked up her plate, placing it beside her father's on the counter. Clara felt the new kitchen curtains, replicas of the one her mother tore. Everything must look ordinary so as not to make her father suspicious of her plans, so she washed the dishes, wiping the counter and the kitchen table. She placed the plates, mug, and glasses on a drying rack.

After washing her hands, Clara readied herself for bed. She stepped up the stairs, gazing down the hallway at her father's bedroom door. It was shut with no light coming from under it. The curtains must be drawn. He was either sleeping or pretending to sleep.

Clara entered the bathroom and stared at herself in the mirror, wearing minimal makeup and a dreary dress. She scoffed at herself; how she disliked the way she looked. Her father put her in this position, and her time was coming to an end. Her father had been working with Oliver to terrorize her and ensure she would be arrested. He left her no choice.

Something was out of place; something didn't seem right. As Clara approached the bathtub to turn the faucet on, a sharp object stuck into the bottom of her foot. She winced, wiping it off and rubbing her foot. It was a piece of tile. There was a chip in the tile—the same tile concealing her makeup. She pulled it up and stepped backward, gasping. Her makeup case was gone. Clara's eyes welled up as she knelt and reached inside of the gap. Her father must be behind this. She returned the tile to its rightful place, washing her face in the sink. Once more, she stared at herself in the mirror a moment longer, then punched it, shattering the glass. Clara's face was fragmented in the mirror, splitting into different directions with fragile cohesion; a web spreading across the center of the mirror before coming to a sudden stop. Her knuckles bled and ached as she washed the broken pieces of glass from them. Clara pressed a towel against her hand, poking her head out into the hallway. No movement or sounds came from her father's bedroom. Hopefully, he didn't hear anything.

She made her way into her bedroom, opening her closet to find no color in any of her clothes. Her teal, violet, pink, and mint green skirts were gone. Her matching shirts, gone. Her bows and ribbons, gone. The lone dress hanging was gray. The rest of her dresses had disappeared. Her father must love torturing her. She envisioned slamming the closet doors so hard they fell off, but she couldn't awaken her father. She turned to her floral jewelry box instead.

Clara opened it, taking out the top compartment. There it was, the small bottle full of Secobarbital from her father's medicine bag.

Tomorrow, it would be put to good use.

23

Carol was finishing her shift as Oliver waited outside Sinclair's for her. Rush-hour streets bustled; sidewalks jammed with pedestrians. Carol might have insider information about why someone was hunting down employees at Sinclair's. She must have seen the young woman at Marcus's funeral. As the door swung shut, Oliver turned.

"I'm ready!" Carol said, holding a light blue purse matching her dress.

Dominic's Coffee Shop was a few blocks away as they navigated around the crowds of people lining the sidewalks. It was a quaint coffee place with black booths on the right side, with shiny silver tables, and black and white photographs of donuts, coffee, and bagels on the walls. On the left, there was a long counter with a display of freshly baked donuts, muffins, and pastries, their sugary scent filling the air. Oliver ordered two coffees and brought them over to Carol in a booth.

"Thank you, Oliver. I should've paid, I feel bad."

"No, it's my treat." Oliver tried to think of a way to naturally ask about Marcus and Sinclair's. Should he bring up the funeral first? He took a sip of his coffee. It was mediocre. "The coffee's good here."

"Yeah." Carol agreed. "This is one of my favorite spots."

"How long have you worked at Sinclair's?"

She squinted and looked at the ceiling. "About a couple years now."

"Do you like it?"

"It's a pretty good gig, not too stressful. My coworkers are nice, and my boss doesn't breathe down my neck like the one at my last job. He kind of leaves me alone, which is nice. I already miss working with Marcus. He was a popular guy there, everyone loved him."

"It was nice how many coworkers came to his funeral."

She took a sip of her coffee. "Oh, yeah. Pretty much everybody came. I'm not surprised, Marcus was such a dedicated doctor. His patients miss him dearly, I'm sure."

Oliver set his mug on the table and took a deep breath. "Have you seen the headlines?"

"Oh, I saw them all right."

"It's unbelievable, isn't it?"

"It is," Carol stopped herself and took another sip of her coffee.

Oliver folded his hands on the table. "You don't seem too surprised."

"I really can't say anything." Her voice grew quiet as she kept her eyes on her coffee.

Oliver leaned in toward her. "Carol, my brother has been murdered. I need to know why."

"The police are investigating things."

"I don't think they're getting anywhere, and it's driving Nancy and I mad. You would be such a great help to us."

"I could get fired, Oliver. And I already told the police one story, I can't go back on it."

"I'm not asking you to," he said patiently. "I won't tell anyone, I promise. It would help me a great deal. I need to know why someone would want my brother dead."

Carol sighed. "We do experimental treatments, the first of their kind. There is a chance of error; a chance of things going wrong. They wouldn't tell me all the details even if I wanted to know everything, which I don't. But not all patients recover, some have their symptoms become more severe or they don't make it."

Oliver's eyes widened.

Carol took another sip of her coffee. "I obviously have no idea if something like that led to Marcus's death. It's just a theory. It's the first thing I thought of when I saw the headlines about murders being connected to Sinclair's. I don't think the hospital handles those situations well, either. No one can probably handle a situation like that well."

It made sense.

"Did you see a young woman around twenty years old with brown hair and a black dress? She sat near Ed Taylor at Marcus's funeral." His description of her wasn't unique enough. Every woman wore a black dress and most of them had brown hair, but it was worth a shot.

"Um, I'm not sure. There were a lot of people from work there. I don't work with anyone around that age, so she must have been a family member. Maybe someone's daughter on the staff?"

"Yeah, that's my guess."

"Sorry, I can't be more specific."

"That's okay, Carol. I appreciate you getting coffee with me."

She gave him a small smile. "Of course. It was nice meeting you."

"Nice meeting you, too."

Carol grabbed her purse and left the booth as Oliver stayed. Maybe one of Marcus's patients didn't make it through treatment and passed away. Maybe it was someone related to the young woman, and she sought revenge against Marcus and the other staff members. After leaving the coffee shop, Oliver stopped before reaching his apartment building. Nancy waited inside, cooking him a warm meal. She would ask about his day, and he would ask about hers. George would run up to him, beaming. They would share dinner on the couch, considering they didn't have a kitchen table. Oliver told Nancy they would pick one out together this weekend.

I don't deserve any of this, Oliver thought, hesitant to go inside. He had watched the young woman leave Marcus's apartment in his trench coat the night he was murdered. Instead of going inside and checking on Marcus, Oliver went home and slept while Nancy had worried all night and waited as long as she could to call him the following morning. All while his brother's body lay on the floor of the apartment with a stab wound in his chest. Nancy wouldn't look at Oliver the same after learning what he'd done. Everything would be over between them, and she wouldn't allow him to see George again. So, Oliver must find that young woman. He must hunt her down, and she must pay for what she did.

Oliver took a few deep breaths and collected himself before going inside. After taking the elevator and walking down the long hallway past Fluffy, he opened the apartment door to the smell of beef stew and George ran to him and hugged his leg.

"Hi, Uncle Ollie!" he said.

"Hey, George!" Oliver picked him up and hugged him. "What did you do today?"

"Lessons, so boring." He sighed. "Then we went to the market."

"Sounds like a nice day!"

Oliver walked him into the kitchen and set him down. George ran to play with his toy car as Nancy stirred stew over the stove.

"Hi, Ollie. How was your day?"

Oliver sorted through his mail. "Very good, how was yours?"

"Good, George is doing very well with counting, aren't you George?"

"Yes, I am," he agreed.

"Amazing, George! I was thinking, do you want to go for some ice cream after dinner?"

He clapped. "Yes!"

"You're welcome to come, Nance, unless you would like a break."

Nancy leaned against the counter, rubbing her lips thoughtfully as she considered it. "You know what? I haven't seen some of my friends in a while. Maybe I'll reach out to them and see what they're up to." Nancy approached Oliver and held his face. Her fingertips were soft and gentle on his cheeks, as she focused on him. She moved closer but stopped herself after glancing at George. Oliver's heart raced. She returned to the stew, pouring it into bowls and handing one to Oliver. "I'm going to make a call."

He sat on the couch and ate some of his stew when a troubling thought overcame him. Would it be wise for Nancy to go out alone? The young woman could be out there, waiting for her. But she might not even be after Nancy after all, and he didn't want to scare her. She looked so excited to go out with her friends; he would hate to take that away from her. Her excitement would turn into confusion then into fear. No, he couldn't witness that; he wouldn't put her through that. She had already been through enough.

Nancy joined them, sitting beside George. "Catherine said she's free, so we're going to the soda fountain and maybe a movie. I haven't been to one of those in a long time."

"That's great!" he said, wiping his mouth with his napkin.

Nancy studied him, tilting her head. "Are you okay?"

Oliver nodded. "Yes, just a long day at work. I'm pretty tired."

She didn't believe him. "Have you heard any updates about the case?"

"Nothing beyond what Benny told me. I was just thinking it over."

"Please keep me updated if you learn anything new."

"I will."

"Well, I'm going to get dressed to meet Catherine!" she said, finishing her dinner. Nancy grabbed a change of clothes and went into the bathroom.

"Ice cream!" George said.

"That's right, buddy, but you have to eat all your stew first, all right?"

"All right," he repeated.

Oliver roughed up George's hair and laughed. They ate dinner together, and Nancy emerged from the bathroom with a bright blue skirt and a white button-down shirt. *Wow,* Oliver thought, staring at her blushed cheeks, curled hair, and pink lipstick.

"You look beautiful, Nance," he said.

"Thanks, Ollie." She blushed. "What do you think, George?"

He looked at her and continued to eat his stew. She giggled then bent over and kissed George on the head, stroking his hair. "I'll see you both in a little bit."

"Take your time!" Oliver said.

"Thanks again, Ollie."

"Of course!"

Nancy grabbed her purse, waving as she walked out the door. Oliver watched the door and told himself he'd made the right call—she'd have a good night and come home safe. George looked about done with his dinner. Oliver gave him a couple extra napkins to wipe his face.

"Why don't you go wash your hands, and I'll clean the dishes?" Oliver said. George agreed, and Oliver washed them in the sink and put away the leftovers into the fridge. As he cleaned the kitchen, he couldn't stop thinking about that young woman. Was Marcus involved with a patient who died from the experimental treatment? The patient must be related to that young woman, and the young woman must be related to one of the staff members. Ed Taylor should be able to give him answers. He picked up the phone.

"Hello?"

"Hi, Ed. This is Oliver, Marcus's brother."

"Oh hi, Oliver. How are you doing?"

"I'm all right, thanks. I was wondering if I could stop by tomorrow and ask you a few more questions about Sinclair's."

"I can't tomorrow, but you can stop by anytime Sunday."

"Does Sunday morning work?"

"Yep, I'll see you then."

"See you then, bye." Oliver hung up the phone as George ran to him, demanding ice cream. As Oliver collected his keys and wallet, someone knocked on the door a few times. Oliver froze. George stared into Oliver's eyes while holding his toy car.

"One second, George," Oliver said, setting his keys on the counter. He stared at the door. Would it be wise to open it? It could be that young woman. He picked up George, carrying him into his bedroom. "I'll be right back, okay?"

"Okay," he replied, as Oliver closed the bedroom door.

Oliver straightened his posture, approaching the door and looking through the peephole. No one was there. He whipped it open, looking up and down his hallway. No one to be found. A folded note had been left on his doormat.

Stop prying or Carol will lose her job.

Oliver was taken aback, looking up and down the hallway again before closing the door with the note firmly in his hand. Someone must have spied on them in the coffee shop.

I'm getting closer.

24

October 1st, 1960, Pocono Lake, Pennsylvania

Clara sat in the tan Chevy station wagon, staring at the cabin. She had to get away; she needed a break. This wasn't her biweekly trip to the grocery store, but she needed to at least go out for a drive. This wasn't breaking the rules. She would be sure to stay away from people. In fact, she would remain in her car and watch them live their normal lives.

Back to civilization.

The roads sloped and wound around the hill to the bottom, and she pressed the gas pedal further down. Clara grasped the wheel, turning it sharply to prevent the car from sliding off the road and plummeting down the hill. Her hair whipped in the wind as she jerked the car around the bumps in the narrow road. If the car were to be destroyed, she would be destroyed with it.

Clara drove to a plaza about forty-five minutes away from the cabin, parking her car in the furthest spot. She turned off the car and sat in silence. Groups of people walked around the plaza, carrying shopping bags. A couple held hands. Two girls smiled while pointing at a store window. Sitting in the car wasn't enough. It would be all right to step outside for a moment. It would only be a walk. No need to look anyone in the eye or speak to them. She would still keep her distance. Leaving the car and passing by the store windows, the first was Melissa's Boutique. Clara stood in front of the window and tried to catch a glimpse inside.

There were colorful dresses lining the racks with petticoats in the skirts and belts around the waists. Clara wasn't interested in those dresses. She didn't care to go inside and touch the soft cotton or try on outfits. The hats and gloves on display meant nothing to her. *I loved clothes*. No interest in clothes anymore. But why?

A couple girls giggled, distracting Clara. One of the girls held the dress in front of the other as she posed. They looked so familiar; she had definitely seen them before.

"Kate and Betty?" Clara whispered. If only she could join them inside. She couldn't interact or make eye contact with anyone, but she had to say hi to them. They must be on a trip here from New York. It had been so long since she had seen them or anyone she recognized. Clara waved and smiled at them, but when they looked at her, their faces turned into strangers. She frowned and put her hand down, continuing to walk through the plaza. She could've sworn those were her friends. *You were mistaken*. The excitement left her as fast as it came. She couldn't have friends anymore. Friends were against the rules.

She continued to the next store which was a charming bookstore. A couple teens walked around, one running her finger along the spines. Another girl sat in the corner by the window, reading. Clara wondered what new novels were coming out, what the latest trends were. In another life, she would've loved to go to college for literature, studying the greatest authors of all time and reading their greatest works of fiction. She could've become a scholar, a literary critic. Her father never liked fiction, always saying what mattered happened in reality. But living in a fiction was much more tolerable.

The last place in the plaza was a bar where girls and guys

mingled. Elvis played as the young people drank and enjoyed spending time together. A man had his arms around his girlfriend and a group of men sat around a table, laughing and chatting. Clara couldn't make out the words they were saying, but they sounded like they were having a good time together. Her mind couldn't envision Sam wrapping his arms around her and swinging her to the music no matter how hard she tried.

Numb and distant.

As she turned around and walked past Melissa's Boutique again, another woman walked out of the store, carrying a large bag full of the latest fashion. She had long auburn hair and green eyes, wearing a blue hour-glass dress with a matching petticoat, pillbox hat, and gloves. The woman stopped and looked into Clara's eyes.

Clara was taken aback as her body froze. She should have stayed in the car, this wasn't following the rules. The woman's lips moved as if she was talking to her, but the sound was muffled and unintelligible.

No matter how hard Clara tried to hear her, she couldn't.

"You aren't... to have... visitors, Clara."

How did she know Clara's name?

What was she talking about? Visitors? Clara stuttered, unable to make a word as she looked over at the shop window. She gasped and jumped backward. The window showed Clara's hair was in disarray, and her face was as pale as the sidewalk. Clara turned away from it, covering her mouth to prevent herself from screaming. The woman who stood before her disappeared, so Clara rushed to her car. She should've never broken the rules; this was all her fault. She slammed on the gas pedal.

The car climbed the hill slowly, winding and turning. The engine roared and struggled. Tears collected in her eyes, and Clara wiped them with the back of her hand. Heat rushed to her face as she gripped the steering wheel tightly. Who was that woman? What was she trying to say to her? Clara never should have broken the rules; she promised she would never break them. But she did, and that woman called her by name.

Once she arrived at the cabin, she sat in the car and stared at it. Shadows moved inside, taunting her. Silence wasn't really silent. Not with her. The breeze picked up, and the chimes hanging from the roof of the front porch clinked together. Clara got out of the car and approached the porch, coming to a halt and almost falling. An ax leaned against the wall by the front door, streaks of blood running around the handle to the rusty blade. She turned, searching the woods for any kind of movement; any sort of shadow. Nothing materialized. Who put the ax there? And was it recently used? No, this wasn't happening. *It's not really there*, she thought, rushing inside, slamming the door shut, and locking it. Clara made her way through the kitchen where she jumped backward and screamed. A knife lay on the floor, also covered in blood, and it chipped some of the wood. The blood spread across the floor toward her. *No, this is only in my imagination*. Clara stepped around it and locked herself in the bathroom.

She opened the medicine cabinet to take some Tylenol before washing her face over the sink with facial cleanser. Closing the cabinet and patting her face dry with a towel, Clara gasped, letting her towel slip through her fingers. She stood aghast, covering her mouth with her hands. SICK was written on the mirror in red lipstick.

SICK.

Your mother's sick.

There's some sick people in this city.

You're sick, Clara.

The back of her legs hit against the bathtub as she leapt backward. Who could've written this? No one was inside the cabin. No one else had a key, and the door was locked.

She grabbed her towel off the floor and drenched it in water to wipe away the writing on the mirror. The water drops ran down the mirror, dripping onto the counter into the sink. She threw the towel at the mirror, causing the contents inside the medicine cabinet to fall.

"I am not sick!" Clara screamed. She held the sides of the sink, hunching over it and breathing heavily. Clara collected herself, squared her shoulders, and washed her face again, then rubbed lotion into her skin.

The contents in her medicine cabinet fell into the sink the moment she opened the cabinet door. Soap, lotions, and bottles of aspirin, Tylenol, and rubbing alcohol. She put them on the shelf in their proper place, closing the door gently.

Out of the corner of her eye, she saw her makeup box sitting on the corner of the counter. She missed dolling herself up with dark eyeshadow, eyeliner, and red lipstick. They had a special bond, she and her makeup. A lot of time spent together, both good and bad. Her victims adored her with makeup; it drew them in, grabbed them by the throat, and didn't let them go. *You are not to wear makeup*, she was told. She had listened. It would be wise to throw the box away, but she couldn't bring herself to do it. They shared so many memories together; it was a piece of herself she didn't want to leave behind. Clara had given up everything else. Maybe putting on a little bit of makeup to wear in the house would be all right. It wouldn't draw more attention to herself if she were the only person in this cabin. Draw attention from who?

As she moved toward the box, music began playing. Clara froze and held her breath. The record player played "Jailhouse Rock," echoing through the cabin to the bathroom. She stared at the closed bathroom door, fearful of what could be behind it. Clara gripped the doorknob for a second and whipped the door open. No one was in the kitchen, and the bloody knife had vanished. Her footsteps were light, and she stepped on the parts of the floor that didn't creak. Clara's heart beat far louder than the record player. She prayed no one would be in her living room.

She closed her eyes and calmed herself. It could be the person whose footprints were in the mud the other day, whose cigar lay on the ground in the woods, whose mouth pressed against the kitchen window, the hand that held her head underwater. Clara craned her neck around the corner from the kitchen into the living room. No one. She stopped the record player and unplugged it, the cord warm. She looked in the front closet and searched her bedroom to be absolutely sure. She was alone. At least for the moment.

Wait a minute. Where did the record and record player come from? They certainly weren't here until now. Clara stepped into the living room again. There was a dust-free spot in the shape of a finger print beside the record player. Someone must have put it there. Probably the man who had been stalking her. Unless she had forgotten about buying them and bringing them into the cabin. That could be her own finger print. No, it couldn't be hers. *I don't know anymore*, Clara thought sadly.

Thunder boomed after a flash of lightning, causing Clara to cower. The rain poured, clashing with the roof and ground. The weather punished her for leaving the cabin. No hike today; she would be trapped inside. Perhaps the rain would make the man go into hiding. Unless he didn't mind getting soaked. She checked the front porch, praying the ax was gone. It, too, had disappeared. *Oh, thank God*. She took deep breaths.

Maybe it would make her feel better to write another letter to her mother. Clara grabbed a piece of paper and a pen, sitting on a stool at the kitchen counter and thinking about what she wanted to say to her. Her eyes welled up as she touched the pen to the paper.

Dear Mom,

I don't think I can trust myself anymore. I don't know what's happening to me. I swore Kate and Betty were at the boutique, but their faces transformed into strangers. Elvis was playing in the cabin. Maybe I bought a record player and an Elvis record. I can't remember, though, no matter how hard I try. And seeing the clothes in the boutique didn't bring me any joy like they used to. Maybe the man brought the record player into the cabin and played it to torture me, just as he did when he wrote "sick" on the mirror. A woman outside of the boutique spoke to me and knew my name, but before I could respond, she disappeared. There was a book lying on the floor in the living room called The Executioners, but I swear I didn't buy it. I know I didn't buy the Elvis record. I don't know how it got there, and I don't know how the book ended up here either.

I want to feel like myself again.

Living in this cabin is beginning to take a toll on me, Mom. I know I deserve it; I know I deserve worse than this, but I can't help but feel sorry for myself. Girls walk around in new dresses, flirting with handsome men, and dancing, while I'm trapped here, trapped in my own skin. I made this bed of knives and now I must lie in it.

Clara crossed her legs and sat straighter. She pressed the pen down and kept writing.

Why haven't you responded to me, Mom? I've written to you every day for over two years, and you've never written back to me. Not once. I need to know you're doing okay, Mom. Please, Mom. Please, tell me you're alright. All of this suffering would be worth it if I could hear from you. I lived my life for you, yet you never write back to me. I know I promised I would never leave you. I'm so sorry I failed you. I regret falling asleep the night before Dad took you to Sinclair's. I should've stayed awake the whole night to make sure Dad couldn't take you away. I'm so sorry. Please, please write to me. I love you.

Love,

Clara

Clara's tears dropped onto the letter as she folded it and held it. Gripping it any tighter, the letter would tear in half. She let it go. Let it fall onto the counter. She grabbed an envelope and tucked the letter inside, sealing it. Clara sighed, resting her head on her hand. The rain splattered against the window, and the branches waved in the breeze. She gazed around the kitchen, stopping at the kitchen window. One of the two blue curtains with oranges on them was torn slightly, splitting one printed orange in two. No memory came to her mind of how that happened. Her fingers ran along the edge of the torn curtain.

The rain continued to pour, crashing against the window. More thunder boomed, and a flash of lightning lit the dark cabin. Clara jolted backward; she steadied herself by holding the countertop. A man stood outside the cabin. The same man from the grocery store. A shadowy man lurking in the woods outside of her home. Spying on her. He was there, clear as day, then vanished behind a drop of water streaming down the window. She knew it was him. The newspaper lying on her doorstep, the cigar in the woods, the word "sick" written on the mirror, the pacing across the floor, the furniture thrown all over the house, pushing her head underwater while she took a bath. It was him all this time. It had to be.

Her time would be coming to an end.

Clara walked slowly into the bathroom and stared at herself in the mirror. She couldn't recognize herself, rolling her eyes at her pale skin and tired, boring face with bags under her eyes. The makeup case sat on the counter, staring at her, so Clara reached for the red lipstick.

25

Gold numbers—*352*—glinted beside Dr. Ed Taylor's door. Oliver knocked on it, feeling the need to pace. He tapped his foot on the floor instead, waiting for Ed to answer. He started knocking again when Ed opened the door and smiled.

"Oliver, hello," he said. "Please, come in!"

Oliver stepped inside, following Ed into the spotless kitchen. Sunlight beamed into his apartment where toys were across the tiled floor in the living room. A Little Richard album spun on the record player by the sofa. Ed went to it, lifting the tonearm off it.

"Pardon the mess." Ed chuckled. "My wife took my daughter to go shopping, and I didn't get a chance to pick up her toys."

"It's no problem." Oliver waved it off.

"Take a seat, Oliver. Would you like some coffee or tea?" he asked.

"Sure. Coffee, please. Thank you." He sat at the dining room table as coffee dripped into the pot. Dr. Taylor poured some into two cream-colored mugs with rigid handles, handing one to Oliver as he sat across from him. The steam rose from the coffee into the hot air, and Oliver pulled his hand away from the mug.

"How have you been holding up?" Ed asked.

"I'm doing my best. It still hasn't hit me yet. I thought it would be at the funeral, but my mind keeps playing tricks on me and makes me believe he's going to come home any minute."

"That's normal. I went to Grayson's Pub the other night, and I could've sworn I saw him sitting at the bar, smoking a cigarette. It was a big shock to the system, especially for you who found him. The trauma of seeing your brother in such a state is a lot to process, but you will process it with time."

"I forgot I was speaking to a psychiatrist." Oliver joked, not wanting to discuss finding Marcus. He tried to suppress that memory as best he could, but it kept rising to the surface like a rash that wouldn't go away. It itched and irritated, keeping him awake at night, but itching made it worse. The best way to deal with it was to pretend it wasn't there.

Ed nodded and shrugged. "Guilty as charged. How are Nancy and George?"

"They're taking it day by day. They moved into my place and seem to be adjusting all right."

"That's good, it's kind of you to take them in."

"They're my family, of course I would take them in."

Ed lit a cigarette, a puff of smoke rising in the air. "How come you're interested in Sinclair's?"

"Have you seen the papers?" Oliver asked.

"It's unbelievable. Four men, two of whom were my good friends, all of whom I worked with. I may have been targeted if I still worked there. Marcus and I actually searched for Peter Donavan a couple months ago. We couldn't find him anywhere and reported it to the police, but they concluded at the time that he had moved away. His family was from the Midwest, he might've wanted to return to them, and he was having trouble in his marriage. Marcus and I agreed he must've gone home. I would've never thought in a million years he would turn up dead."

"I wanted to ask you whether any of Marcus's patients were killed or their symptoms became more severe from the experimental treatments. I spoke to the receptionist, and she made it seem like it's happened more than once. I'm wondering if any of them involved Marcus, and if the patient was also related to a staff member at Sinclair's."

Ed sighed, unsurprised by Oliver's question. It was almost as if he was anticipating it. "Yes, there was a patient who died while receiving treatment, an absolutely tragic story. I left the hospital a few months before it happened, but Marcus filled me in. It had to do with Dr. Haggard's wife. A severe case. Hallucinations, paranoia. She heard voices. She had fits of rage. A difficult patient to treat. She responded poorly to an experimental treatment and passed away."

"Oh my God." Oliver gasped.

Ed nodded grimly.

"When did this occur?"

"About four months ago. Marcus said Chris was depressed, never the same after that. I couldn't imagine having a wife who battled such a condition, only for her to die when you try to treat her. He even debated quitting being a doctor."

"Marcus never said a word to me about this, and usually, his work was all he talked about."

"The only reason I'm aware is because Marcus started babbling after getting drunk at Grayson's Pub one evening."

"What happened to the hospital?"

Ed hesitated, taking a sip of coffee.

"There must have been an investigation of some sort," Oliver said, leaning toward him.

Ed avoided eye contact for a moment. "Chris didn't want anyone to know about his wife and her condition. And the hospital wouldn't make it through..."

"There was no investigation?"

He took a deep breath. "No, the records state that Chris's wife was released from the hospital and died two days later. The official cause of death was that she fell down the stairs in her home and hit her head."

Oliver sat back in the chair and crossed his arms. Dr. Haggard's wife was killed by experimental treatment, probably administered to her by Marcus.

And it was all covered up.

"Does Chris have any children?" Oliver asked.

"Yes, a daughter."

Oliver's eyes widened, feeling a jolt in his chest. He had a daughter. "Do you know anything about his daughter?"

"Nothing, really. All I remember is Chris had a picture of her inside his wallet. I could tell he cared about her very much."

"Do you remember her name?"

"I don't. I wonder who was given the senior role of the hospital, Marcus's old position. I wouldn't be surprised if it's Chris's job now. He had been wanting that title for a while now and was passed over for Marcus. Chris also cared about the place and the patients, working long hours. He was a talented physician."

Oliver took a sip of his coffee. The murders started about a month ago, and Dr. Haggard's wife died about four months ago. *Too much of a coincidence.*

"You think Chris had something to do with it?" Ed asked, tilting his head.

Oliver debated whether he should admit who the murderer was. It sounded outrageous, a teenage girl murdering full-grown men. But it had to be true. Marcus and the young woman walked into Marcus's apartment building, and only the young woman walked out in his trench coat, leaving behind Marcus, lying on the floor with a stab wound in his chest. It was Dr. Haggard's daughter. "I think it's his daughter."

"Daughter?" he said with skepticism, raising his mug to his mouth.

"The bartender at Grayson's Pub saw him leave with a young woman."

"I find it hard to believe someone of her stature could take on grown men, but I guess it's possible. Especially if she's anything like her mother." Dr. Taylor set his mug down and inhaled smoke from his cigarette again.

"Did you see her sitting with Chris at Marcus's funeral?" Oliver asked.

"Yes, I did. That's the first time I ever saw her. I didn't meet her. She and Chris came and went without saying a word to anyone." He inhaled more smoke and exhaled it. "Maybe you're right, it's her. You would think Chris wouldn't be spared if this killer was targeting the staff at Sinclair's. Maybe he will be spared since the killer is his daughter. Only time will tell."

Oliver agreed. "Did you tell the police about Chris's wife?"

"Yes, Detective Howard came again and asked me about Sinclair's as you did. I told him exactly what I told you."

Oliver sat back in his chair. Maybe the evidence was insufficient to get a warrant for her arrest, but at least the police were aware of the motive. "I should get going," Oliver said, taking a sip of coffee.

He and Ed stood, shaking hands. "I would tread carefully, Oliver. If Chris's daughter is the one behind these murders, there's nothing Chris won't do to protect her. She's all he has left."

Oliver nodded. "I understand, thank you."

"Anytime," Ed said, walking him out.

Oliver waved goodbye as he walked down the hallway to the elevator. He could almost see his reflection in the gold doors, a shadowy figure outlining his frame. The floor indicator arrow swung to the right as the doors opened. Oliver didn't give any thought to his movements or the world around him—only about Dr. Haggard and his daughter. That must be her motive. She sought revenge against the doctors and other staff who had failed her mother. She hunted them down one by one and killed them. How many more was she capable of killing? How long will it take Detective Howard to get off his ass and arrest her?

Oliver stepped onto the subway and took a seat, staring out onto the blackness beyond the windows. He looked away from his reflection. Married couples and their children sat together, one wife trying to prevent her toddler from running away, while a few single men laughed, talking about the Dodgers and how they would make the World Series this year. An elderly man sat alone, fanning himself with a newspaper. The headline read: ***FOUR MURDERS CONNECTED TO SINCLAIR HOSPITAL PSYCHIATRIC WARD***.

Oliver folded his hands in his lap, trying to avoid scratching the itch. It would be too late to go to the police now. Detective Howard might not believe his story, thinking Oliver was lying to cover something up. The last time Oliver saw Dr. Haggard's daughter was at Marcus's funeral, wearing a black veil and matching dress. He widened his eyes and sat up. Everyone at the funeral signed a book with their sympathies. Maybe Dr. Haggard signed it on behalf of himself and his daughter. Nancy kept the book on his bookshelf, her name could be inside. He would have to make a stop at his apartment.

The subway came to a sudden stop, and the doors slid open. He got off and climbed the stairs in Brooklyn. As he turned the corner across the street from his apartment building, a couple of police cars were parked in front of it with flashing lights but no sirens. He stopped in his tracks. *Please, God, no.* He bolted into the building and climbed the stairs to his apartment. Oliver burst through the door to find Detective Howard standing in his kitchen with a police officer as Nancy sat with George on the couch in the living room.

"Hello, Mr. Anderson," Detective Howard said, wearing a black suit and holding a notepad and pen. The other officer had his hands in his pockets, staring at Oliver with a blank expression.

"Hello, sir," Oliver said politely, trying to catch his breath.

"We're continuing the investigation into the death of your brother, Marcus, and we would like to ask you some more questions."

"Of course." Oliver sat on the couch with Detective Howard sitting across from him on a chair.

Detective Howard turned toward Nancy and George. "Could

you please leave the apartment for a little while? I would like to interview Mr. Anderson alone."

Nancy looked at Oliver first before agreeing, taking George by the hand and leaving. Oliver folded his hands on his lap, as Detective Howard readied his pen.

"Where were you again on the night of Marcus's murder?" he asked, staring at his notepad.

Shit. Detective Howard's eyes narrowed at him, staring through him.

"My apartment," Oliver responded.

"Where did you go after finishing work that day?"

"I went to Marcus's and Nancy's apartment to visit them and George. I brought George a pizza for dinner. I went to my apartment. Then, I went to see what Marcus was up to at Grayson's Pub. He told me he was seeing a girl named Melissa."

"What happened there?"

"I went there to try to convince him to go home. I said it wasn't fair to Nancy and George. I found his behavior unacceptable."

"We have a witness who said you were arguing with him out back, and you pushed him backward. Your voice was raised, and at one moment, your faces were nearly touching, then you stormed off. Is this correct?"

Who saw that? "I wanted him to return home to his wife and son in one piece. He would go out, get drunk, get into fights... I didn't want anything happening to him. I told him to go home and spend time with his family instead of cheating on Nancy."

"So you were doing all of this for Nancy?"

"Yes," Oliver stuttered. "And George."

Detective Howard seemed to write every word down. "What did you do after that?"

"Marcus told me no and walked back into Grayson's Pub, and I went home."

"You went home?"

"Yes."

"Hm, now that is where we diverge." He smirked at Oliver, sitting back in his chair. "Miss Nancy claims she saw Marcus and a young woman leaving Grayson's Pub from down the street. Did you see her there?"

"No, I walked down the alley to the street. I must have missed her."

"You must have missed her," Detective Howard repeated, nodding.

"I didn't know Nancy was there that night. I learned that at the same time you did."

"The witness also said he saw a man matching your description walking into Marcus's apartment building that night about an hour after Marcus and a young woman left Grayson's Pub."

"I went home," Oliver said defiantly. "Marcus said he was going to sleep with Melissa, if that's her real name, and unfortunately for his family, he liked to keep his word."

"Such disgust when speaking about your deceased brother, Mr. Anderson."

"What?" Oliver asked as the detective continued writing down notes. "Was the young woman seen entering the apartment building with Marcus?"

The officer gave no indication whether he knew if the young woman had been seen entering the apartment building.

"I do not think you are being honest about when you went to your apartment that night, Mr. Anderson." He raised his eyebrows as Oliver clenched his jaw, avoiding eye contact. "The lady next door to Marcus's apartment named Marilyn said she heard someone fall."

"She told me the same thing when I spoke to her the following morning."

"Yes, but when she knocked on the door and asked if everything was all right, someone responded, 'I'm okay.' It was a man's voice."

Oliver sat rigidly, every muscle tense and tight. He had to keep a poker face. These accusations lacked any evidence. Detective Howard analyzed him, studying his movements. Oliver wouldn't give him anything to work with. "She's an old lady; she probably hears things. I never went into the apartment building that night."

Detective Howard couldn't be serious. An old lady imagining things couldn't be used as evidence.

"Did you meet Miss Nancy before or after she started dating your brother?"

Oliver's titled his head. Why was he asking about when he met Nancy? "Before, we met at a social event for Marcus's work."

"You two dated prior to her dating your brother, yes?" Detective Howard looked at his notepad, continuing to write.

"Yes." Why did he care about whether Oliver dated Nancy?

"How long?"

"Five months." *I answered too fast.*

"And she broke it off after falling in love with Mr. Marcus."

"She didn't fall in love with–" Oliver stopped himself as a smile crept up on Detective Howard's face.

"Why did Miss Nancy break up with you?"

Oliver grew restless on the couch. "Nancy wanted to please her father. Her father wanted her to marry Marcus; Marcus and her father worked together."

"Did Miss Nancy love Mr. Marcus?"

Oliver hesitated. He didn't want Nancy to be seen as a suspect if he answered no. The answer must be no. Detective Howard nodded as if Oliver's nonanswer was an answer.

"You visited Sinclair's and met with the receptionist. We do not need any outside help in solving this case, Mr. Anderson."

Oliver shook his head, having enough. He couldn't take it anymore. "Have you spoken to Dr. Haggard's daughter?"

He sighed. "Mr. Anderson, I am handling this investigation and am working around the clock to figure out who did this. It does not happen overnight."

"She's a suspect, right?" Oliver asked, trying not to raise his voice. "Right?"

"We are doing our due diligence, Mr. Anderson," he said,

putting his notepad and pen inside his jacket pocket. "That's all for now, thank you. You have been very helpful."

They both stood, and Oliver led him to the door. Oliver opened it for him, and Detective Howard and the police officer left, walking toward the elevator.

Oliver closed the door, shaking his head and clenched his fist, ready to make another hole in the wall, but resisted. The detective knew Oliver lied about going home after confronting Marcus at Grayson's Pub. He inquired about Oliver's relationship with Nancy, seeking a potential motive. It would make sense. A man murdered his brother for stealing his to-be wife. Oliver was the one who found Marcus dead and called the police. Detective Howard didn't trust him from the start.

And now a man supposedly saw Oliver arguing with Marcus at Grayson's Pub and entering Marcus's old apartment building. Who was that man? Ed said there wasn't anything Dr. Haggard wouldn't do to protect his daughter. Maybe Dr. Haggard was aware of his daughter's crimes but didn't want her to suffer the consequences. He might have spied on Oliver and Carol inside the coffee shop and left the note to stop prying. If that were the case, not only was he aware, but he was trying to pin Marcus's murder on Oliver.

Oliver rushed to his bookshelf in the living room, pulling out the sign-in book from Marcus's funeral. He ran his fingers down the page before gliding to the next one. Dr. Haggard signed his name but neglected to add his daughter's. And Dr. Haggard didn't write anything else. Oliver slammed the book shut, shoving it onto the shelf.

After a few minutes of pacing, he stopped at the mail pile on his kitchen counter. The envelope on top didn't have a return address and his address was written in sloppy handwriting. He picked it up, opening it to find a sheet of paper, reading ***LEAVE HER ALONE, OLIVER***. It slipped through his fingertips, landing on the floor, as Oliver clutched the top of his head.

He continued pacing in his apartment, from the living room to the kitchen, from the kitchen to the living room. Oliver must admit he lied to Detective Howard about going straight home from Grayson's Pub. He must tell him the truth of what he saw the night Marcus was murdered. It was the only way to prevent more people from dying. With the two threatening notes in his hand, Oliver left his apartment for the police station.

26

March 15th, 1958, Brooklyn, NY

Hours after Clara discovered her mother had died, her father drove her home. The drive home from Sinclair's lasted longer than Clara's entire existence. She leaned her head against the car window, inconsolable. Her father glanced in her direction every few seconds, but she stared out the window, not seeing anything. She could never be happy again. The world was cruel and unrelenting. The clouds hovered over them, ready to pour. Clara wished her father would crash the car. Her mother had been dragged into that shithole and left to die. Clara had known deep down her mother would never return home after being committed to a place like Sinclair's. Now, her suspicions were confirmed. The only option from here was to burn it all down.

The silent car ride came to an end with Clara jumping out of the car the second her father parked it and sprinting into the house, slamming her feet on the ground with each stride. Her father followed her, closing the door and approaching her. That was a big mistake. He would be better served to leave her alone for a while.

"Clara—"

"I knew she would die in there!" She could barely manage to get the words out. Mucus burned in the back of her throat. "I told you, but you wouldn't listen! You as much as killed her–"

"You think I liked your mother being in there?" he yelled back, startling her. It was the first time he ever yelled at Clara. He had spoken sternly with her before but never yelled. "I did everything I could to keep her at home and protect her, but I wouldn't be able to live with myself if anything were to happen to you. When you're an adult, you have to make hard decisions no matter how sick they make you!"

Clara stared at him with her mouth open, her shoulders rising and falling.

That was four months ago.

July 27th, 1958, Brooklyn, NY

It was a new Sunday morning. The birds chirped, the air was hot and sticky, and the sun beamed down relentlessly. Clara made her father a cup of coffee and eggs. He sat at the table, reading the newspaper. His glasses perched on the edge of his nose, looking as if they could slip off at any moment. He wore a gray suit although he didn't have any plans that day. Clara matched him, wearing a gray dress, the last dress in her closet. The color suited the mood, anyway.

Silence. The only noise was the sizzling of the butter in the frying pan, and the ticking of the grandfather clock. No words were spoken between them. Her father must have known about her victims. The question was how long had he had known about her murderous behavior? He must know she loved knives, considering the knife set disappeared from the kitchen counter and no butter knives remained in the drawer.

Clara whisked the eggs and poured them into a frying pan. Eggs were her father's favorite breakfast food. Her mother would make them for him every morning along with coffee, and Clara continued the tradition after her mother's passing. After the eggs cooked, she slid them onto a plate and set them in front of her father on the red placemat. Once the coffee finished dripping into the pot, she poured it into a mug and set it next to his plate.

No 'thank you' from him. He took a sip of his coffee and began eating while reading the paper.

Clara stood at the stove, her back turned to him, and started making eggs for herself. His fork clinked against the plate, and he took sips of his coffee. The eggs sizzled in the pan; steam rose from it. She moved the spatula around, trying to prevent the eggs from sticking to the pan. Clara closed her eyes and took a deep breath. The questions burned in her chest. This was the last opportunity to ask them.

"How long have you known?" she asked, continuing to cook the eggs.

He kept eating, not acknowledging her question, while flipping the newspaper page.

She turned to face him. "How long have you known?"

He looked at her with wide eyes and a straight face, dropping his fork onto his plate. He never looked at her that way before. "Clara—"

"Are you scared of me, Dad?" Clara whispered.

"What were you burning in the fire pit, Clara?"

"Marcus's trench coat."

"Is this because of your mother?"

"Yes, they deserved it," she said, as he moved his chair backward. "They killed her, and I'm sure she's not the only patient who has ever died from their treatment. They deserved it, Dad. I wouldn't have murdered them if they didn't deserve it."

His eyes became glossy. "I failed your mother, and I'm sorry. I thought I could cure her. Dr. Anderson was a brilliant physician, and we worked together to create a treatment plan with the goal of eliminating her symptoms. I've been angry at him for failing your mother, but he did the best he could. It turned out to be a disaster. We only had good intentions, Clara. I do put my patients first, especially when one of them is my wife. It is something I carry with me every day."

"Don't lie to me!" Clara snapped.

Her father stood but lost his balance, holding onto the table and shaking it as he attempted to steady himself. After struggling, he sat again in defeat. "What did you give me?"

His speech began to slur, but she understood him fine.

"I'm sorry Dad, I really am." She turned toward the stove, focusing on the scrambled eggs again. They started to burn, so she moved them to a plate.

"I've protected you, Clara. I've suspected you were the culprit this whole time, but I could never turn you in, don't you understand? You're my daughter."

"You're working with Oliver to imprison me." She turned, making eye contact with him again. "I saw the two of you out on the sidewalk, discussing your plans to turn me into the police. You must think I'm stupid to believe you would protect me. Look what you did to Mom! You want to commit me next."

"Clara, that's not true. I—"

Clara took out the Saran Wrap from the drawer, grasping it in her hand. "You're the last two people who know about what I've done. Since you're incapable of speaking clearly, I'll pry it out of Oliver, what you two discussed about me. Marcus's brother will be taken care of next, and I can put all of this behind me and move away. Maybe I'll go to our cabin in the Poconos and find peace there. I'll live a quiet life knowing the people who murdered my Mom are six feet under just as she is. I'll have to make certain he never told Marcus's widow, Nancy. That would be a real shame."

She shrugged. "But don't be afraid, Dad. I'll wait until you're passed out. You won't suffer like the others did."

Her father mumbled, not making any sense, as Clara watched him, trying to keep her emotions out of it, but it was challenging. His body shook, a tear streaming down his cheek. Clara had never seen her father display any emotion before. It sent a chill down her spine. His body was shutting down, he couldn't communicate, but he knew what was going on. His daughter whom he loved and raised was killing him. Clara would reunite him with his wife. Her mother's mind shouldn't be burning there.

Her father closed his eyes and drifted off to sleep, and Clara unwrapped Saran Wrap, holding it over his head. She hesitated. But this must be done. It was the only way for this madness to come to an end.

"Dad," Clara whispered, staring at the Saran Wrap in her shaky hands. "It must be done, Clara. It must be done." She told herself.

And so, she wrapped it tightly over his face, around his head. Over and over again. Around and around. Tighter and tighter. The Saran Wrap ensured his mouth and nose were unable to get any air. His body remained perfectly still.

Clara ripped off the Saran Wrap, setting the box on the kitchen table, kneeling on the floor next to her father and holding his hand through the last moments of his life. She would give him the courtesy he didn't give his wife. After a few minutes, she pressed her finger against his neck to take his pulse. Nothing. No heartbeat. His chest was quiet. She unwrapped his head and threw away the Saran Wrap, putting the box in a drawer. Clara stared at her father's body slouching in the chair, his chin resting on his chest. The newspaper lay on the table, never to be flipped by him again. His half-empty mug sat beside a half-eaten plate of scrambled eggs. The fork was upside down on the table. The only sound came from the ticking of the grandfather clock.

Clara could only think of one place to move him, the cellar. Trying to lift him from the chair and onto the floor, she stood behind him and wrapped her arms around his body. She grunted, moving him with all of her strength, yet her father remained slouched on the chair. Clara tried to catch her breath. She didn't possess the strength to carry him, so she pushed his body over onto the floor, holding his head to prevent it from slamming onto the tile floor and making a mess. He lay on his side with the chair tipped over. Clara picked up the chair, before dragging her father by the ankles across the floor to the cellar door. She opened the door, walking backward down the stairs. His head thumped on each step like a bowling ball slowly rolling down the stairs, dropping from one step to another. She took a step. Thump. Another step. Thump. Her father's head collided with the cement floor, as Clara dragged him behind stacks of boxes, the opposite corner from the washing machine, dropping his ankles and allowing his legs to fall onto the floor. Clara took deep breaths, looking at the staircase and the beam of sunlight glistening down it, providing most of the light besides a couple of lightbulbs.

Her mother fell down the stairs, carrying laundry. She slipped on the top step, causing her to plummet down and hit her head on the cement in the cellar, cracking open her skull. The blood gushed out too fast. By the time the ambulance arrived, it was too late. It was an accident; it could happen to anyone. Yet no one feared the stairs. The darkness in the cellar, the imaginary monster waiting for you, the imaginary man with a gun, pointing it at you. You couldn't see anything but blackness, but he could see you perfectly. He would make a noise, causing your body to freeze and all your hair to stand at once. He would reveal himself at last, taking the shot and watching you bleed to death. Yet, what was more likely to happen? You being shot by a shadowy man hiding in the darkness of your cellar, or you taking a tumble down the stairs and cracking open your skull?

Her mother didn't fall down the stairs and wasn't murdered by a shadowy man. She was murdered by men in white coats, matching the white floors and walls. They didn't need to conceal themselves in the darkness; they could do whatever they wanted in the light. The light didn't protect people like her. The staff didn't protect her mother, so they deserved her fate. Who knew if any of them would be good enough to enter the gates of Heaven, but she would send them to their judgment day before God's schedule.

Peter Donavan rotted in the attic of an old restaurant, being feasted upon by rats. Bernhard Altenhofen, Marcus Anderson, and Dean Caraway were lying underground being eaten by worms and insects. Peter Donavan would be joining them soon now that his body had been found.

Trapped.

Oliver would be next; the last loose end to tie up. He had to have his own little investigation, scheming with her father to arrest her and send her away. Clara turned to see her father's dead body one last time before climbing the stairs and shutting the cellar door. The phone rang in the living room, a shrilling sound Clara refused to answer.

Clara approached the living room window. Cars drove by, going to and from errands, work, or play. Her father never let her drive. The passenger seat or the backseat were her only two options. She learned how, but her knowledge was rusty by now. People were laughing and talking, going about their day, while Clara pulled out a cigarette and lit it. The voices should calm down after Oliver was killed. Oliver wouldn't be able to stalk her anymore, and her job would be finished at last.

A police car parked in front of her townhouse with its lights on but its siren off. Clara backed away from the window, putting out her cigarette, and rushing into the kitchen to clean the dishes. Her breaths became short and her hands shook as she scrubbed the plates clean and washed her father's mug. The house looked to be in perfect order, no one could possibly tell a murder had been committed there ten minutes ago.

Someone knocked on the front door. Clara set the burnt pan into the sink, soaking it in soap and water. She dried her hands and collected herself, taking deep breaths and pushing her shoulders back, approached the door, and answered it. There stood Detective

Howard, wearing a black suit with another policeman in uniform standing behind him. Both wore straight faces.

"Hello, sir," Clara said, holding the door with one hand.

"Hello, Miss Haggard," Detective Howard said. "Is your father home?"

"No, he went out to run some errands."

"Do you know where exactly?"

"No, I think he said something about a hardware store." She shrugged.

"Do you know when he'll be back?"

"No."

"May I come in, please?" he asked. "I have a few questions for you."

"Of course," she said. *For you*. Detective Howard and the police officer entered her home, and she closed the door. "Please take a seat. Would either of you like something to drink?"

"No, thank you," Detective Howard said, as the police officer shook his head. Good thing because the coffee pot needed to be cleaned. The police officer stood next to the window, while Clara sat across from Detective Howard in the living room. He took out a notepad and pen from his jacket pocket. He clicked his pen and readied it. "So, Miss Haggard, have you heard about the murders of the staff members at Sinclair Hospital Psychiatric Ward?"

"I have, I read the papers."

"Do you remember where you were the night of July 11th, a Friday?"

Clara looked at the ceiling, squinting. Of course, she remembered. That was the night she killed Marcus, plunging a knife into his chest and watching him fall backwards, smashing his head against the floor and bleeding out to death. However, answering too quickly would look suspicious, as if she had rehearsed her answers. She also had to remember to use the present tense when discussing her father. "Um, my dad works late on Friday evenings. I think I went grocery shopping and put the groceries away, then I cleaned the floors and kitchen. I made dinner for myself and my dad, putting his portion in the fridge for when he came home. That's about it, I think. A pretty boring evening."

"I spoke to Elizabeth Sanders and Catherine Peterson..." he said, reading from his notepad.

Kate and Betty. He spoke to Kate and Betty. *Shit.*

"...Who said they stopped by your house right before six o'clock, wanting you to join them for the evening. You said you could not because you had plans. Miss Peterson said she assumed you were meeting a man. Did you?"

"No, I didn't want to go out, and they didn't leave me alone about it. So, I lied and said I already had plans. They usually go to bars and get drunk, and I don't like doing that."

The corner of his lip curled. "It is interesting you say that. All they did was go to a local hall to dance."

"Well, you're a detective. They're not going to tell you the truth."

"Like you?" he asked.

Clara was taken aback. "I am telling the truth. I told them I wasn't interested, and they kept pressing me about having a date. But that wasn't true. I wanted to stay home, and I did."

Detective Howard took notes. "What did you wear on that night?"

"A dress, I'm sure."

"What color?"

Clara shook her head. It was a black dress. "I don't remember. That was over a couple of weeks ago now."

"I also spoke with your next-door neighbor, John."

Shit. The little boy next door who asked for brown sugar on the same night. "Oh yes, he came over asking for brown sugar."

"Yes, that is true. He said you looked messy and distraught with your hair all over the place and your eyes red and teary."

Clara squinted. "He said that?"

"He did."

She shrugged. "I mean, I guess I was tired. I don't know why he would use the word distraught. You wouldn't think a small boy would use a word like that."

"He did. He said you stopped him from opening your front hall closet." He pointed to it.

"No, I came back with the sugar and gave it to him, and then he left."

"And his father found it odd you would light a fire in the fire pit out back on such a hot night."

"Well, I was smoking a cigarette, and I dropped it into the fire pit."

Detective Howard's eyes narrowed. "John's father said he saw you pour gasoline into the fire pit first."

"I like to light fires, even in the summer." That lie was weak, but she couldn't come up with anything better. That was true, though, she liked fires. She enjoyed watching the wood become engulfed in flames. It was nice to watch something else get burned and feel like they're on fire, for once.

"Your mother was checked into Sinclair's for a brief period this past year, correct?"

"Yes, she was there for about four months."

"And, she returned home and passed a couple days later?"

"Yes, she received treatment and her condition improved. Unfortunately, she slipped down the stairs into the cellar." Clara repeated the lie. "I miss her every day."

"I am sorry for your loss, Miss Haggard. May I see these stairs?"

"Of course," she said without hesitation, standing and leading him to the cellar door. The rooms were blurry around her as she had to keep a straight face and not show any of her nerves. Her father's body should be hidden behind the stacks of cardboard boxes. Hopefully Detective Howard wouldn't want to go down the stairs and look around. She opened the door to the cellar.

"I would like to walk down these stairs," he said.

Clara nodded, walking down first and standing with her arms

crossed behind her back. The police officer remained upstairs by the door as Detective Howard stepped thoughtfully down each step before turning and studying them. He gazed around the cellar.

Clara could've sworn she heard movement behind her. The sound of nails scratching the concrete, clawing their way closer to her. A chilly breeze pushed against the back of her legs. Her father had woken up, crawling behind her and reaching, grabbing her ankles, wearing the Saran Wrap and gasping for air.

"Can I take a look around your shed?" he asked, as Clara snapped out of it.

"Certainly." Clara climbed the stairs at the correct speed, not too fast like she was hiding something, and held open the back door for them. They walked past the fire pit, and Detective Howard stopped and looked into it. Thankfully there was nothing but ashes. Clara waited with the police officer in the backyard while the detective looked around the shed. Good thing she bought a hammer and an ax to replace the ones she used on Dean.

Detective Howard emerged, making notes. "Thank you for your time, Miss Haggard. We may be in touch again if I need any more information. Please answer the telephone when I call, all right?"

"Yes, sir, I will." Clara smiled. He was the one who called earlier.

They walked through the house once again, and Clara opened the front door to let them out. She climbed the stairs to her bedroom and approached the window, watching them get into the police car and drive away. Time ran out. Clara was officially a suspect, and her father's body lay in the cellar. She wasn't safe here. When Detective Howard returned, it would be with an arrest warrant.

One person was left: the person who worked with her father to get the police to suspect her.

Oliver Anderson, her stalker.

Then she could leave for the Poconos.

27

Nancy barged through the apartment door, running into Oliver. George let go of her hand and rushed to his corner of toys. Her face was bright red. Oliver closed the door, following her into the kitchen with Dr. Haggard's threat in his hand.

"The nerve of Detective Howard to come in here and demand that I answer all of his questions! And then he wouldn't leave, even though I told him I didn't know when you would be coming back! I don't like him."

Oliver didn't like him either. "I know, but he's doing his job. He is trying to solve who did this to Marcus and his coworkers."

"Yeah, you're right, but I don't like being treated as a criminal."

"What kind of questions did he ask you?"

"He asked questions about us, which was strange. What does that have to do with anything?" Her eyes widened in realization. "He doesn't suspect you had anything to do with this, right?"

"I'm not sure. He asked me similar questions about how long we dated before you dated Marcus. Someone must have told him."

"I could understand if Marcus was the only person killed, but the motive has to do with Sinclair's. There were three other men killed, all staff there. It's too much of a coincidence."

"I agree. I think he's looking at it from all angles. I've heard from many people that he's an expert in this, and if anyone could figure out who's responsible, it's him."

Nancy leaned against the wall and crossed her arms. She stared at the envelope he held in his hand. "What's that?"

He wanted to lie to her; tell her it was nothing important. But she would know better. She knew him better than he knew himself sometimes. Nancy could always tell when he was lying; it was no use to lie now. "I spoke to Ed Taylor this morning. Dr. Haggard worked with Marcus at Sinclair's, and his wife was committed there and died from experimental treatment. He has a daughter, and I think she's the one you saw leaving Grayson's Pub with Marcus."

Nancy's mouth dropped. "She's targeting the staff at Sinclair's in revenge for her mother?"

"That has to be the motive." Oliver looked at the envelope. "I think Dr. Haggard is threatening me to leave his daughter alone. He might be the one who told Detective Howard we dated before you married Marcus."

"He's trying to pin this on you to protect his evil daughter?" Nancy gasped. "Did you tell Detective Howard this?"

"That's where I'm heading now."

"Does Detective Howard know about Dr. Haggard's daughter?"

"He does. I'm hoping he finally arrests her after I show him this letter."

Oliver turned for the door, but Nancy held onto his arm. "I can go with you."

"No, stay here with George. I'll come back after showing this to Detective Howard."

"Please be safe, Ollie."

"I will."

Nancy pressed her palm against his cheek. Her glossy brown eyes were full of worry, and her hand shook against his skin. He gently wrapped his hand around her wrist to steady it. Her eyes drifted between his eyes and lips before she stared at him again.

"Promise you'll be safe," she whispered.

"I promise," he assured her.

Oliver left his apartment for the police station with the letters in his hand. He took the elevator to the first floor, leaving the building and walking a few blocks to the precinct. His surroundings went unnoticed: the crowds of people walking on the sidewalk, the cars racing by and honking at other drivers, the newspaper stands and other street vendors. The only building that stood out clearly was the police station a block away. As Oliver tried to cross the street, another man held out his arm and prevented him from doing so.

"It's a red light," he said.

He was right. "Thanks."

Oliver counted the seconds until the light changed. Once it did, he crossed the street and entered the precinct. An officer sat behind the receptionist desk on the phone. A pinboard with portraits of missing persons hung on the wall, along with their identifying information and posters about protecting your belongings. A police radio sat at the desk, humming.

"Thank you, sir... Okay, goodbye." The officer hung up the phone and looked at Oliver. "Hello, sir. How may I help you?"

"Hello, I would like to speak with Detective Howard. Is he in?"

"Yes, what's your name?"

"Oliver Anderson."

"I'll see if he's available."

"Thank you."

The officer went down the hall as Oliver tapped his fingers on the desk.

A few seconds later, he returned. "Mr. Anderson, you can follow me." Oliver trailed after the officer down the hall until they took a corner and he waved Oliver into Detective Howard's office. The detective sat behind his neat wooden desk with stacks of papers, a black telephone, a lamp, and a cup of coffee on a coaster. He leaned back in his chair.

"Hello, Mr. Anderson. Please close the door."

Oliver nodded, closed it, and sat on the chair across from the desk. He took the envelope containing both threats from Dr. Haggard and handed the first one to the detective. "This note was left on my doorstep right after I met with Carol, the receptionist from Sinclair's." He handed Detective Howard the second note. "I received this in the mail yesterday. I opened it after you left. Dr. Haggard sent it to me, threatening me to stop suspecting his daughter of murdering my brother."

Detective Howard stared at the letter for a moment longer before placing it back into the envelope and putting it into a drawer in his desk. "How do you know Dr. Haggard sent this to you?"

"Dr. Haggard must have been spying on me while I was speaking with Carol in the coffee shop on Friday. Then, you came to my apartment and asked me about my relationship with Nancy before she married Marcus. Who told you about that? I'm guessing it was Dr. Haggard. I'm also guessing he was the witness who claimed to see me arguing with Marcus behind Grayson's Pub and walking into Marcus's apartment building the night he was killed. Then, I get this letter. The 'her' in the letter is his daughter. The sick individual responsible for the deaths of four men. The motive is clear, she's avenging the death of her mother who died while in the care of Sinclair's."

Detective Howard tilted his head impatiently. "Thank you for providing these notes, Mr. Anderson, and thank you for bringing them to my attention. I will keep them as evidence. But this is your final warning to stay away from my case. I will be in contact with you if I am in need of contacting you."

Oliver restrained himself, clenching his fists and resisting the urge to shake his head. How dare he be treated this way? Dr. Haggard was attempting to frame him for murdering his own brother, and Oliver was supposed to sit back and take it? There was plenty of evidence at this point to arrest Dr. Haggard's daughter, and yet, the detective sat here on his ass and lectured Oliver instead. If Oliver told him the truth about seeing that young woman the night Marcus was killed, Detective Howard wouldn't believe him and twist it into getting an arrest warrant for Oliver. He couldn't say another word, or he would end up in one of their holding cells.

"Understood," he said through gritted teeth.

"Good day, Mr. Anderson."

"Good day." Oliver left the office door open although he felt the urge to slam it shut. He exited the police station and headed back to his apartment. He wanted to go to Dr. Haggard's townhouse and punch him in the face. If Oliver had a daughter who had murdered four men, he sure as hell wouldn't be protecting her and concealing information from the police. But he wouldn't be going to Dr. Haggard's apartment—he would go back to Nancy and George as he had promised. Oliver entered his building, pressing the button for his floor. Dr. Haggard might have thought he was safe, but Oliver wouldn't be surprised to learn that he was the next victim. He stepped off the elevator and continued to his apartment. He turned the doorknob, but it was locked. Nancy must have been more nervous than she was letting on. He unlocked it and stepped inside.

"Ollie, thank God!" Nancy cried, hugging Oliver as soon as he entered. Her eyes were swollen and her body shook.

Oliver held her arms for a moment. "What happened? Where's George?"

"He's in your bedroom. A young woman stopped by, looking for you. I think she was Dr. Haggard's daughter! She kept knocking on the door, saying your name, my name, and George's name. I didn't open the door, but I saw her through the peephole."

He widened his eyes. "What did she look like?"

"Brown hair and brown eyes, and she was wearing a gray dress. I can't believe she said George's name! I can tell something isn't right about her just by looking at her. She kept repeating our names and knocking on the door..."

"What happened next?"

"Eventually she left, and I called the police."

"How long ago was this?"

"A couple minutes, maybe."

Dr. Haggard's daughter must be in the building.

Someone knocked on the door, causing Nancy to hold on to Oliver tightly. Oliver moved toward the door as Nancy backed away into the kitchen. He braced himself for the worst, approaching it vigilantly and checking through the peephole.

"Hey, Oliver! Are you there?" It was Benny.

Oliver let out a sigh of relief. *Thank God*, he thought, then turning to Nancy. "It's Benny, my neighbor."

She placed her hand on her chest as he opened the door.

"Hey, Oliver! Is everything all right?" Benny asked. "I thought I heard crying."

"Can you stay with Nancy and George for a few minutes?" Oliver asked. "I'll be right back. Nancy will explain everything to you; it has to do with my brother's case."

"Sure, of course." Benny entered, and Oliver left, closing the door.

The hallway was empty and quiet. Dr. Haggard's daughter left right before Oliver arrived. She couldn't have taken the elevator, or he would've run into her. Oliver raced down the hall toward the stairwell, swinging open the door and heading down the stairs. Something pressed against his back, pushing him forward. He tripped over a step, freefalling, the edges of the stairs digging into his arms, legs, and back and bruising them. His head hit the floor, his body aching. Oliver closed his eyes, and the world faded to black.

* * *

Oliver's eyes opened, his eyesight blurry with black dots flickering in front of him like a film on a silver screen. A throbbing pain in the back of his head. Twinges in his back sending shooting pain down his spine. He tried to sit up, but his wrists pulled him back. They were handcuffed to the radiator. He rubbed his eyes, trying to clear his vision. Eventually, the room came into focus again. Oliver was in a maintenance closet in his apartment building. The closet was tight with cleaning supplies, tools, mops, and buckets. A single lightbulb dangled from the ceiling. The young woman, Dr. Haggard's daughter, stood still and stared at him, tilting her head, as if she waited for him to wake up. Oliver gasped, yanking at his wrists to free himself to no avail. It was no use.

"Hi, Oliver," she said like it was an ordinary conversation under ordinary circumstances. Oliver stopped struggling, pressing his feet against the floor to prop himself on the radiator. His hands shook. Trapped with the woman who killed four men, including his brother. He tried to catch his breath and was unable to swallow. His head felt fuzzy. Dr. Haggard's daughter looked far worse than she did when he ran into her at the newsstand. She had bloodshot eyes with bags under them. Her hair was disheveled.

"What's your name?" he asked.

"Clara Haggard," she answered, not blinking and standing emotionless. Her face was pale. She looked as though if you were to stick her with a pin, she wouldn't feel a thing. She would take the pin out of her arm without flinching and stick it in your eye. Murdering four people in cold blood, Clara must be unhinged and unable to feel empathy toward others. Oliver must choose his words carefully, or he would end up like his brother.

"Do you know what happened to my mother?"

Oliver drew in a deep breath. "Yes, I'm so sorry. I couldn't imagine what it must be like."

"You're right. You have no idea what it's like, and your brother carried on his life as though nothing had happened." She sighed. "I'm sorry for beating you to it."

He furrowed his eyebrows. "What?"

Clara leaned toward him. "I saw you watching Marcus and I, following us to the apartment. I saw your face, and I know it well. You were going to kill him."

"I wanted to kill him after seeing he didn't sell the car or the apartment—"

"No," she interrupted him. "You didn't just want to kill him, you were planning on killing him. You were going to wait for me to leave the apartment before murdering him."

"No, I would never murder my own brother."

Clara smirked, rolling her eyes. "I'm not speaking in hypotheticals."

Stay calm. I'm not dead yet. Keep her talking.

"You're right," he said, playing along. "I wanted revenge."

Clara raised her eyebrows, her face lighting up at the word revenge. That had to have caught her attention; he was speaking her language. "You wanted revenge?"

"Yes, I was planning on killing my brother."

"I saw you at the end of the hall, pretending you lived there by trying to unlock another apartment's door. I saw you when I left the apartment after killing Marcus. I knew you would be disappointed. I beat you to it."

None of it was true, but he had to keep her talking. Every moment she was engaged in conversation was another moment Oliver was alive. "He stole my girlfriend from me and married her, and I'll never forgive him."

"Are you talking about Nancy?" she asked innocently, like she had stopped by his apartment for a chat.

Oliver clenched his jaw and swallowed the words he wanted to say. She was trying to get a rise out of him. He couldn't let her. The idea that she might go after Nancy next... if she dared to hurt a hair on Nancy or George's head...

"I tried to meet her today when I stopped by your apartment. I could hear George inside, playing with his toys. I wanted to visit them, but Nancy refused to answer the door. You weren't there unfortunately; I missed you. Lucky I waited in the stairwell, I figured you may try to come after me. Her son is adorable. I saw him and Nancy walking down the street the other day."

He must resist taking the bait.

"My brother was a piece of shit who didn't deserve her," he said, returning the conversation to Marcus and away from Nancy and George. "He ran around behind her back, having affairs. I understand why you killed him, Clara, and I'm not mad at you, I don't hold it against you."

She pointed at Oliver. "You're full of shit. Where were you going alone just now? Were you going to the police station to turn me in? Is that what my father asked you to do?"

What her father asked me to do? Did she think he was working together with her father? Is that why she wanted to kill him?

Clara continued. "You know everything about me and my family, and you were about to go to the police. You came to my house, speaking to my mother, asking about me and my father. I saw you go into Sinclair's to meet with my father; I saw you talking with my father outside my house..." Her voice grew louder with every word she spoke. Her fists were clenched, her body tensed up, and blood rushed to her face.

Oliver shook his head. Her mother was dead; it was impossible for him to have met with her. He had never met her father. They hadn't spoken, and Oliver had never been down her street, let alone stood on her front door. He stopped himself before responding. That wasn't the answer she wanted to hear. Dr. Taylor's words rang in his ear. Hallucinations, paranoia. She was correct in seeing Oliver entering Sinclair's, but he didn't speak to anyone other than the receptionist. Her mind must create visions convincingly. Clara must not be able to determine what was real and what was fiction. She would never believe the truth, so Oliver had to handle her another way.

"I met with your father one time. He wanted to ensure I

wouldn't say a word. Your father is protective over you, and the last thing he wants for you is to get caught. I agree with him."

"Yes, I know!" she yelled to her right, like she was having a conversation with a ghost. Clara turned toward Oliver again. "You're lying to me!"

She hears voices.

"No, I'm not! Your father has been trying to pin the murders on me. He sent me two threatening notes to stay away from you. I haven't seen you since Marcus's funeral."

"You followed me on the subway, and you watched me murder Dean. You've been stalking me for weeks now!"

Paranoia.

"No, that's not true!"

"I know what I saw!" Clara took a hammer off the shelf and gripped it so firmly her bones looked like they could break through her skin. Her eyes watered.

Hallucinations.

"George is a sick child. Nancy can't take care of him herself. She doesn't have a job, she can't afford the rent or his medical bills, I care about them far too much to rat you out to the police."

"I'm not sick!" Clara said, tearing up.

"No, you're not. I never said you were."

She stepped closer to him.

"Please, Clara, please!"

"Don't say my name!" she screamed, her eyes becoming bloody and her teeth grinding together. Oliver flinched, pushing his back against the wall.

Fits of rage.

"I promise I will keep my mouth shut."

"I'll make sure you do."

"You're going to destroy our family. Nancy and George have never hurt a soul. They haven't done anything to you. I never told them anything because I want to protect them. Whatever you do, please don't hurt Nancy or her son. Please, promise me."

Clara steadied her hand by holding her wrist with the other.

"Please don't let Nancy find me like this! It will kill her!"

She raised the hammer, ready to strike, when the piercing sound of sirens penetrated the walls. Clara lowered the hammer, leaning against the door of the closet. Nancy had called the police several minutes ago, and police cars must be at the entrance.

"You must leave now if you want to escape the police," Oliver said, as Clara stared dead into his eyes. She shifted her gaze to the hammer then looked at him again. Nothing would probably please her more than to murder him. The urge to kill again must be strong, addictive, like a cigarette sitting in front of a chain smoker.

The next moment, Clara was gone, the door left open a crack.

The hammer sat among the tools.

Oliver would be the first and only of Clara Haggard's victims to survive.

28

Clara approached the stairwell, pressing her ear against the door. Loud footsteps pounded up the stairs, passing by her floor and going up one more floor to Oliver's apartment. There must've been around five police officers. The stairwell door slammed above, then everything went silent. Clara opened the door, peeking around it before racing down the stairs to the first floor, opening the side door and running down the alley to make it to the street. She blended into the crowd, put on her sunglasses, and walked casually among them. More police cars drove down the street with sirens, causing people to stop, stare, and point. Clara needed to get home. She needed to talk to her parents. They would be able to help her.

Turning down her street, she walked a couple more blocks. No police cars there yet, but it wouldn't be this way for much longer. Clara ran through the front door.

"Mom?" she called. "Mom? I need help!"

No response. The townhouse was clean and neat. The throw rugs were folded under the coffee tables, the books on the bookshelf, and the furniture was upright. For once, Clara wouldn't mind if the house was a mess. It would show some semblance of life. The air was thick; she had trouble breathing. Her eyes welled up as she wiped them with the back of her hand.

"Mom! Mom, are you here?" she yelled. "Mom!"

Why wasn't her mother responding? Why wasn't she home? Clara needed her, but she was nowhere to be found. Clara climbed the stairs and searched the bedrooms. No one. The beds were made, and the curtains drawn. She returned downstairs, walking through the living room into the kitchen.

"Mom, please! I need you!" Clara was breathing so heavy it felt like bricks had been stacked on top of her chest. Why couldn't her mother respond and comfort her?

"Dad?" she called. "Dad, are you home?"

Her father was the one to watch over her when she had a cold. She remembered him bringing her a cold Coca-Cola from Sandy's. How good that felt on her burning throat. He would also take her out for her birthday to a movie of her choice. One year they saw *Cinderella*, another year *Singin' in the Rain*. Maybe he could help her. He should be reading the newspaper at the kitchen table, drinking a cup of coffee and smoking a cigar. She would love to make him lunch, and they could eat together. He would tell her about how he disliked Elvis's music, and she would roll her eyes, thinking he was old and out of touch.

Clara stepped into the kitchen over a small piece of Saran Wrap. She took it off her shoe, feeling sick. *No, it was only a nightmare.* The newspaper lay flat on the kitchen table, and the burnt pan soaked in the sink. The chair was tucked under the table. *No, please, please.* It had been a nightmare. She swung open the door to the cellar, and a sense of dread overcame her.

She stepped down the stairs slowly, gripping the railing.

"Dad?"

The left corner had stacks of cardboard boxes. *Please*, she thought, moving the cardboard boxes out of the way. Maybe nothing was there. Perhaps her father was running errands, stopping first at the hardware store, as she told Detective Howard. But when the boxes were out of the way, she had to face the truth: what she had done. Her father lay on his back, lifeless. Clara collapsed onto her knees beside him, ignoring the sting of the concrete against her bones.

"I'm so sorry, Dad!" His heart no longer beat in his chest. His life had ended, his soul leaving his body and meeting with God. His jacket moved, revealing a piece of paper sticking out of his inner pocket. Clara picked it up and held the photograph. Her mother wore a silky white dress hugging her silhouette and had long lace sleeves. Over her curly hair, she wore a gorgeous lace veil. Her smile radiated as she posed next to Clara's father. He looked dashing, wearing a tuxedo. He grinned as they held onto one another.

Clara covered her mouth with her hand and sobbed. He had tried his best with her mother. He did everything he could for her. He kept her at home as long as possible, even when she hit him and falsely accused him of being unfaithful to her. When she threatened the life of his only child, he knew it was time to take her into a facility. What other choice did he have? He did the best he could with a difficult situation.

"Oh my God!" Clara cried, barely able to breathe. She rested her head on his arm. "What have I done? I'm sorry, Dad! I love you!"

Sirens blasted outside. Clara returned the picture to his pocket and ran up the stairs. Flashing lights poured into the living room and kitchen. She bolted out the back door, ran through the neighbors' yards, and burst onto the street.

Clara had nowhere to go, no one to turn to. Then, it came to her. Father Benedict. He would know what to do. She wiped the snot off her face with her elbow, walking quickly down the sidewalk through crowds of people, trying her best not to draw attention to herself. She looked at her hands, covered in blood. She swallowed a scream, and no one around her seemed to notice. When she looked at her hands again, they were clean.

Clara stopped at the last street corner before St. Catherine of Siena, as she breathlessly awaited the light to change. The same newsstand where she spoke to Oliver the first time was beside her. The newspaper's top headline read: ***NEW DETAILS IN THE SINCLAIR'S MURDERS.*** Portraits of Marcus, Bernie, Dean, and Peter were printed below.

Her body count was five.

She had killed five people.

Clara fiddled with her hair, waiting for the light to change before looking at the newspaper again.

Blood poured from their smiling mouths, pooled on the sidewalk, and ran into a storm drain. Clara gasped, backing away and feeling like she was going to be sick. She closed her eyes and opened them again. The blood disappeared as the worker at the newsstand squinted at her. The light changed, and she ignored him, running across the street and up the steps into the church.

She ran into Father Benedict's office. The color drained from his face, and his mouth dropped the moment he looked up at her. Clara wondered what she looked like.

"I need help," Clara said, as Father Benedict stood alarmed, offering to speak to her in the confessional. He handed her a veil to wear, and they entered the cathedral. The faithful kneeled before the altar in prayer, scattered in different pews. The Sanctuary Lamp flickered on the altar. She walked past St. Catherine of Siena, wearing the crown of thorns and holding flowers. Maybe this was a mistake.

I don't belong here.

Father Benedict waved her inside the confessional, where they sat face-to-face as they always had. "Let me grab you some water and tissues, all right? I'll be right back."

Clara nodded as the door was closed. Her thoughts were incoherent. She didn't know how she would put a sentence together. The walls of the confessional latched themselves onto her chest, pressing against her rib cage while her lungs pressed against it in the opposite direction. She covered her eyes with her hair.

"What's wrong, Clara?"

Clara gasped, opening her eyes and hitting her back against the wall. Father Benedict appeared before her, sitting across from her. She wiped her eyes and nose, gripping her gray dress and taking a deep breath.

"I'm scared, Father. I'm going to burn in hell."

He tilted his head, leaning toward her. "Why do you think you're going to hell?"

"I've done such horrible things." Clara tried to stop crying, so she could speak clearly. He handed her a tissue, so she wiped her eyes and blew her nose. "The burning never stops. My mind is always racing, no matter how much I pray it goes away. From the second I fall asleep to the moment I wake up, it burns. Maybe that's why I didn't mind watching over my mom; she felt the same way as me. She would destroy the house and hit my dad. Once, she almost murdered me by holding my head underwater when I was taking a bath. I always cleaned the house and took care of her at her worst. I watched my friends have normal parents and normal lives, going on dates, dancing with men, and going to the soda fountain, while I had to stay home with Mom and make sure she didn't kill herself. I blamed my father for taking her away from me, but there wasn't anything he could do. I should have realized that sooner. My God, I wish I had realized that sooner.

"I hated you when you always made me say she was dead every week. I miss her so much it's unbearable sometimes, and my anger flares up, and I can't control it. I wanted to make the doctors pay for abandoning her, so I killed them one by one. Peter, Bernie, Marcus, and Dean. They all loved to cheat on their wives, so I pretended to be interested in an affair so they would take me to a secret, quiet spot where I could murder them. I can't say it didn't feel good to end their lives. Their wives are better off without them, even if they won't admit it to themselves. They had to die; I'm sure my mother isn't the only patient the staff has killed. I had to protect the other patients. It was so easy for them to cover up her murder; they must have done so with others."

Clara put her head in her hands and stared at Father Benedict again. "I didn't mean to kill my father. I really didn't! But he and Oliver were working together to try to have me arrested and killed. He made me do it. But now my family is gone. I've always felt alone and now I am.

"I wanted to murder Marcus's brother, Oliver, but the police came, and I had to escape. But how badly I wanted to put a hammer through Oliver's skull and how good that would feel. I shouldn't be feeling that way; that's not how this started. I wanted to help the patients at Sinclair's. It got out of hand so fast."

Clara paused, blowing her nose. "The police are hunting me down right now, and you're the only person I could turn to. What I did was wrong, and I know I'm going to burn in hell and I'm scared. I never wanted it to go this far, I don't know what's wrong with me. I don't want to die, though, Father. They're going to kill me if they find me, and I don't want to end up like Mom. God abandoned me long ago, I'm afraid. I prayed and prayed He would protect my mom, and she's dead. I prayed the burning would stop, and it hasn't."

Father Benedict leaned toward Clara, unafraid of her. "God did not abandon you, you abandoned God with what you have done. You have done evil things. Do you want to get better?"

"More than anything, Father! I don't want to burn anymore!" Clara cried.

"This will be your purgatory, Clara. You will go to your father's isolated cabin in the Poconos. You will live there alone. You will not go into town. The only store you can go into is the grocery store, and you cannot look at anyone. You can't wear any flashy clothes or makeup and you can't talk to anyone or ask anyone any questions. You cannot draw any attention to yourself."

Clara listened intently.

"You will live a life in solitude and pray to the Lord for His forgiveness. You are going to need it, Clara."

"I'll follow the rules," she said. "I'll do everything."

"If you break any of the rules, I will tell the police where you live. I can't tell them any of your confessions, but I can give them your location. The Church is a place for the sick."

Clara wanted to stand and scream, *"I'm not sick!"* but she was weak and exhausted. She stayed quiet instead. "Thank you, Father. I won't let you down, I promise."

"This isn't about me. You have let the Lord down, Clara, but you can earn His forgiveness if you are truly sorry for your sins and repent."

The door opened and Father Benedict stepped inside, holding tissues and a cup of water. Clara furrowed her eyebrows when she saw that the seat across from her was empty. Wasn't she talking to Father Benedict? Yes, she was. She knew she was. He sat down across from her as Clara pushed her back against the wall.

"Please begin, Clara," he said.

Clara shook her head and shot out of the confessional instead and ran out the backdoor, ignoring Father Benedict yelling her name. She walked down a side street, and a police car turned down the street in her direction. Father Benedict's car was parked beside her, a tan Chevy station wagon, so she sat in the driver's seat and watched the policeman's car approaching in the side mirror.

She put down the sun visor, turned her head away, sunglasses and veil partially hiding her face. The car crept closer and closer but passed her by. After it was out of sight, she searched for the keys. Nothing inside except for some pennies, glasses, and a couple of prayer cards. She stepped outside again, walking down the side street and turning onto a main road with a crowd. People walked on the sidewalks while the traffic was at a standstill. The light turned red a block away from the newsstand. The worker talked with police, pointing at St. Catherine of Siena's Cathedral. The light remained red, and cars drove by. If she were to run through the intersection, cars would beep and the two police officers would look in her direction. It would be better to wait.

Her heart hammered in her chest as the two police officers

stopped at the street corner opposite her, also waiting for the light to change. Clara couldn't walk past them, so she went down the street again beside the church, reaching another street corner. She couldn't go onto the subway around here; she needed to get out of Brooklyn first.

"Officers!" The newsstand worker shouted, pointing at Clara.

"Shit!" she whispered as they chased her. She ran through a red light, causing cars to slam on their brakes and beep. A police car pulled up behind her, putting on its lights and siren, so she ran between two buildings into a back alley. She concealed herself behind a building, grabbing her knees to catch her breath. The police car stopped as the siren didn't fade off in the distance. They were probably calling for backup. So Clara ran again, down the alley. Another patrol parked at the end of the alley on the street, its lights flashing. Clara turned to run between two buildings and ran across the street into a park.

Clara leaned against a large oak tree, relishing the respite from the relentless heat. She closed her eyes and she tried to slow her breathing. The rough edges of the bark pressed into her spine as the breeze picked up. Her legs gave out, and her body slammed against its roots. She couldn't run anymore. It would only be a matter of time before the police came and took her away. *When you're an adult, you have to make hard decisions no matter how sick they make you.* Clara opened her eyes again. Her purgatory wouldn't be in her beloved cabin, it would be in a prison cell.

Bernie, Peter, Marcus, and Dean walked toward her, wearing white lab coats. Blood gushed out of Peter's back, out of Bernie's and Marcus's chests, and out of Dean's head. Their bodies decomposed before her eyes and turned into ash. Their eyes were black, lifeless, and hollow. Clara wouldn't run anymore. She would accept her fate, so she stood. Her mouth was dry and sweat trickled down her brow. Her time had run out.

Someone pushed her from behind, her nose slamming against the harsh, dry ground. A police officer put handcuffs on her, holding her shoulders and forcing her to stand upright. Blood traveled down from her nose and dripped onto her dress; it must be broken. He walked her to the police car surrounded by a crowd of people, staring at her and pointing. He opened the door, and she climbed inside. Her reflection stared at her in the rearview mirror. She understood now why Father Benedict looked at her the way he had, like she was a monster. Clara looked like she had been through a war. A war of her own making.

Two police officers sat in the driver's and passenger's seats.

"Yes, Detective Howard, we have her," one of the officers said.

Clara could picture the cabin, pretending it existed before her on the side of a large, majestic hill full of trees. She could drive on the winding dirt road and park in front of the covered front porch, cutting herself off from society for good. She could have fires in a fire pit, grow a vegetable garden in a sunny spot, read, and draw. Clara could take hikes around the property, sit on the porch and take in the view. Peaceful and calm. She could be good; she could live a good life away from others. No one had to come into contact with her ever again. No one had to be her next victim. There would never be a next victim. The police car moved, and the cabin disappeared into the abyss.

Clara would never make it there.

29

Oliver winced, trying to free his hands from the handcuffs. His back and head ached. He learned her name after all this time. Clara Haggard, the young woman who left Marcus's apartment wearing his trench coat the night of his death. It had been her the whole time, killing men who worked at Sinclair's and avenging the death of her mother under their care. She almost put a hammer through his skull, but thankfully Nancy called the police in time. His hands shook as he reached toward the petite shelf for something to stick inside the keyhole, but his fingers didn't come close. His throat was dry, and he felt too weak to make a sound. Footsteps came down the hall along with the jingling of keys.

"Hello? Anyone there? I need help!"

A man who looked to be in his thirties poked his head through the crack in the door. He stared at Oliver's handcuffed hands, puzzled.

"Can you get one of the police officers down here so they can unlock these?"

"What?" he asked, looking like he was trying to process the scene.

Oliver's head kept ringing from being pushed down a flight of stairs, and he was running out of patience. "Can you please go to my apartment, 706, and tell the police officers I'm handcuffed to a radiator?"

The man left without a word. Hopefully, he would head to Oliver's apartment instead of ignoring him and returning to his own. Oliver tried to sit straighter to no avail. He wanted to hold Nancy and hug George tightly, ensuring no harm would ever come to them. Protect them from Clara Haggard, who knew their names and faces.

He looked at the hammer on the table again. Clara came close to striking Oliver's head. He looked away from it, his body shaking. *She must be caught if she has not been already.* Clara would kill whenever the urge returned. The redness in her eyes, her strong grip of the hammer, the talking to someone who wasn't there, and the screaming...

And so Oliver waited for help. He closed his eyes.

"Ollie!" Oliver flinched when the door was pushed open, but took a deep breath when Nancy ran to him and knelt beside him. Her soft hand felt his cheek as her face was full of worry. "Are you all right?"

Oliver nodded with a smile, grateful that he lived to see her again. "I'm fine."

She moved aside so a police officer could unlock the handcuffs. As the officer attempted to free him, Oliver kept his eyes on Nancy. She swayed from one foot to the other, holding her chin with her hand, staring into his eyes, and tearing up.

"I'm okay, Nance, I'm okay," he assured her.

She took deep breaths and nodded. The handcuffs were unlocked, freeing Oliver from the radiator. The police officer helped him stand as he was unsteady on his feet.

"You need to see a doctor," Nancy said.

"Detective Howard is in your apartment and would like to ask you some questions first," the police officer said to Oliver. Oliver was too tired to roll his eyes, so he nodded. The officer supported him as they followed Nancy to the elevator. The doors opened again, and they walked to his apartment, finding Benny sitting on the floor next to George as George played with his toys. Detective Howard watched from the kitchen with a police officer leaning against the wall.

"Mr. Anderson, I have some questions for you," Detective Howard said, taking a seat on a chair. Oliver sat on the couch, his back and neck stiff and sore. Nancy brought Oliver a glass of water, and he thanked her. The water brought relief to his dry throat.

Detective Howard took out his notepad and pen. "Please describe what occurred."

"Has Clara been caught?" Oliver asked.

Detective Howard tilted his head, looking displeased with the interruption. "Not yet, but I have officers all over Brooklyn. We will find her, I assure you. Now, please describe what occurred after you left the apartment. Mrs. Anderson has told me about Miss Haggard's visit here."

"I went into the stairwell, and Clara pushed me down the stairs. I blacked out, and when I woke up, I was handcuffed to a radiator in a maintenance closet downstairs. Clara has been having hallucinations of me working with her father to imprison her. I've never met Dr. Haggard, and she grew furious when I told her the truth and was about to kill me with a hammer..." Nancy gasped, causing everyone to glance at her. Her hand covered her mouth. Oliver wanted to assure her he was fine, but Detective Howard stared at him impatiently. "...The police came in the nick of time, and she fled."

"Did she say anything else?"

Oliver widened his eyes. "She admitted to killing Dean Caraway. She said she saw me there, watching her kill him, which, of course, isn't true. Clara spoke to thin air in the closet like a person were standing beside her. Ed Taylor said her mother had hallucinations and paranoia, and it seems Clara does, as well. She's dangerous and will kill again without a second thought.

There is nothing there behind her eyes. No emotion and no remorse."

Detective Howard clicked his pen and put it into his jacket pocket, along with his notepad. "Thank you, Mr. Anderson. Two officers will remain in front of the building to ensure Miss Haggard does not come back. We will notify you when she is in custody."

Detective Howard nodded at the police officer, and Nancy walked them out of the apartment. Benny stood, shaking Oliver's hand. "Glad to see you're doing okay, buddy!"

"Thank you for watching over Nancy and George."

"Don't mention it!"

Nancy smiled at Benny, showing him out next. "Thank you, Benny, for keeping an eye on George."

"He's an awesome kid. He can come over anytime!"

Nancy giggled, waving goodbye and closing the door. Once everyone had left, Nancy sat next to Oliver and held his hand, staring into his eyes. Oliver wiped the tears off her cheeks.

"I'm so relieved you're okay!" she said.

"I am, Nance, I am."

"I couldn't bear to lose you, Ollie. You're the only person that's ever understood me."

Oliver pressed his hand against her cheek and stared into her eyes. "Sometimes, I think you know me a little too well."

Nancy giggled again, smiling at him the way she did when they were dating. She loved him; she still loved him after all this time. He leaned forward, and she did the same. Oliver kissed her softly for a moment.

Nancy leaned her head against his shoulder and wrapped her arm around Oliver's stomach. As she held onto him, the guilt ate at Oliver for not telling her the truth of what happened the night of Marcus's death. He must tell her, despite the possible consequences.

"Nance, I was there by your old apartment building the night Marcus was killed. I followed Marcus because I was so angry at his behavior, furious that he kept cheating on you and furious that he didn't sell the car or apartment when George needed money for treatment. I waited for Clara to leave, so I could tell him off..." He stopped briefly. "She left the apartment in Marcus's trench coat, and I didn't go inside. I left and went home. I didn't even try to follow Clara and chase her down. I went home... I even hoped he would face some consequences for his actions. I fell asleep while you stayed up all night, worried about Marcus. Then you called the next morning, telling me he never came home. I knew deep down something terrible had happened. I never wanted to be more wrong in my life, but I tried to retrace my steps the next morning so the police wouldn't suspect me."

Nancy sat straighter, locking eyes with him and sighing. "You're too hard on yourself, Ollie. Marcus wasn't your responsibility; he was a grown man. You never could've guessed when you left that he had been killed. I couldn't imagine what it was like for you to find him the next morning." She shuddered. "You need to let whatever guilt you have go. I can't thank you enough for all you've done for George and I—"

"You don't need to thank me."

Nancy smiled at him. "You took care of everything for me, and I am so grateful." She took her hand away from his cheek and held his hand again. "I got into a major argument with Marcus before you stopped by that evening. I told him I would leave him if he cheated on me again. And all he did was laugh. He knew I was trapped. And I said some terrible things to him; called him some terrible things. I told him I never loved him. I don't blame myself for saying it, but I hate that those were the last words I would ever say to him."

"I'm not too happy about the last words I spoke to him, either. It was frustrating to love Marcus, but I did. I'll never forget how great of an older brother he was after my parents passed away. He helped me move on and focus on the future."

"Marcus was comforting after George's doctor appointments. He always reassured me that we would find what was wrong with him and fix it. He always gave me hope. I'm grateful for our marriage; George is the best son I could've asked for."

"He is my favorite nephew."

Nancy laughed, looking at George who was playing with his toy car and turning to Oliver again. "He loved my father like my father was his own. I wished my dad respected me, as he respected Marcus."

"You deserved that." Oliver said as Nancy stared at the floor. "You know, I forgot to tell you. Ed Taylor told me Marcus went into debt to help a patient stay in Sinclair's and get the help they needed."

Nancy nodded. "He loved his patients. He was a brilliant man."

The phone rang, startling them. Nancy helped Oliver stand before picking up the phone in the kitchen. "Hello?"

"Is this Mr. Oliver Anderson?"

"This is he."

"This is Officer Barnes. Detective Howard wanted me to inform you that Clara Haggard is in custody."

"Thank you." Oliver let out a sigh of relief, hanging up the phone. He turned to Nancy, who approached him with her arms crossed. "They arrested her, it's over."

"Thank God!" Nancy said, touching her chest. Oliver winced, feeling a twinge in his back. He leaned against the counter. "Ollie, you have to see a doctor. We should go now."

Nothing would come of it, but he would go to make her feel better. "All right, let's go."

"Come on, George! Are you sure you can walk, Ollie?"

Oliver nodded, collecting his belongings.

They left the apartment, stepping into the elevator. George jumped, clutching his toy car.

"Do you want to pick out a kitchen table tomorrow?" Oliver asked. "We could go to Marty's Furniture Store and see if anything sticks out."

Nancy wrapped her arm around Oliver's. "I would like that very much."

The elevator doors opened again, and they exited the building, heading toward Oliver's car. People gathered on the sidewalk, lining the street as sirens wailed in the distance. A couple of police cars with flashing lights sped down the street as the other cars on the road pulled over. Nancy and Oliver waited on the curb, and Nancy held George's hand. A couple more cars went by with no one in the backseat.

"That killer will be driving by!" a woman whispered to another standing beside her. "They're taking her to the station to book her."

None of this should be exciting. Four people were dead, and their families mourned their loss. Nancy looked at the woman with a frown briefly and turned her attention to the road. A car passed by with a passenger in the backseat. Clara Haggard sat in the back, scanning the crowd watching her. She didn't look at Oliver, must not have noticed him. When the car was out of sight, people moved on with their day.

"Ready?" Oliver asked.

"Yeah," Nancy said, interlocking her arms with Oliver's. "Murders shouldn't be a spectacle."

"I agree. Are you all right?"

"I'm fine."

* * *

Nancy was right to insist on going to the doctor. Oliver had a concussion and stayed in bed for the rest of the afternoon. It was Tuesday now, two days later, and Oliver was almost done with another day of typing obituaries. Taking one card off the pile, typing it up, and placing it on the completed pile at his tiny desk with his mug of steaming coffee. Alex came and went, bringing new cards and chatting about the Dodgers. Only a few minutes left as

Oliver finished his last card for the day. He picked his briefcase and left his desk.

"See you tomorrow, Oliver!" Alex said, waving to him.

Oliver waved back. "See you tomorrow!"

He waited behind a few of his coworkers for the elevator to arrive. Once it dinged and the doors opened, as many men as humanly possible fit inside. Oliver wrinkled his nose and tried holding his breath. Someone could use more deodorant in this heat. The doors opened, and Dorothy perked up at the sight of Oliver, giving him a wave.

"Have a nice evening, Oliver!" she said with a smile.

"You too. See you tomorrow!" He waved.

Once he stepped outside, Oliver inhaled the fresh air. Time to pick up a pizza for Nancy and George to enjoy for dinner.

Oliver passed by the newsstand and came to a sudden stop. His mouth dropped at the headline as he picked up the paper.

DR. HAGGARD FOUND DEAD IN HIS HOME

Dr. Christopher Haggard was found dead in the cellar of his home on Sunday evening. Foul play is suspected. Being employed as a psychiatrist at Sinclair's and father of the accused murderer Clara Haggard, Detective Howard links his death to the other four victims. His daughter, Clara Haggard, is now in custody. New York will seek charges of first degree murder for each victim.

If you have any information about Clara Haggard or this case, do not hesitate to contact the New York Police Department.

Oh my God. Clara did kill her father after all. Even he wasn't safe from her murderous rage. Her body count was now five people. Oliver put the paper back, taking a deep breath. Hopefully justice would be served, and Clara Haggard would pay for her crimes.

Oliver tried to clear his mind as he continued toward Leo's Pizzeria, approaching the counter. Leo wiped his sweaty brow with his elbow, resting his elbows on the counter and readying his pen. "Hey, Oliver! How are you holding up?"

Oliver shrugged. "As well as I can."

He turned around and picked up one of the boxes behind him. "Here you are. Tell Nancy and George I said my prayers are with them, all right?"

"I will, thank you."

Carrying the box, Oliver headed home. He took the elevator to the seventh floor. He passed the cat on the landing. "Hi, Fluffy!"

He unlocked the door and stepped inside, setting his briefcase on the floor and the pizza on their new circular metal table with four wooden chairs. Both traditional and modern. Nancy picked it out; it was her favorite.

"Hi, Ollie. How was work?" she asked, approaching him.

"It was good. How was George?"

"He did well today; we went through a few of his lessons. He should be up from his nap any minute now—"

George came running out of the bedroom with messy hair. "Pizza!"

"That boy can sense pizza from a mile away." Nancy laughed, as George sat at the kitchen table. "I'll grab some plates and napkins."

"Hey, buddy!" Oliver patted George's head.

"Hi, Uncle Ollie!"

Nancy brought three plates over, placing a piece of pizza on her and George's plates. As she filled a few glasses of water, Oliver picked out a slice and sat next to George. Nancy handed Oliver his glass and put two more water glasses on the table for her and George, along with a stack of napkins. Nancy sat next to George, and they ate dinner together. Oliver tried to conceal his smile, gazing at Nancy and George. He took a bite of his pizza.

"Did you hear the news about Dr. Haggard?" Nancy asked.

"Yes." Oliver nodded. "He probably made the error that he was safe from his daughter's wrath."

"I know what he did and how he protected her, but I can't help but feel sorry for him."

"Me too," he whispered.

Nancy sighed as she continued to eat.

"Marcus and her other victims will receive justice, Nance. Clara will be proven guilty."

Nancy agreed, reaching out across the table. Oliver held her hand, gliding his thumb over her knuckles.

"How's the pizza, George?" she asked.

"Good!" he said with his mouth full.

Oliver chuckled. The three of them ate the rest of their meal together as a family. Oliver wanted to be the best uncle he could be to George; taking him to his first baseball game and to his first movie; going for bike rides in the park; going to the soda fountain; and spending quality time together. He was planning a trip that the three of them could take to Lake George. Nancy deserved a quiet, relaxing vacation after all she had been through. Nancy and George would be well taken care of.

Oliver promised this to Marcus.

30

October 13th, 1960, Pocono Lake, Pennsylvania

I am not sick.

I am not sick.

I am not sick.

Clara wrote the words over and over with her sore hand, scrawling in red lipstick across the living-room wall of the cabin.

I am not sick.

I am not sick.

I am not sick.

"Your mother's sick, Clara," her father explained.

"You're sick, Clara," Marcus taunted.

"You're a sick child," Oliver said.

"There's some sick people in this city," the newsstand worker said.

"The Church is a place for the sick," Father Benedict said.

"I'M NOT SICK!" Clara threw her lipstick onto the floor. The red color stained the floor and spread against the walls.

She took out each book from the bookshelf, breaking each

spine, flinging each one into the air behind her. Book by book, shelf by shelf, until no books remained to ruin. She shoved the shelf; it slammed down, scattering the wood-fire tools. She tossed the throw blankets, tipping over the couch, chairs, and end tables. She tore down the curtains and flung a lamp to the floor. The bulb and ceramic base shattered on the hardwood.

She turned to the kitchen next, yanking the plates, bowls, glasses, and mugs out of the cabinets and breaking them one by one, their pieces of glass scattering across the floor. Clara moved to the bathroom, shattering the mirror and turning on the bathtub faucet. The water rose and rose, steam filling the room. It overflowed onto the floor as Clara left. A black hair clip sat on the kitchen counter. She picked it up, squeezing it. The sharp ends pierced her skin. The calendar hanging on the wall confronted her. Today was the circled day.

Clara returned to the living room, looking at the mess she had made. She stepped backward until her body hit the wall. She slid down it as her eyes watered, and heat rushed to her face.

The front door swung open, and Clara's father entered the cabin, approaching her. He picked up the chair and sat across from her, taking out a cigar and lighting it. Puffs of smoke spread through the air between them. His glasses sat on the edge of his nose, and he wore his favorite black hat and matching suit. Clara tried to smile. She couldn't remember the last time she had. It was nice to see him again; it had felt like an eternity. Her father stared into her eyes with a straight face, crossing his legs and slouching his back. He didn't speak, but Clara's mouth opened as she tried to collect her thoughts.

"I'm so sorry, Dad," Clara cried. "I'm sorry I killed you, I never should've killed you. I think about it every day, the memory of what I did to you suffocates me. If I had duct tape wrapped around my head, I wouldn't feel any differently than I do now. You must know how much I loved Mom; I gave up everything for her. I always made sure you came home to a clean house and a calm wife. Then all of that went down the drain when you took her away from me. I know now that you did what you thought was right; she almost killed me. I try not to think about it, but my mind loves to remind me. I just couldn't let her death go. I feel guilty for killing them sometimes, but I shouldn't. I should be glad they're dead; Brooklyn should be glad they're dead. But it was wrong, maybe that's why I punish myself for what I did to them. Maybe that's why I torture myself. It's all so confusing sometimes. Then I think about you again and I lose control."

Clara stopped, two questions gnawing at her. "Are you afraid of me? Do you think I'm sick?"

Her father didn't say a word, continuing to smoke his cigar.

"You are scared of me, I can tell. Maybe I am sick after all, even my own father is scared of me and Mom would be too if she had known what I had become. I prayed every night that this sickness would go away, but my mind has always been on fire. There's nothing I can do. It's always reminding me that it's there, no matter how hard I try to distract myself. I know I deserve to die for what I've done, but I'm scared I'll be burning in hell."

She took a deep breath.

"Sometimes I ask myself why I did all of this because none of it has made me any happier. My happiness is buried deep into the earth, lying beside my Mom."

Her father didn't react.

Clara opened her eyes. The luminescent lights glared down on her, forcing her to squint. Her breath hitched—were they real or not? Her arms, legs, and chest were bound with ropes. She was strapped to a wooden chair, too weak to struggle. Where was the cabin? Where did her father go? The room smelled like cigars, and chairs creaked.

A group of people watched her. Father Benedict sat in the front row, doing the Sign of the Cross. Oliver sat in the back, holding a notepad and pen and wearing a wedding ring. A man sat next to him, exhaling cigar smoke before whispering into Oliver's ear. He, too, held a notepad. About a dozen other people faced her.

Clara always had the sinking feeling in the pit of her stomach that she wouldn't live a long life. And today she would meet her maker. She had a lot to answer for.

Someone put a mask over her face from behind. Men whispered words from behind her that Clara couldn't understand. She closed her eyes and brought herself back to the cabin.

Clara sat on the floor across from her father who exhaled cigar smoke.

Tears streamed down Clara's cheeks. "I hope I can see you and Mom again."

A jolt surged through her body, and the cabin shook.

Her father dropped the cigar, causing the rug to catch on fire, before he vanished. The flame grew, spreading to the couch, the books on the floor, and the wood on the walls. The curtains became engulfed, and the water from her overflowing bathtub flowed into the living room. Clara stood and stared. There was nothing she could do. This cabin was never under her control. It was merely a figment of her imagination. She ran outside, staring at the whole cabin engulfed in flames, a heavy and thick gray smoke rose into the atmosphere. As Father Benedict said: *It is important to accept reality. Only then can you heal.* Her little sanctuary in the woods. Her little sanctuary all to pretend she wasn't in a prison cell waiting to be electrocuted to death. It was nothing but ashes now.

Clara tried screaming but making a noise seemed impossible. Her skin was on fire, peeling off her muscles, and she lost control of her limbs as the thick straps held them in place. And the next moment, it was over.

The burning had stopped.

THANK YOU FOR READING!

I hope you enjoyed reading Clara and Oliver's stories as much as I enjoyed writing them!

Please consider leaving a short review on Amazon or Goodreads. It would help this story find more readers!

Thank you again!

ACKNOWLEDGMENTS

So many wonderful people helped me get *Until Your Father Comes Home* to where it is now!

Emily LeVault, my editor, helped me take this story to the next level. Her feedback was insightful and encouraging, and she always gave thoughtful answers to any questions I had. My beta readers, Marlee, Jennifer, Lydia, and Leila helped me transform my first draft into a sound manuscript at the developmental level. Their constructive criticism was invaluable.

My parents and brother, William, for their continued support of my publishing dreams.

And you! Thank you for reading. It really means the world to me.

ABOUT THE AUTHOR

Meaghan Dwyer writes suspenseful and twisty mysteries, thrillers, and horror. Sign up for her newsletter to be the first to know about upcoming releases, and signed copies are also available at:

meaghandwyerbooks.com

instagram.com/mdwyerbooks

tiktok.com/@mdwyerbooks

www.ingramcontent.com/pod-product-compliance
Lightning Source LLC
LaVergne TN
LVHW091253150826
845673LV00006B/1404